Inside the trailer, floating in the epsom salt solution was a naked man-form, head covered with an opaque helmet, Simon Boyle's artificial Billy the Kid. Simon lifted Billy's head out of the solution and turned off the holograms of Billy's dreams. He pulled the helmet off gently so the nasal tubes wouldn't bruise Billy's nose, exposing a long jaw, buck teeth, narrow eyes, light-colored hair between red and blond. *A replication of Billy the Kid—no, a replica of Billy-the-Kid legends, made from stolen parts.* Boyle lifted the chimera out onto a wheeled stretcher and dried him, then rolled the stretcher outside. If the optical transformer still held after this seventh death and reconstruction, Billy wouldn't see the twentieth-century car and trailer.

Billy woke up and said, "Where am I? What happened?"

Boyle began fixing a pot of coffee. "We're heading for Texas, Billy."

Billy looked at the trailer and said, "That's funny."

"What?"

"At first I wasn't sure if it was a rock or a house."

Boyle wondered if he'd left Billy in the conditioning tank long enough this time.

THE
ILLEGAL REBIRTH OF
BILLY THE KID

REBECCA ORE

A TOM DOHERTY ASSOCIATES BOOK
NEW YORK

THE ILLEGAL REBIRTH OF BILLY THE KID

A Tor Book
Published by Tom Doherty Associates, Inc.
49 West 24th Street
New York, N.Y. 10010

Cover art by Dean Morrissey

ISBN: 0-812-50672-3

First edition: March 1991

Printed in the United States of America

0 9 8 7 6 5 4 3 2 1

Acknowledgments

With thanks to Patrick County Sheriff Jay Gregory, for permission to use him as an example of modern professional law enforcement.

This is an alternative alternate history.

CHAPTER ONE
The Maker and His Man

Let us fake out a frontier—a poem somebody could hide in with a sheriff's posse
after him—a thousand miles of it if it is necessary for him to go a thousand miles.

Jack Spicer, "Billy the Kid"

SIMON BOYLE'S CLIENT INVITED HIM TO A PLACE in Wyoming where the present was almost invisible so her holiday would be as authentic as possible. The European *ricos* who controlled the place loved their antiques.

After Boyle registered his destination with the CIA resident in Cheyenne, he thought how ironic it was to be so honest about where he was when he was playing with an illegal construct. Why hadn't Langley asked why a fat, fifty-three-year-old DNA technician who built and conditioned spies would spend so much time riding horses?

Maybe they know? That was a thought as nasty as the highway between Cheyenne and Denver. Simon drove all day and turned off I-90 at Sundance to pick up his entry permit at the Devil's Tower Preserve Gate. The warden there found his invitation from Lisa Auschlander and gave Simon a map. "Lisa's real curious," the warden said. Simon wasn't quite sure how the guy meant that, but nodded and walked to the truck.

After 4.3 miles Simon turned off Route 14 and went down an almost stainlessly preserved dirt road. His pickup pulling the horse trailer wiggled through the ruts and vibrated on the washboards, resonating with the ripples, making them deeper. Boyle was sweating slightly, wondering if wagon ruts in the nineteenth century would have been deeper than these anachronistic car-ground ruts, the washboards quite so bad. The sky was back to the same blue. He steered the truck to the left toward a boulder.

The wheels squirmed in the ruts as if not wanting to leave, but finally came out. He slowed down when he felt them get good traction, careful about the horse trailer behind him, easing it out onto the praire.

When his heart beat faster than a hundred beats per minute, an almost subliminal voice, a monitor wired to his left mastoid process, counted off the beats. It chirped, "100, 101, 2, 103 . . ." high but not pushing it. Boyle felt a twinge of guilt.

On the surface, the rich who controlled this area demolished all human structures built later than 1910. Underground was different: tunneling machines ground the substrate, analyzing it for suitable chemicals, calling for the larger extracting and refining machines.

Always the machines below us, Boyle thought. In the meat-robot spy games, few real humans died, just a lot of spliced DNA lysing from lethally disrupted biomechanisms. His creations replaced human defectors. Soviets and Africans made their own chimeras out of DNA factions, phaged together, computer-assembled. We real humans just live to make things that make things, Boyle thought, *Homo faber* expanded to the ridiculous, and now, in Billy, I've got my own lithe and active little surrogate.

Devil's Tower was to the west, behind him as he unloaded the horses, first the chestnut mare with the receiver and vocal-cord player, then the gelding with the neural cutout to the hind legs. The horses seemed spooked by the tower, wheeling around to see what it was. Boyle looked at it, too, a mocking symbol of both the past and a future that couldn't happen. *Not a sign of aliens out there, no way around Einstein. It's a universe for what humans can make of it.* He got the saddles and packs out of the third stall, one thing at a time. His monitor fussed at him when he tried to lift a saddle topped with one of the smaller packs.

Then he went into the fourth horse stall. An isolation tank almost filled it, the fiberglass hull vaguely resembling an unturned antique bathtub. The biodisplay framed in brushed chrome ticked out a REM sleep pattern. Simon pulled at the lid, which opened sideways, not counterweighted, so he had to struggle with it, wondering if his heart-monitor messages went anywhere but to his own ear.

Floating in the Epsom-salt solution was a naked man form, head covered with an opaque helmet, Simon's artificial Billy the Kid. Simon lifted Billy's head out of the solution and turned off the holograms of Billy's dreams. He pulled the helmet off gently so the nasal tubes wouldn't bruise Billy's nose, exposing a long jaw, buckteeth, narrow eyes, light-colored hair between red and blond. *A replication of Billy the Kid— no, a replica of Billy-the-Kid legends, made from stolen parts.* Boyle lifted the chimera out onto a wheeled stretcher and dried him, then rolled the stretcher outside.

180 beats per minute.

As Simon pushed the gurney over the bunchgrass, he wondered if he could have more easily carried Billy. He laid Billy on blankets by the horses and covered him, then put the gurney back in the trailer.

After spreading a bedroll for himself, Boyle built a little fire and waited for Billy to wake up. If the optical transformer still held after this seventh death and reconstruction, Billy wouldn't see the twentieth-century car and trailer.

Billy was illegal, beyond being stolen. The DNA laws forbade reconstructions of criminal personalities within the United States. *Not precisely Billy. No one really knows enough about him*, but Boyle knew how judges interpreted the DNA laws.

Billy woke up and said, "Where am I? What happened?"

Boyle began fixing a pot of coffee and said, "We're headed for Texas, Billy."

The chimera sat up and began looking for his clothes. Boyle threw him jeans, a shirt, boots, and a leather jacket, then went to the trailer for Billy's hat and mohair plaid scarf.

Billy said, looking at the trailer, "That's funny."

"What?"

"At first I wasn't sure if it was a rock or a house."

Boyle wondered if he'd left Billy in the conditioning tank long enough this time.

Simon Boyle rode ahead of Billy the Kid, his own thigh tendons achingly stretched over the chestnut mare. Now he'd become Pat Garrett, start the game for the woman who'd fuck a legend made of chimera. To the creature riding behind him, Boyle said the cue words, "Arizona is always Arizona." Now he *was* Pat Garrett, tall and lean in Billy's eyes only. Boyle wanted Henry McCarty, Kid Antrim alias William Bonney, alias Billy the Kid, to be conceptually blind to anything that didn't fit the nineteenth-century concepts wired to his visual cortex.

Billy said, "Shit, I hate Texas and Arizona both."

Each time I fish him out of the rebuild vat, he believes the whole history.

The wind blew against them from fresh glaciers eating into Canada. If the cold continued, global power would shift south.

"Ain't it a little too damn cold?" the chimera said as it wrapped its buffalo robe tighter. The gelding between the chimera's legs grunted as though the saddle girth had been cinched tighter.

"We're pretty high up," Simon said.

"It's colder than it was last year," Billy said. "Pat, when I'm hid, go tell Governor Wallace I never killed no twenty-two men. Six, maybe. I'm not like those damn reporters say."

The chimera sounded weary and stared at Simon as if seeing behind the Pat Garrett image. Simon wondered if reality leaked into the chimera's perceptions, if he had developed a rudimentary personality that fought the conditioning. He said to Billy, "I could see Governor Wallace."

"Don't know, asking for that man's goodwill. He's not much better than a dime novelist himself."

Boyle didn't say anything, just wondered how well this variation would play out. *Maybe I should start a fresh corpus. Maybe the chimera mind isn't washing clean from time to time.* But the chimera was still riding with Pat Garrett, trusting him.

Boyle saw the cabin his client had noted on her map, and knew that he'd be warm, snugly underground, soon after he put the chimera to sleep.

"I've seen this before," the chimera said. Boyle stiffened, but Billy continued, "I don't know. All outlaw shacks look alike."

They looked at each other then, the chimera's large round chin looking even rounder, stupider, since Billy let his lower jaw dangle, the moist interior of the mouth looking like a wound. *I can fill his sensory systems with false signals, but I can't be all the way inside that head and still operate my own body. The CIA's classic problem.*

Billy said, "It's the damn telegraph and railroad make it hard on a man trying to get some peace these days, telling everything so quick. New York papers had stories on me."

"I haven't seen either around here," Boyle/Garrett said. He wondered if the visual transform always worked—when he was Pat Garrett, he should be thin and tall, not fat and balding. They rode up to the cabin—when Billy rode, Boyle liked real space to move the horses through, but sometimes Billy had to travel imaginary ground. Lisa and her rich friends didn't own all of Wyoming.

"So, Pat, what do we do next?" Billy grinned and swung off his horse.

"Let's eat dinner and get some sleep. There's a dance tomorrow."

After dinner, Boyle reached in his pocket and turned on Billy's sleep inducer, lightly at first, so that Billy could put himself to bed. Then heavily.

That done, Boyle went out to the horses. His mare lifted her muzzle from the water bucket and said, "Lisa wants to know if she can sleep with him more than once before the shoot-out."

"Don't talk to me through the horse unless—"

"He's asleep, isn't he?"

"I haven't put a cutout in his aural centers, okay. How do I reach you?"

The horse's voice didn't change. "Hi, Simon, Lisa here. We'll send the tunnel 'vator up."

Boyle heard the grinding beyond the corral and hurried toward it, his heavy flesh shaking, his heart monitor whispering warnings in his ear. *Rich bitch, that's all Lisa is.* The tunnel escavator buzzed up through the ground like a silver drill. Soil cutters fell to the side like steel petals, each twelve feet long. Simon climbed between them, the petals refolded around him, and the escavator sank.

Showy bitch.

The steel flower opened again. Simon stepped out, barely able to see in the subterranean room. Then three hologram walls cut on and he was almost blinded. *Holograms of glaciers— what a statement.* But then the ice age never completely left Switzerland. Lisa Auschlander was sitting on what looked like a slab of ice hovering in the air. She wore jeans, not authentically nineteenth-century, and a silk blouse. Her hair was cut in bangs in the front, sharp-angled cut that touched her right eyebrow on one side and disappeared against her temple on the other—a constant-care cut, the slanting edge beveled perfectly every time Simon had seen her.

Lisa said, "So I meet him at the dance?"

Simon replied, "You'd better wear a dress."

"Wouldn't he interpret jeans in a nineteenth-century way?"

"He sees, but he doesn't know. But . . ."

She said, not asking, "Cognitive blindness isn't perfect."

"If I make them smart enough to be useful or interesting, I'm always fighting their brains. It's a bitch."

"Constance said he was fun. Is he still the same one?"

Simon nodded.

"What do you get out of it?"

"He could kill me and escape."

"Really?"

"I made him more than smart enough, except he gets caught up in the story."

She didn't giggle; he'd expected her to. Simon continued, "He likes his life, the romance. He doesn't remember getting shot."

"You edit the death memories."

"No, shock does that."

"Oh. Then it hurts when you kill him."

"I suppose so."

She lowered her head, the bangs swinging neatly away from her face, then she tightened her lips and raised her head. Her hair, slightly mussed, looked better than the earlier perfection. She sucked her tongue off her upper incisors—*t'kek*—and asked, "When do I meet him and who does he think I am?"

"Celsa Gutierrez."

"At Pete Maxwell's? Are we near the end, then?"

"I'll jump-cut him to New Mexico."

"Doesn't he get confused?"

"Reality jump-cuts for him. Bet he thinks it happens to everyone."

Billy woke up in a cabin on the road to Pete Maxwell's. He felt dizzy, his tongue thick in his mouth, as though he'd been hanged and cut down the night before. He thought he remembered riding to Texas with Pat Garrett, but now Pat was hunting him, only Pat hadn't been too active about it, stayed in Lincoln after the Kid escaped.

Killed that bastard Olinger always poking my belly with his shotgun—too bad about Bell, but the law had a death warrant on me.

Across the room was a nightstand with a blue clay pitcher and bowl. Billy reached under the bed for the chamber pot—empty, that was odd. He opened the door carefully and saw the plains glittering with frost, tried to remember the month. *Must have got drunk.* He pissed out the door and went back inside the room. He thought the room smelled like someone else had been there the last night.

He went back out to wind up a bucket from the well and took it back inside, then sniffed around for soap—there, in the nightstand cabinet behind the door. He pulled the glass knob, got the coarse yellow soap out, and washed his narrow hands, smiling at them, so easy to slip out of irons. He soaped the scars—cuff and rope burns—duding up for Celsa.

Maybe I'm just going to get shot by her jealous husband? He laughed out loud at that foolishness, then cleaned under his nails with his pocketknife, shaved the nails short enough not to snag her pretty skin.

They love me at Fort Sumner. He wondered if he would also spend time with Deluvina, little Navajo pet of Pete's. If Pat got him, all the women would be weeping, tearing their hair. He could imagine Deluvina raking her nails down Pat's face, ripping out his mustaches.

Pat's an old woman hisself. Billy knew that he was going to call Pat that, maybe he had called Pat that, and Pat would get real ticked.

Suddenly he felt jarred, didn't know why, like an earthquake had shook just him, leaving the ground and cabin alone. Then he saw the camera in the corner of the room—an old big black box with the hood dangling down behind where the plates slid in. Odd, he hadn't remembered the camera being there.

"He sees it," Lisa said, pulling back from the screen.

Simon said, "In nineteenth-century terms. It looks like a big ground-glass-backed tripod camera to him."

"But it just suddenly popped up."

"He does seem a bit startled."

"But he is cute, despite the jaw and the teeth. Or maybe because of them."

"You like, then?"

She nodded. The chimera started to touch the camera. Simon took out his pocket controller and pushed the button that released a short-term memory wash and brought the camera down.

. . . jarred. He started and picked up his gun, whirled to see who was watching, if anyone was watching. Old Woman Garrett's getting to me, he decided as he sat down on the bed and field-stripped his pistol, dropping the heavy .44-caliber bullets on the *jerga* blanket. He sat cross-legged on the floor, checking the firing pin, the cylinders, remembering the joker who'd been so eager to buddy up to him or kill him, the one whose gun had two empty chambers. Billy had spun the cylinder to fire on an empty chamber and the fool did draw on him after Billy made it plain they weren't going to be buddies. *Click*, and Billy shot the fool in the throat before he could cock again.

It wasn't all that funny, actually. Billy decided he wanted to sneak away from his dime-novel reputation, someday. But the whole United States had him down in those novels. Maybe Mexico? He spoke Spanish *muy bueno*, but Mexico was as gun-happy as New Mexico— better see if his friends could help him.

Damn dime novels—I'm a real man. He put the pistol back together, making sure all the chambers were loaded except for the one directly under the hammer. There he put an empty shell so the revolver wouldn't fire if he tripped. *I'm tired of dying.* He held that thought in his head and mentally walked around it, wondering how he got it. *I'm tired of dying.* Something was awful real about that thought *. . . tired of dying.*

Billy shuddered, then looked over in the corner of the room where the camera had been. He remembered something, almost, like a name lost when he could visualize the face. Maybe he'd read about himself dead in a dime novel? But he didn't think that was precisely it.

"How can you keep Billy from seeing what's real?" Lisa asked Simon.

"I gave him a set of concepts and block new ones. You can't see something you don't have a visual concept for, not immediately. You have to learn to see it. Except face recognition. Face recognition's neuro-programmed."

"But he—"

"He sees faces, but not always as a particular face. And the other concepts—I researched his era—amazing what I could fit in his head. Get changed." Simon handed her the Mexican-replica clothes. He realized he'd spoken a bit sharply to this rich woman, but she collected the long skirt and lacy blouse from his hand, her eyes lowered. This moment tended to em-

barrass the women who played with the Kid—
changing into a poor nineteenth-century Mexican.

"Does this have to be the last night?" Lisa
sounded anxious behind her poised face. The
face was beautiful, but a trifle immobile—
surgery, genetics work? Lisa's parents were
rich enough for either, but Simon noticed a cer-
tain stiffness to Lisa's expressions, perhaps
from surgical damage. DNA, even now, could
still fool designers.

She was still looking at him with her almost
inflexible eyebrows, so he said, "I need to kill
him. Job stresses."

The eyebrows twitched, slightly. "Oh."

Billy remembered he'd come for a dance, with
Celsa, and later? All he could remember right
now is that everyone at Fort Sumner loved Billy
the Kid under all his aliases. Whatever was my
real name? Billy wondered. State didn't know
for sure, why should he. He strapped on the
holster, put the .44 in it.

Vaguely, he wondered where Old Woman
Garrett was tonight. He drew his pistol and his
body remembered how the gun bounced in his
hand when he shot people.

"Sexy bullshit with the gun," Lisa said.

SImon looked at her and smiled. "His life was
very dangerous, so he keeps checking his equipment. He thinks that gun has saved him more
than once."

16

Lisa didn't reply. She and Simon rode down the tunnel in an electric cart, then she stepped into the escavator and rode up. It returned for Simon, but by the time he loaded his resuscitation equipment and the brain growth factors and got to the surface, she was gone into her Celsa bedroom. Billy was riding into Fort Sumner.

This would be the simple legend—no deputies tripping over their spurs, a body model in Pete Maxwell's bed, Simon as Garrett, and the woman as Celsa. Not historically accurate, but then Billy's life wasn't exactly accurately recorded, was it? Some Mexicans signed affidavits that Billy the Kid lived until the 1950's, a shy old man, much scarred, the buckteeth gone and that weird dumb jaw shrunk by senile bone atrophy. He died of a heart attack after stepping out of obscurity to find that no one really believed him.

Maybe? Maybe not. Simon didn't use Brushy Bill's claims when he built the Billy chimera consciousness. But as Simon set up the resuscitation equipment, cleaned the carotid-artery trocars, he wondered if knowing about Brushy Bill's claim subliminally affected the brain and story design.

Billy'll have three minutes to be dead. Simon fingered the switch boxes for the micro chem hitters he'd planted all over the Kid's brain. *Then burn memory back, hit those little mammillary bodies with a precise dose of alcohol,*

17

induce a little Korsakov's syndrome, retrograde amnesia, stop memory formation, then rebuild.

Simon wished he could play with a real human brain—Lisa's, any bitch who'd wanted sex with a taste of Billy's death. He told himself again that the chimera had no memory of earlier uses, of being killed and killed over again.

When I kill him, I bring him back, like a god. He liked that part, Pat Garrett treating Billy's gunshot wound, outside both Billy's history and his own. No politics, just seeing his chimera firm up again, mentally and physically, as Billy the Kid, the charming sexy outlaw.

But Simon didn't have much time. The Agency expected him to rig memories for a false *federales* colonel as soon as this leave was over. So many dead chimeras, minds he'd built to specification. Why should the government worry about him having one to play with himself? He sighed deeply and dragged his hands through his balding hair, then switched on the small camera in Celsa's room.

They were chatting in Spanish. He hadn't known Lisa spoke it. She touched both of Billy's wrists, then grasped them, squeezed. He pulled out of her grasp, saying *"dedos meniques,"* then caught her by her own wrists and pulled her in for a kiss.

They began dancing and taking their clothes off. The older women who'd fucked Billy had moved sultry and slow, knowing Simon watched. This dance was innocent and bouncy, but more erotic than any half-closed painted eyes glancing at the monitor. Simon was almost embarrassed to watch; it was as if the woman, not just the chimera, were pheromone-enhanced. Billy was more excited than Simon had ever seen him.

Then Billy said, in English, "So much better than dying." His cock sagged.

They both stopped, naked now, and Lisa stroked his brow, then licked his sweat off her hand. He grabbed her close—Simon wondered if he ought to intervene—and shivered against her, not sexually at all. Scared.

With Billy still in her arms, Lisa moved around so Simon could see her face through his camera. Her eyes were wide, brimming with tears. *Damn the bitch if she's going to feel guilty about this.*

Then Billy moved her toward the bed, murmuring to her in Spanish, then just murmuring.

Simon watched it all, his own groin knotted with blood.

Pete Maxwell's bedroom, July 14 going into the fifteenth, 1881—1981, 2067—almost two hundred years of legends. Pete Maxwell lay in bed; Pat Garrett sat with the .44-40 Frontier Colt he'd take from Billie Wilson at Stinking Springs. The gun Simon held was an exact replica, heavy against his thigh—*don't think this phallic bullshit*—a slight gleam on the barrel, worn trigger guard, the grip's open-pored grain all pointing at the cylinder, splinters smoothed away by handling and sweat.

* * *

Billy heard something. Steps. An old-woman man hunting him. Steps, spurs catching in the boardwalk, shadows. He pulled himself away from Celsa, who looked up at him, frightened.

"No, ya no, no vayas."

"Celsa, es necesario."

She sat up. Tears glinted in the dim light. Wordlessly, she stretched out her arms to him.

He told her in Spanish, "If it's nothing, I'll come back."

"No es nada sino tu muerte," she told him.

My death, he thought, knowing it was so, pulling on his pants and taking his Colt out of its holster. He walked out, poised on the balls of his bare feet, his toes curling down, feeling each crack in the boardwalk, sweat chilling on him, cold against his groin.

A man sat beside Pete Maxwell's bed.

"Quién es?" Billy asked, gun in his hand. He made one cross-the-body move with the other hand—the gun was cocked now—then touched Pete on the shoulder. *"Pete, quién es?* Pete, who is this man?"

Simon slowly raised his gun. Billy jumped back—deadly, deadly, his gun loaded with real bullets, a working replica—and asked again, *"Quién es?* Somebody answer me. *Quién es?"*

Someday, Simon thought as he fired, I'll wait too long.

Lisa came up to the door, tears streaming

down her face, dressed as a Mexican, wailing. Simon asked, "Do you want to do it again?"

"Simon, he's all bloody. Stop his jerking."

"You knew that was coming."

She shuddered, then said, "He was too innocent."

Simon watched the resuscitation equipment. A bell rang. He moved quickly to thrust the trocars up the chimera's carotids, then washed out the recent memories.

Lisa watched, then said, in a very rich girl's voice, "I'll take care of him after he's out of the regrowth tank." Simon knew that she'd make an issue of this, and she could do it, and he needed to finish the *federal*-colonel chimera for implacement by the Rome Summit.

Billy was wet all over, naked. His head ached. Celsa came up to him and asked, "What do you remember?"

"Drunk?" He looked up at her rigid face, pissed stiff at him. "Blackout drunk, I bet. I can't remember a damn thing."

Celsa, her face oddly smooth, began to cry.

"Hey, baby, I'm sorry. I think I remember a dance. Your husband catch us?"

Celsa shivered. He sat up and felt sore around the middle as if he'd been stomped. "Tell me who stomped me when I was drunk and I'll get him, them. The whole of Dolan's gang, the Fort Stanton brigade ..." He suddenly wondered why he and Celsa were talking in English.

"Billy, I don't want to give you back," she said.

Simon and Burton from Operations brought the defecting *federal*, Colonel Julio Navarez, into the room behind the one-way mirror. On the other side, the *federal* colonel's exact physical duplicate sat slack-faced in a wheelchair.

"What happens if they link up with each other—your chimeras, the Russian chimeras?" the *federal* colonel asked. "They duplicate so many of the second-level hierarchy now."

"We gene-mark 'um. If they get their own ideas, we turn them in," Simon said. "He's built. Now we just need to fill in the mind."

The Mexican colonel sighed and said, "Must I tell you my entire life with my voice or have you ways to get it out of my brain tissue?"

Simon said, "A little of both."

Navarez shuddered. Billy had shuddered like that. Simon wished he had a human brain to play with. This man? But Burton from Ops said, "Colonel Navarez, we promised you a protective identity, facial rebuilding, and we'll make good on that. You'll keep all your memories, sense of self, but it would be less boring to be drugged while we take your life story." Burton looked at Simon and added, "And I'll be at your side at all times. You trusted me enough to bring you out."

Simon bobbed his head and thought how tedious remapping always was. His teachers had told him intelligence chimera work was creative. *God, what a world.* If a glacier appeared in the east, he hoped someone would piss on it while it was just an August snow patch, hidden behind a Mount Marcy rock. Piss them all away, get the weather back to normal, defuse the tensions.

But then who would I be? Simon knew most jobs were even more boring, and the ice wasn't to blame for that. He thought about war, but these days it was mostly fought with chimeras smuggled into high places. Someday, either the Russians or the Americans would test everyone for gene markers; the government chimera makers would stop using the markers, would make chimeras totally indistinguishable from humans down to the molecules. Like a twentieth-century nuclear standoff, Simon thought.

Then chimeras could take over. Simon fantasized about that chimera future, mere humans their slaves after they could control their own recombinations—a cruel, beautiful, gaudy future where his Billy the Kid gunned him down over and over.

"Quién es?" he asked when Burton came in the room.

"Colonel Navarez in a can," Burton said, handing Simon tapes and ROM chips.

Simon began working, fitting the colonel's memories inside his imitation's skull bones. Tonight, he'd see what was happening with the Kid.

At five, he drugged the Navarez chimera and led him to an isolation tank filled with Epsom-salt solution, heated to body heat. The chimera seemed vaguely bewildered as Simon strapped his head in and taped the vital-signs monitors to his chest.

"Good night," Simon said as he closed the lid. On the underside of the lid was a digital holo-display. Simon found the colonel's home-ground tape—his neighborhood, his usual routes through Mexico City to his mistress's apartment, his wife's parents, his office, the proving grounds—and loaded it for an all-night display. The chimera would have memories of all these routes by morning.

As Simon left, he told the night officer where he'd left the Navarez and headed downstairs for the executive-level maglev trains.

Looking like ten gargantuan 1953 Porsches, the train braked, rolling off its magnetic cushion. The doors slid into the car walls, though, nothing as fragile as a hinge.

Simon stepped in and sat down on one of the cultured leather seats, sighed with the boredom of it all. The car was only half-full—four men and two chimeras playing poker under the fiber-optic light diffusers. One chimera, the one shuffling the cards, was a serpent-skinned girl; the other was a fuzzy with a face like a tapir's, but the trunk was more mobile. The chimeras played along with the humans, all of them seeming tired, bored. The tapir-faced one seemed to be trying to snap the pseudofingers wiggling at the end of his trunk.

I could have brought out material for another

Billy, Simon thought; I wasn't searched when I left. He speculated briefly about how the girl chimera's scales would feel against his belly, then leaned back and slept briefly until the train reached his station in Richmond. He rode the garage elevator up to his parking deck and stared at his car long enough to wish the little fiberglass thing with the plastic disposable engine was a centuries-old Porsche, dangerous to drive. Then he got in and slipped his card in the ignition. The car drove him home.

Simon lived alone with an enhanced bulldog and, sometimes, Billy the Kid, who hid his identity from visitors as if Governor Wallace's bounty was still in effect. He owned a town house on the edge of the city—bought it himself with salary—and inherited a James River farm that his family subdivided half of to save him from a state education. Not rich enough, not poor either, though, was how Simon described his condition.

The car pulled into the subterranean garage and popped the key card back at him. Jake, his bulldog, was waiting, grinning, the red tongue lolling out, curled at the tip. The dog drew his tongue back in and said, "Welcome home, boss."

Like a parrot, Simon thought. He knew precisely how he'd wired the brain. He bent over the dog's head and popped out the speech cartridge. The dog looked confused, then gently slapped his tongue over Simon's hand. Simon scratched the dog behind the ears and asked it,

25

"And what are you fighting for, dog?" If the Company was listening to his garage tonight, the listener might not think that statement was too despairing. He walked up two flights of stairs to his bedroom, his heart beating fast from the sudden exertion. The dog panted up the stairs beside him. Simon looked down at him. He hated to see that his dog resembled him so much, that dumb cliché.

What had Lisa done with Billy? Simon wanted to know. At the replica Fort Sumner, he'd patched observation instruments into a signal scrambler and then on through the postal-system net. Upstairs in his study now, he turned on the decoder and called up his signal.

Nothing. Fort Sumner was empty. He said, "Lisa, you fool," and transferred to voice message. His fingers fumbled over the keypad, punching in her private number before the chip voice came in. I am numerate and literate, which is more than many people today can say, Simon thought.

A deep male voice told him, "Lisa Auschlander wants you to leave a message. She'll get back to you as soon as it's practical. Speak or key in, now. . . ."

Simon didn't think the bitch would be fool enough to steal the Billy the Kid chimera. He said, "Lisa, I hope you're enjoying yourself," and went to activate Billy's body surveillance instruments. If the readings were correct, Billy was dead in New York City. Simon's abdominal muscles writhed.

The Agency didn't care what Simon did, really, as long as its rules weren't broken. Broken rules meant possible disloyalty. Simon told himself that all he'd stolen were DNA fragments, time on the Agency recombinant computer, a storage vial for the zygote. He'd grown the Kid in a private force tank—semi-illegal.

Better for Billy to be dead than loose, but Simon would have to go to New York and find the body.

But he had to finish programming the Navarez chimera. Maybe it was better if Billy's body was mistaken for human, buried, or tested chimera and left a mystery. "Not my chimera," Simon said to his bulldog, who looked up at him and huffed.

The next night, the chimera seemed to be still dead, but moved to a garbage barge out in the Hudson waiting for processing. *They check garbage for corpses more carefully than that in Manhattan. That's just his monitoring device.* Simon's abdominal muscles began their slow twist again.

He tried to call Lisa again, but her phone-answering machine still spoke in that low male voice. Simon worried now that he'd called her enough to trip the Agency phone monitor. He had no prearranged code for this, no innocuous words to exchange with those women if they tried to steal Billy.

Poor bastard, he thought of Billy. *Next weekend, I'll go hunting. Maybe Allesandra can help?* He'd meant to forget Allesandra after the

Agency fired her. *Seventeen years ago, Jesus, has it been that long?* But since she wasn't precisely legal, he might be able to get her to find which surgeon fixed ladies' secret chimeras.

Allesandra—he knew he'd have to report seeing her, though. And how had she aged after all those years? He hoped he wouldn't be aroused, knew she'd mock him if he were.

Billy woke up and felt the bullet hole—bullet dug out now, the hole patched. Celsa and a strange doctor sat watching him. The doctor got up when he opened his eyes—maybe I opened them too quickly, Billy thought, not taking time to listen while they thought I was asleep. He tried to lick his lips, but his tongue got stuck in his mouth. Celsa came over—she'd cut her hair—maybe passing for a man? She took a gourd and wet his mouth.

For a second the gourd looked transparent, like bendable glass, but then it was a solid gourd with a drinking straw in it. He sipped and got his tongue working again. "Thanks, Celsa."

"I'm not Celsa, really," she said.

Billy felt like a private earthquake twisted the bed. Not Celsa? He looked at her; maybe she wasn't Celsa? Her nose seemed to shift under his eyes, the skin tone lightened. "If you're not Celsa . . ." He wondered if he was dead and his mother right—demons about to torture him, but this was damn faint torture, except for the bullet hole. He tried again: "Who are you?"

"You don't need to know my name. Are you sure you're Billy the Kid?"

"William Bonney, Kid Antrim, whatever." He smiled at her rather than adding "so what?"

"Did it hurt when you died?"

Shit. He scooted back away from her even as doing that pulled at the wound. "Did I stay dead?"

"No."

He'd heard of premature burials, women mostly, scratching through the coffin boards to thrust a hand out of the grave dirt before they died for good. "Thanks for not burying me." He remembered something like floating in blood, though. "Is Old Woman Garrett still looking for me? Does he think I'm dead?"

The doctor muttered something at the woman in another language. German. Billy remembered Tunstall's cook speaking like that. The woman answered Billy, "You made a deal. You'd stay away. He'd say he'd killed you and collect the reward."

"He really shot me?"

The woman's eyes seemed to shine. "Yes." She barely breathed it. "He'll kill you if he sees you again. And his friend will kill you, too." She showed Billy a photo of a fat man with a high-bridged nose, sharp chin under the fat. Her hand went to Billy's shoulder, heating his skin through the sheet.

Billy smiled up at her and held the smile. He knew he was a charming bastard when he smiled and kept his lip down.

29

* * *

Simon spooled vast tracks of Colonel Navarez's memories into the imitation *federal*'s brain, hoping that he worked as alertly as ever. The chimera began to take on a grave but slightly confused courtesy when it was untanked—the real Navarez was back in Mexico City, detuning himself, becoming slightly scattered. Simon almost hoped they'd find out about Navarez's side trip to Washington. Then this chimera would be scrapped and Simon could go hunting Billy in New York. I'll go hunt him anyway over the weekend, Simon thought. He set the Navarez chimera back in the isolation tank for the weekend, for a weekend full of synthetic conferences with his Russian advisers—Andre Shchevek, Tomia Astrokova, Migma-fusion-generator specialists.

Two wiry marines checked Simon for contraband before he left Building 86. A cold world closing in on us, Simon thought as he boarded the New York City train in Langley station. He knew that the agency wouldn't understand that he'd always be loyal if they discovered that he'd broken their rules. He never broke the Agency's own rules, just those imposed on it by strangers.

I'd have to rent time on a DNA compiler to make a new Billy, can't chance using the Agency machines again, he decided as the train skimmed over Maryland, a hundred thousand greenhouses wheeling by outside the windows, flashing in the sunset. Then Pennsylvania dark—all tunnels, then night was outside. New Jersey refinery lights, twenty-four-hour culture vats glowed a second before the train fell back belowground.

Simon got out in New York's electric glare and stood on the cold pavement, wondering if Allesandra would even talk to him. As he hailed a cab, he realized he'd be safer if he abandoned the chimera and forgot about rebuilding a new Billy.

Billy wondered if he was drugged—Pat had told him about cactus buds Indians ate for visions. Somehow, this woman who held him locked up while he recovered from his gunshot wound fed him cactus buds—or was this whole episode just fever burning holes in his mind?

The woman smiled at him, but the smile seemed forced. She had her knees crossed high as if protecting her cunt. The light in the room was wrong—harsh yellow coming out of an oil lamp sitting by his bed. An insistent light, he thought.

"Where am I?" Billy asked. "You promised you'd tell me."

"New York City."

"Hell, I think I was born near New York City, Brooklyn, somewhere like that."

She looked like he'd said something wrong. The doctor came back in and pulled off his bandage. Billy looked at the wound, too, as he was familiar with them—healing nice, thanks, ma'am, and I must get going.

The woman said, "I thought you'd be different."

"I've been shot," Billy said, wondering why he couldn't remember how it happened, but then Pat had told him about the time he'd been shot, dumped against rocks, and lost two days—jostled in the brains. "I'm lots different when I'm not getting over being shot."

"Sure," the doctor said, fingers against his wrist. He then laid a tape against Billy's skin and seemed to read something off it while the woman got up and paced. "Lisa," the doctor said to the woman, "why don't you put him back where you found him?"

"Simon might make a scene."

"A $50,000-a-year government technician. Who cares?"

Billy felt insulted. Maybe they didn't realize how much better he felt. He moved and felt restraints at his wrists, waist, and ankles, bands of heavy cloth like linen canvas. Startled—*hey, these weren't here before*—he stiffened, then forced each muscle limp, a smile back over his teeth. Then he realized, $50,000 a year, that's a damn lot of money and these people were sneering at it. Better pay more attention, he thought, wondering if they were Europeans so rich that they joked at what Americans made. Tunstall—he was a damn rich Englishman before that sheriff's gang gunned him down.

Tunstall—that's why Billy was an outlaw. He felt almost as though he'd cry, confused by these people, his eyes hurting from the mad yellow light. "Who are you, Lisa? What do you do?"

"I'm rich," she said as if that explained everything.

Boyle stood by Dr. Allesandra Aul's buzzer on Mott Street, ginkgo trees half shading the entrance. Two small Chinese girls leaned against each other while they watched him, the stranger. Boyle wanted to flash his CIA card at them, call on the Secrets Acts, but on his business, he couldn't. He pushed Aul's buzzer and smiled at the two girls, who giggled.

Aul's lean wrinkled face appeared on the screen. She jerked her chin down when she recognized Boyle. He felt shocked to see how she'd aged. She could have preserved her skin. "Why and for what, Simon?"

"Can I come up? Or do you want to have lunch?"

"Come on, Simon, you haven't made this official." She smiled as though she knew what she'd do with that fact.

"I'm looking for someone who cut out a chimera's locator box. Personal service for a friend."

She said, "I don't believe you."

"Allesandra, I don't want to discuss this on the street."

Allesandra buzzed the door open. He decided he was stupid to even bother trying to find the Kid through outlaw surgeons. The KGB couldn't twist him; still he didn't want to have to explain to his superiors why he'd made Billy.

Allesandra's elevator, like a lady's glass phone booth, waited for him. He squeezed in on the little wire and blue velvet chair, breathing through his mouth to avoid the violet stink.

The cab rose through a Lucite tube, through three empty floors, the tube blackened on the third floor, then came up through the fourth floor and stopped. Simon opened the door and worked his way out while Allesandra watched from a desk. She wore pants.

"Simon, I wouldn't have thought you'd go illegal."

"Allesandra, I haven't."

"I've been running your voice through the breaker." She waved her hand at the gray metal box with three cathode tubes running sine waves every time she or he talked or breathed hard. Simon clicked his teeth together—if he had brought out a voice tamer, the marine guards would have found it and pried it none too gently off his vocal cords.

"It's an illegal chimera." Simon knew he could, bare-corded, beat some stress analyzers.

"A real problem?"

"I don't know yet."

"Oh, and you, not the Agency, needs my help. Simon, I only help other outlaws. So you're one now. And you cost me my job then."

He wouldn't reply to that. Coming to see her had been a big mistake, a huge mistake, more than building Billy.

She grinned suddenly like a little girl. "An illegal of who?"

"Billy the Kid. I did a lot of custom neuro-wiring. He's conceptually but not perceptually blind to anything like this." Simon waved his hand around the room, meaning it, the city, the twenty-first century.

She laughed. "Damn, Simon, not Colonel Oliver North, not anyone interesting like Idi Amin, just a dumb country killer faggot."

"He sired children on Mexican women."

"And you want to watch, you dumb bastard. And you came to me for help—me, after all you did to get me driven out of the Agency for—"

She'd built faces on the side, humans into other humans, and used the Agency files to build them new identities. Simon said, "Stop. Please, Allesandra."

"Can you deal for me if I find your chimera?"

Outlaws drag you down, Simon thought, into their stupid limited worlds. "I'll reward you if you find the chimera."

She turned off the breaker and said, "I'll hold you to that, Simon."

He said, "I'll keep in touch. Sedate and hold the chimera if you find him." Then Simon turned his back on her, the hairs on the nape of his neck stirring as though his body thought he'd done a dumb thing. He shrugged, knowing that she'd read the movement as tension reducing, and got in the elevator.

"Doing you a favor will be worth a lot to me,"

35

she said as the elevator sank down, carrying him away from her voice.

Simon remembered when she was a friend inside the Agency, when they'd worked together on imitations of women who'd had plastic surgery. Then, the Agency would have liked them to marry—security. Now, security considerations again, he shouldn't have come near her. But he'd done it. He bought jeans and a shirt on Fourteenth Street, held the bag away from his body until he could burn the clothes he had on when he went to see Allesandra. She had a fondness for tiny robot bugs. Then he showered. While he dressed, he considered using an encephalo-mixer, pins under his scalp around the hairline, the broadcast unit tucked in his jeans pocket. She couldn't track him by brain waves now, but he'd have also disappeared off the Agency map if they did a spot check, tapping his booster for a location check.

Simon went out again and took a cab to Rockefeller University, stood by the gate looking at the buildings, then went in to see the Agency resident.

As he walked toward the resident's office, he thought how stupid he'd been to build Billy, how trivial that seemed now.

It was his old boss Turner sitting in the office. Then Turner looked up at Simon; his narrow face seemed like a parchment mask. *Why are they all aging?* Simon knew Turner had applied for a transfer. "Turner, I didn't know you were resident here."

Turner said, "I like to keep up with the research without getting into the work myself."

Simon said, "I went to see Allesandra. I want to report myself."

"We know. Glad you came in. Sit."

"She tell you?"

"No, we tracked you. Random check."

"I miss her sometimes." Simon visualized her breasts as he spoke to control his voice. His heartbeats ticked faster in his ear.

Turner said, "There are other women in the Agency."

Simon sighed and asked, "Will this go on my file?"

Turner's eyelids drooped slightly but he didn't confirm verbally. Simon sighed and walked out.

Simon walked west. It's like a boy's game, Allesandra had told him before, when she trusted that he wouldn't turn her in—wrong, Allesandra, Simon thought. He began to look around him at the sleaze on this cross street, pasty-faced white girls—keyboard entry clerk, probably, marginally numerate—and the Europeans in silk and real wool grown on cultured sheepskins, buying up what of the island the Arabs and Japanese didn't already own. Two Jamaicans babbling in patois and eating Kung Po chicken out of plastic boxes nearly tripped him. *This I defend?* No, really, he wasn't working for them, but was he working for Turner?

He worked for the Agency, for the best of his kind. But he wanted to kill Billy, right then, on the street. An outlaw chimera, he could do it, too.

He should have resigned after he turned Allesandra—just wanting to be with her meant he was infected. She'd corrupted him seventeen years ago and the rot had been eating at him ever since. But Simon didn't want to give up being part of the Agency, knowing the facts behind the newscasts, seeing how long his creations fooled the other side.

A multisensory image of Billy the Kid filled Simon's mind, Billy asking *Quién es*, the smell of his sweat, his body lit by the gun flash. Falling, dead for real and forever.

Simon fought the idea that he'd gone rogue. *When the KGB come sniffing, if they come sniffing, then I'll see if I'm rogue.*

Billy decided Lisa and the doctor were insane, set upon him by Old Woman Garrett. Lisa teased him with hand strokes that he couldn't confuse for nursing touches, her bangs swinging down to her eyebrows, her gilded nails denting his skin at the end of each stroke.

"Can I walk around some?" he asked her. He told himself, Look sad.

She sighed and looked at the door as if a whole posse waited outside, then loosened the tapes holding him to the bed.

Billy sat up cautiously, feeling the wound pull, then asked, "Pants?"

She handed him long white cotton drawers and he pulled them on, then stood up and smiled at the notion that he needed to be modest before her. "And you're Lisa."

"No, I'm—"

"You're not Celsa. That's a fact we settled earlier." She looked at him as if a jealous husband stalked her. Billy added, "I'm quiet about my women."

She laughed. Insane, Billy decided as he walked up and down the floor. But he wasn't strong enough to leave quite yet.

Allesandra and Simon walked through Little Italy in a light rain, both of them in micropore suits, Simon still sweating. Allesandra wore an eye screen like a blown stretched bubble, both the nosepiece and the ear bows as transparent as the dome over both eyes. The windows were filled with *finocchio* stems and white cheese, chrome pasta machines, and avocado-and-blue-enameled microwave ovens. They didn't talk on the street, just walked. Allesandra led Simon to Ferrara's, neon glowing on a window full of cannoli, vats of gelato guaranteed to be made of true cow cream.

Simon sighed and smiled as he followed Allesandra through the Lucite door that slid into the wall for them. The mechanism was invisible, hidden with mirrors.

Allesandra bought an Italian ginger soda, then said, "I haven't heard anything. Perhaps you'd better forget him."

Simon looked at the pastries, thinking she'd brought him here so he couldn't press her, so he'd remember when they'd come here before. "They didn't have gelato before."

"It's excellent," Allesandra said. "Made out of honest cows."

"Clonal udder milk is biologically indis—"

She cut him off with, "I'd rather buy something from a happy beast than a brainless hunk of flesh."

"We can feed more people."

"I'm not 'more people.' I'm unique. I want my cream from an individual cow, Simon."

He thought, I'm the one eating ice cream. He told the clerk, "Two scoops of chocolate."

The clerk, a young man growing wispy black hairs on his upper lip, cut the gelato with a laser, two trapezoidal chunks. "That will be six dollars."

Simon could remember when it was two dollars, even more before the currency was adjusted. And laser chunking was techno-glitter overkill. He paid, then said to Allesandra, "I feel old."

"The Europeans sell cloned bodies," Allesandra said as if that wasn't done closer.

"You can't help me?"

"You want me to ask, draw attention?"

"You should still remember how to do that."

"Simon." She touched her eye shield, which immediately turned dark, reflecting a distorted Simon staring at her, and behind Simon, a man watching them. The next instant, Allesandra touched the shield back to transparency.

Simon felt hungry again. He wanted to shoot

Billy again. He wanted to go back in time to when Allesandra was innocent, at least by Agency standards.

"Okay, Allesandra," he said. He got up and left her there, hoping it was an Agency man watching, not KGB, especially not a chimera.

Outside Ferrara's, he caught a cab and went back to his hotel near the park and called his answering service. Lisa had left a New York number. He punched it, stomach cramping around undigested gelato.

"Hello?" It was Lisa's voice.

"Simon here." He almost punched the Agency code that would trace the number, then stopped himself.

"Oh, hell," she said, and hung up.

Simon knew she was having trouble with the chimera. He stripped to his shorts and sat on the edge of the bed, holding his knees.

The phone rang again, as Simon expected. He answered. Turner said, "Who was that?"

"Rich girl named Lisa Auschlander."

Turner didn't say anything immediately, a pause long enough to run several database scans. He finally said, "Too rich. Auschlander family bought free from media availability when they immigrated in the twenties."

Media invisibility created a haze of distorted information around the unavailables like the Schwartzchild radius around a black hole. Well, then, no newsbody would be likely to accidently find out Lisa had stolen a Billy the Kid—she wasn't a licensed target. Simon went through the exercises to control the vocal muscles, then said, "I don't know why she called me. I've done a little phallic engineering on a couple of rich women's chimeras, though."

Turner paused a long time. Simon visualized Turner's bony fingers keyboarding that datum against Simon's file, logging extracurricular activities when he found Simon had no permission for outside work. "Simon," he finally said before he hung up.

I can explain myself, Simon thought as he laid the phone back on the nightstand by the bed. He needed a bath now. His sweat had congealed to oil.

Billy's skin went to goose bumps when he looked out the window, but he didn't understand why—too foggy out there to see. Lisa was sleeping, curled up against the pillows as if they were his body. I'm in New York City, Billy's mind seemed to realize for him. Billy watched his thoughts as if they weren't his after that— *drugged, that must be it.*

Fog outside, drugs inside. He tried to open the window—something terribly wrong with opening the window. His hand cramped when he tried to pick up something to break it. *I have to go through the door.*

Billy opened the door and saw the doctor, gun in hand. The gun seemed to squirm when Billy grabbed it, shot at the doctor. No blood, Billy thought he'd missed, then the doctor began babbling, "Overdose, you fool, get Lisa . . . don't want to die," as he sank to the floor.

Billy felt as much as heard Lisa coming up behind him. Still holding the gun, he jumped over the doctor, found the exit, and went running downstairs while alarms rang like a million bells strung to the steps. He never knew there could be so many floors, so many stairs, so much noise. When he reached the ground floor, he stopped behind the door, hurting where the doc had taken the bullet out. Now, Billy felt stupid, shooting that doctor. *I lost my patience—I don't want to get hanged for losing my patience.*

But Lisa and the doctor had strapped him to the bed long after when he wasn't going to roll out wound-groggy. The noise stopped, but Billy stayed put.

A man stuck his head in through the door and Billy grabbed him, rammed the man's head against the wall. He didn't remember pulling up the zipper when he switched clothes with the man. Suddenly he was dressed. He walked quickly through the door into a huge hotel lobby, more lights than he'd imagined there was kerosene for, blow out all the air burning that much gas. He saw the street and walked out into it.

Billy hired a carriage with the money from the man he'd stripped and went down a roaring stone road.

* * *

Lisa, hysterical, called Boyle in Richmond on Tuesday and said that the chimera had hired a carriage in Central Park and then disappeared above Harlem. Boyle thought New York, massive cognitive dissonance, would drive the chimera crazy.

The Kid got between an Anglo man and his woman as they got to the streetcar, knowing the man would push by him. The dip would have worked easier with a partner, but he managed to get the man's wallet and wiggled between the Indians and Mexicans to get off. Let the lard-ass sweat it. Now he looked for a train, saw lots more telephones than there'd been in New Mexico. Odd thing, telephones. He picked one up and asked the woman to connect him with the train station.

"Amtrak, can I help you please." The voice sounded the same as the operator's—expressive, but the same expressions.

"I want to go to Albany," Billy told her.

"Trains to Albany leave from Grand Central . . ."
Upstate, the Adirondacks, Canada. One of the train stations the woman mentioned wasn't far, 125th Street. He opened the wallet he'd stolen and got rid of the identification, then began walking.

On the way to Albany, his mind kept cutting in and out, but his body knew how to handle everything.

CHAPTER TWO
Found As a Transient

Mr. McSween wrote a note to the officer in charge asking what the soldiers were placed there for. He replied saying that they had business there; that if a shot was fired over his camp or at Sheriff Peppin or any of his men he would blow the house up; that he had no objection to Mr. McSween blowing up his own house if he wanted to do so. I read the note; Mr. McSween handed it to me to read. I read the note myself. I seen nothing further of the soldiers until night. I was in the back part of the house when I escaped from it. Three soldiers fired at me from the Tunstall store—from the outside corner of the store. That is all I know in regard to it.

The Kid's testimony
The Dudley Inquiry; May 25, 1879

BILLY NEVER HAD A HOME FROM THE DAY HE broke jail over stolen laundry when he was still Henry. But I managed, Billy thought. He closed his eyes as soon as the train left the Bronx. If law was on the train, or waiting for him in Albany, nothing to do about it right now. Before he went to sleep, he realized that this was the smoothest train he'd ever been on. Making progress in the east, obviously. He sighed, remembering blown sand gritting up his town clothes. He always preferred to change from workclothes to a linen suit and straw hat when he came into Fort Sumner. As fresh as a bandbox, Paulita Maxwell told him, her a friend of his and Pat Garrett's, scared of him the first time they met until Billy smiled.

She was warning him now in his dreams, saying, *Billy, Billy, you don't really even know Pat.*

His half-Mexican daughters looked up from the grinding stones their mothers trained them to.

Billy woke with a start and saw mountains on the other side of the river. Wrong side of the river for Albany, he thought, and sat in the seat wondering if he'd been tricked. *I've never really been to New York as a man. Things change.* Out on the river, he saw goose decoys and men in rowboats behind brush, waiting. *It was so cold in Texas.*

And the train hardly touched the rails. Didn't touch the rails at all.

Billy sweated when he realized that, but then relaxed. Too many people on the train for it to be a trick. A new eastern thing, quiet-running trains. He remembered a black soldier, one of Colonel Dudley's men, singing a minstrel song, "Pompey Smash, the Ever-living and Unconquerable Screamer," or was it "Unconderable Skreamer"? What did those people mean in secret by going at the letters that way? Billy could identify with "ever-living" and "unconquerable," but he didn't understand "unconderable" and the "k."

And had Pat shown him the music or had he taken him to the show? David Crockett was involved. One of his Mexican women said that Crockett had tried to talk his way out of being killed and her kin had wanted to let him live, but another Mexican pushed a saber through

Crockett's belly and so what was there to do but finish the old guy off? Billy had never heard such a story from Americans.

Shit, my folks came over from Ireland just before I was born. How did I get fucked up in these American legends? That damn Wallace with his eye on the eastern press, riding west in dead-silent trains.

Billy jerked and realized he'd almost fallen back asleep. He stretched and looked around. Somehow he knew the town the train was going through was Hudson, then he realized a voice was whispering the town's name through something like a telephone.

Fog masked Hudson. The train ghosted through. Billy saw some clear patches of red-brick buildings, an odd fog at their bases.

Pat once said something about Irish always being the ones for cattle raids. *I don't want to be caught in a damn-fool Irish legend, either.*

The telephone voice whispered, "Albany–Rensselaer station in five minutes. Passes to the Adirondack Preserve needed for further travel."

Billy jerked when he heard that, turned, and saw the grille the voice came from. Passes in America? Or did some rich eastern man own all the Adirondacks now? He'd have to find folks in Albany to tell him how to get around the patrols. Nobody was rich enough to fence one-fifth of a whole state.

The train stopped inside a series of hoops. Billy wondered if anyone was going to notice that he had no luggage. He opened the wallet he'd stolen and saw that he had about five dollars, some cards made of celluloid, but better, flexible, and coins so fake it was embarrassing that he'd used them earlier—celluloid, rigid this time.

Five dollars, he thought, should hold him a couple of days. He got off the train and looked for a stagecoach. His body twisted him away from the buses. Other people were walking. He began walking, mind cutting in and out, but that didn't seem unusual to Billy.

His visual cortex found the bridge but didn't relay any information to his consciousness until it identified the pedestrian and bike way. Billy began walking toward Albany, small trains whizzing by him on the bridge. Where do you get on those? he wondered.

And Albany's towers looked so far away, then suddenly close and preposterously huge, surrounded by small buildings. Billy shuddered and didn't quite know why. He walked off the bridge and began trudging up the hill toward what looked like a capitol building. He was so hungry now he had a headache. His eyes didn't seem to want to look at the huge towers. He went to the right of them, by the state house, looking at the policemen, one on a horse, chatting around it, feeling very lonely. *Maybe I should have stayed with the woman?*

He went in the first scruffy-enough bar with lots of glass windows, sat where he could see what was happening on the street, and opened the menu—a steak was $6.98. *Oh, shit, I'll have to do something.*

The waitress, a fat woman in white, stopped in front of him and he ordered a ham sandwich on rye, with lettuce and cheese, no tomato. That was $2.59. She put a cup of coffee in front of Billy. He hoped that was free. If the waitress had been younger, he'd have tried to talk his way into more food, a place to stay, but fat and that age, she'd be mean.

"Where does a man find a room around here?" Billy said when she put the sandwich in front of him.

"What can you afford?"

"Not much, judging from these prices."

"You a man?"

"Yes." He gave her what had always proved to be a woman-snagging smile. Maybe he could manage with her.

"Go to the Sallies if you're human and broke."

"Sallies?"

"Salvation Army."

Billy ate his sandwich without replying. Salvation Army—religious people would turn him in if they knew he was wanted.

Another man came in, ragged and smelly. He didn't sit down on a stool, but said, "Sis, you have anything?"

The waitress pulled a bag out of the icebox and handed it to the man, who opened it and said, "Thanks."

"Don't mention it," the waitress said in an

almost nasty voice. Then she said, "Maybe you know where someone can sleep if mention of the Sallies makes him nervous?"

"Him?" The ragged man looked at Billy. "You?"

"Yes."

"I don't want to see you in here again," the waitress said as she took Billy's money and gave him back change. "Only Al comes in here. Understand."

Al said, "Bad for business."

Billy said, "Looks like a dive to me," but he was on his way out.

Al opened the bag again and pulled out a half-eaten roll and began eating it. He thrust the bag toward Billy, who was still hungry but not for what looked like pig slops.

"I'm fine."

"How much you get?"

"What?"

"Got, then. Sis knows a wrong wallet when she sees one. So do I, but I'm short registered transients this week."

"What are these good for?" Billy slid the celluloid cards out of the wallet and showed them to Al.

"Dumb," Al said. "They're credit cards. You want to throw them off with the wallet 'cause sometimes the cops can track with them." He took the credit cards and melted them with a little torch he had in his pocket. "Stealing cards looks good short-term, but ... what is your name?"

52

"William Mayo," Billy said, substituting one Irish County for another. "Billy."

"Okay, Billy. I ain't gonna map your jeans and I don't want to know anything. But you don't steal from us, and you throw wallets straight out."

Al didn't look like he had enough for a pack-rat to steal. "I can live with that. And I can handle punks." Map his jeans indeed.

"It's gone get damn cold soon," Al said.

"I'm trying to get to Canada."

"Canada's all froze."

"I need a horse."

Al stopped and stared at Billy. "A horse? What kind of horse?"

"Getaway horse. To the Adirondacks and then to Canada."

"If they thought it was a moose, might get through the sensors." Al started walking around a block, then around it again.

Billy said, "Nobody following us."

Al said, "Good. I don't want another transient boss to pick up the squat." He swung up three boards and sidled through sideways. Billy came in after him. City backside—all tiny windows, boards, alleyways, and manholes. Al pried up a ground-level grate and went down it. Billy heard a sound like water splashing, looked down, heard Al breathing heavy just beyond the square lit by the grate hole. There was a creek down under the city. He lowered himself, fingers holding the edge of the hole, then dropped, splashing. Al nodded and put his pointing finger to his lips. *Shush.*

Moss grew on the walls as far as the light went. The water chilled Billy's feet through his thin shoes. Al began walking upstream. Just as Billy worried about moving through the dark, Al opened a door and motioned Billy through.

"What can you do for us?" Al asked after he locked the door and lit a lamp.

"Do for you?" Billy said.

"Work. There's a day hire in Colonie, breakdown work."

"I've got—"

"Nothing." Al sucked his teeth and looked at Billy a minute. Billy remembered Windy Cahill beating his head on the floor of that bar in Camp Grant and calling him a pimp. He may have blubbered like a girl first, but he killed Cahill for that.

Al looked away, then said, "We don't just run a charity here. If you can't help one way, then there's another."

"I had a misunderstanding with the law."

"We've all had misunderstandings with the law. You had stolen credit cards. If that's what you want to do, we can improve your craft."

"Pickpocket."

"You need a bit more . . ."

Billy's ears didn't pick up what the man was saying, something about . . . telephones. "Sorry."

"Com . . ." and Al's voice turned into babble.

"Don't make fun of me."

"Where are you from?"

"New York City."

The door opened and a middle-aged man came in leading an old one. "Al, who's this?" the middle-aged man said.

"Billy," Al said. "Billy, this is Sid and Frank."

"Okay," Sid said. "What does he do?"

"Boosts, but real sloppy."

"Oh, shit." Sid, the middle-aged man, eased the old man, Frank, into a ratty chair and caressed his shoulder before putting down a bag that clinked.

Billy froze. Had he or hadn't he seen men who . . . pimp? He said, "I can do some carpentry."

"You alone?" the old man Frank said.

"Yeah."

"It's rough when you're alone and my age." He turned blued filmy eyes toward Sid.

Sid said, "We try to take care of each other, stay out of the home, don't take refuge with the damn Buddhists. They make you sit half a day, break your knees. But safer to work honest than to steal."

"If folks will let me," Billy said.

Al said, "He doesn't have cards."

"Cards?"

"No ID. No identification."

"Looks like a man," Sid said. "Sosha's not back yet?"

"It's her hospital day," Al said.

"Damn, I am a man," Billy said.

Al said, "He thinks he's a man."

Sid said, "Al, can you get him checked? Or

55

would it be safer to tell the pound we have no way to type him if he does turn out to be a dog-meat robot."

Billy sat down on the damp floor and hugged his knees. What was this gibberish, *dog*, *meat*, *ro* . . . He heard his lips going *bup*, *bup*, *bup*, softly, air exploding between them in little bursts. He was scared and couldn't understand why.

Frank said, "I think he's like Sosha. Get him registered with Out Services."

Al said, "Billy, we'll try you on the labor pool, okay, but we've got to get you a usable ID card. We'll take out for that from your first check."

Billy knew he'd get gypped, but nodded. He needed a few days to figure things out. Then someone banged on the door and he heard a woman's voice saying, "Damn key got away from me. Damn key."

Sid unlocked the door and a skinny woman with black hair too bright and uniform to be a natural color and black paint around her green eyes came in. She looked to Billy like an aging whore, skin on her face dried up to fine wrinkles, not grooved deep yet. "They wouldn't give me Mohawk Electric credit, but I got stamps. My God, they've sent a spy."

"No, Sosha, it's Billy."

"Billy the Kid, oh, my damn."

Billy stiffened, then cursed himself for showing sign. The men stared at him as if he had suddenly grown a wolf's muzzle. Al asked, slowly, "Do you think you're Billy the Kid?"

"I told you I was Bill Mayo."

Sosha said, "He's got that jaw, the eyes. I've seen pictures." She sounded disturbingly educated.

"Billy, it doesn't matter." Al smiled, but his face muscles moved phony.

Frank said, "What kind of Billy the Kid does he think he is?" He frowned at Sid as though the younger man had betrayed him somehow.

"Okay, I am Bill Antrim. I've got lawyers in New Mexico, but Governor Wallace—"

Sosha said, "We'll be happy together, Billy. You're psychotic, too."

"Don't believe the damn newspapers."

Al said, "But, Billy, now, do you think you might could try . . ."

. . . and it all turned to gibberish. He signed something in blood, more gibberish.

When Al, Sid, and Billy went to clear the rubbish in Colonie, Billy picked up trash that the machines missed. The boss paid them in food stamps and a Mohawk Electric credit letter, scrip it appeared to Billy.

Al took the credit letter and said to Sid, "Now we can get the lights back."

Billy wondered what they were talking about, but the next night, after another day of work in Colonie, he noticed ten kerosene lamps burning, odd lamps that seemed to shift form when you looked at them.

"I've always had funny eyes," Billy said, sitting around a table with them eating lentils and rice.

Al asked, "How so?"

"The lamps look funny. The cookstove. Fuzzy outlines."

"You're getting cataracts," the old man Frank said.

Sosha, who'd taken care of Frank while they worked, said, "Nonsense, he's just a little crazy."

Sid chewed his lentils.

Sunday, nobody worked. "Why do you live here?" Billy asked Al. "With them."

"They're my people," Al said. "Just like you are."

"Haven't been anybody's people since Tunstall died. People were mine."

"Well, Billy, this is the way it works in Albany."

"I've got to be moving on. To Canada, Mexico."

"Billy, I don't think you understand what was done to you if you're not crazy."

"What do you mean what was done to me?"

"It isn't the 1880's."

"Yeah. When is it?"

"2067."

All his being nice comes to this. Al was trying to drive him crazy. "You think I'm like Sosha?"

"Yeah, and you'd bring a little more to the arrangement if you registered with Out Services."

"Well, Al." Billy started out to see if he could find a horse, saddled and bridled, then a gun. Al watched him leaving without saying more.

The alley was full of snow. Billy stared at it and wondered how much worse it would be north. He came back in and said, "It's snowing already."

"Billy, you want me to take you to Out Services. You don't know Albany."

"I guess."

"In the morning, then." Al stared at the floor as he spoke. When he looked up, his eyes dodged around. Billy knew how to keep his face innocent. *Al's going to betray me. I need a gun.*

Sosha came back then carrying dresses and pants. "From the church," she said.

"I guess we could do worse," Al said.

Sosha said, "Al, why aren't you doing better?"

Al shrugged. Billy thought about the snow in the alley, snow falling all the way to the North Pole. He went up to Sosha and began picking through the clothes she'd brought, looking for the warmest pants. Sosha put her hands over her ears and started muttering to some demon talking only to her.

Sid and Frank didn't come back that night. Al said, "Probably won't be working in Colonie tomorrow."

That's okay, Billy thought, I'm going to find a gun and move on.

Billy walked out into the grinding blizzard full of boxcars and balloons. He shivered, then the snow dropped, clearing the sky. There were blimps in the sky and steam machines off rails shoving the show aside with push blades. *Damn fool to stay with these people so long*. He looked behind and saw holes in the snow where he'd walked.

Al came out behind him and stopped about fifteen feet away. Billy wondered if he was looking vicious now, because Al pulled his hands out of his pockets and didn't say anything.

"I'm stir-crazy," Billy said.

Al said, "We're not holding you prisoner."

"I don't think you could," Billy said. He turned and listened hard between his own steps for snowflakes shifting in boot-rim-sized masses.

"Billy," Al said, "what are you looking for?"

"Horse."

"You must know you can't get a horse."

"Aren't there any livery stables?"

"Billy, people don't ride horses in Albany."

Billy turned and saw that Al hadn't moved. "Cops have them. I saw."

"Billy, I like taking care of people. But I can't take care of you if you're going to act crazy."

"Why can't I act crazy if everyone thinks I am? And if Pat Garrett's coming to try to kill me, how you gonna stop him?"

"I had you tested, cheap test, doesn't say anything except if the man's full human. You aren't. Some people feel like they can shoot things like you at will."

"What kind of test? You calling me a thing?" The word "test" wobbled in Billy's mind— testing a man's nerve, then some weird chemical meaning bubbled up like something he shouldn't remember. Blood in glass vials— screams. A metal tube with edge honed to glitter coming at him, eyes froze open.

"Billy, you're not . . ."

And Billy couldn't hear what Al said, couldn't make it out, and was terrified of the words he couldn't hear.

"A block, I guess," Al said.

"What did you say to me, pimp?"

"You can't hear what I said about the test."

"You mumbled. You're trying to drive me crazy."

"Billy, it's all right. You work like a man. Don't you remember who shot you? Where it happened?"

"What's all right? Driving me crazy, *puto?*"

"Billy, I won't turn you in for the bounty."

"Damn Wallace. Damn federal marshals, journalists. Garrett shot me. Celsa saved me, got me to a doctor."

"Come on. We don't need this out in public."

Billy walked on. He looked back and Al had disappeared. Suddenly he felt very lonely, cold. He saw a Catholic church and wondered how many Mexicans and Irish lived in Albany. His family had been Irish, had they been Catholic? A hundred years back?

White blank.

* * *

Billy watched three policemen on horses by the state house, not quite sure when he realized where he was. One of the mounted police came toward Billy. The gelding he rode stopped to knock its hoof tips against the ground as snow balled up in its feet. "Lost?" the black policeman said in a voice that didn't sound like a freedman's even though he was in his forties.

"I'm okay."

"ID."

Billy handed him the card Al gave him to show to the bosses at Colonie, wondering if Al'd reported him by now. *Which is when, now?* He couldn't remember how long he'd been walking. The black cop looked at the card. The other cops had gotten their horses' hocks under them, ready. He wondered if the gelding would manage good under a new rider.

"Drifter, registered for transient work?"

"Yeah, I guess." Billy felt pissed at Al.

"At Al's. So we know where to look for you."

"How did you know that?"

"Code on it. You wanta freeze, staring at us."

"I really like horses."

The cop handed Billy back his card and said, "Al sure picks some funny ones."

Billy faked a stumble, flop into the snow. As soon as the cop swung off his horse, Billy grabbed him and kicked for his balls, swinging up, and grabbed the reins as the man jerked. As Billy swung into the saddle, the two other cops pulled out nightsticks and said, "Freeze." Billy whipped the horse, but it wouldn't move. *Damn horse to hell freeze.* The cop he'd kicked stood up, darker than ever. The other two cops pulled out nightsticks and rode up to him.

"He did it, didn't he?" one of the other mounted cops said.

"Yeah."

The nightstick grazed Billy as he ducked. Still it jolted him out of the saddle. Billy didn't understand why. The cop he'd kicked slammed his nightstick between Billy's legs, an ordinary pain, then twisted the nightstick handle and blew Billy away.

When Billy woke up, he wasn't shot, but he was back at Al's, Sosha wiping blood off his head. Al sat in a chair, not giving straight eyes to the black cop. "Explain to him we don't jail drifters in Albany," the black cop was saying.

Billy said, "You shot me."

"No, shocked you, but you have been shot recently, haven't you? We got no record of gunshooting problems on the cop net. You work, you collect crazy stamps, I don't care, but don't you ever try to steal even a slice of bread in Albany or we'll break both your arms. Al, where did you get this one?"

"Asked me for help off the street. I was lowhanded."

"You bonded for him if he ain't human?"

Billy's brain threw him pictures he couldn't remember seeing—weirdly shaped railroad cars, metal and glass, rolling on fat rubber tires in the street, a big metal car with wings, a glass holding a glowing wire. *Maybe I am crazy, just like Sosha*. Insanity explained enough, too much. He felt suddenly humbled.

Then Billy looked at Al and realized he hadn't answered the cop's question.

Billy licked his lips and said, "I'm not even sure who I am."

The cop said, "And you don't smell quite right."

Sosha said, "He's putting sex hexes on me, but the medicine saves me."

"Al, don't suppose you've run his DNA?" the cop said.

Al said, "He's got a drifter reissue ID, doesn't he?"

The cop stood up, leather belts creaking. "Appears like it." He pulled out his nightstick and added, "If he is chimera, he ought to go to a Dharma refuge if he doesn't want the pound to pick him up." Billy saw blood dried on the stick's metal tip.

"Shaka, that's bad as jail," Sosha said. "He's just crazy like me."

"Well, register him at Out Services." The cop stared at Billy as though he was a dog, then left.

Billy began sweating worse after the cop left. He didn't want to know what a Dharma refuge was, was terrified someone would explain it to him and drive him to screaming.

Al said, "I don't know what I'm going to do with you now."

Sosha said, "You're so scared, Billy. People hunting for you that did that?" She pulled down the sheet covering him and stared at the scar.

Billy heaved himself up on his elbows and looked at his own flesh twisted like he'd been melted in one spot. "Don't really know. Al, I ought to leave."

Sosha said, "Billy, psychosis hurts more than the drugs do. But you didn't shoot yourself and stitch yourself up, did you?"

"You both think I'm crazy even if I was really shot?"

They nodded. Al said, "If the cops don't have a record of a recent shooting, it was too private to be safe for you, Billy."

"Shit." His balls ached, his head ached. "What is Out Services? Do we have to go right now? Can they help me?"

"They just stabilize you," Sosha said as she shook her head. Al didn't look at him, but instead pulled out a bottle and poured shots for each of the three of them.

"You've done that lots. Were you a bartender?" Billy asked.

"Once," Al said.

The sounds outside had disappeared as though snow completely covered the walls. Sosha brought Billy's glass over to him and he sat up to drink it, feeling it bite, a shudder going up. "What sort of refuge? Why's that like jail?"

"Buddhist," Al said.

Billy trembled. "No."

Al said, "You've got a block against that, don't you, you poor bastard?"

I'm crazy, gone crazy, and what can I do? Mexicans screamed. Pat Garrett kept him in irons. And the train kept rocking down to the hanging ground. Billy looked back outside his memories and saw Al and Sosha waiting for him to start screaming. The scream came up his throat and he wanted to step outside his body and deny any of this was happening.

Frank and Sid came in then, so snow-covered that Billy stopped screaming, wondering for a second if they'd died and were ghosts.

"Al, you've got to get rid of him," Sid said.

Billy thought Sosha would speak up for him, but she nodded. "He's scary. Too scary."

"I'm just . . . Jesus, Mother Mary, you can't just throw me out."

Sid said, "Nobody is supposed to re-create outlaws."

Al said, "Billy, I don't think I can explain this to you." He poured himself another drink, wrist twisting just so to stop the drips. "But, since you worked good for me, I'll try."

Billy's eyes seemed to refocus. Wires in glass, carbon arc lights, celluloid floors. Al's words burbled out as though his lips had been knifed. "Dog-meat robot . . . Buddhist temples . . . only place that makes sense for you, Billy. We can take you there."

Images of smoky idols, knives, screaming blood spouts out of Billy's throat. He vaguely heard Al say, "Damn, he's been conditioned or wired against it."

Billy began running through the snow, seeing metal shapes on the roads that he felt had always been there, then they twisted into buckboard wagons and coaches with carbon arc headlamps.

Slow down, Pat Garrett seemed to be saying inside his head, *or you really will go crazy.*

Lies, all lies, Al's lies, Pat's lies. He took out the identity card Al'd gotten for him and tried to tear it up, but it wouldn't tear, instead bloodied his fingers. He found a tree near the gray mass of the capitol building and leaned against it, taking deep breaths and trying to calm himself down. The Helderburgs, I saw them from Colonie. I can walk to there, hide until I can steal a horse. He straightened up, wiped his fingers on the snow, and dropped the identity card in a post box.

Then he began walking west, on cleared sidewalks, slush between them and the road, straight up Western Boulevard. The sun was rising and he realized how tired he was, how his bloody fingers scared the shop owners as they came to open their shops. He stopped in front of a store full of furniture he thought he recognized and was shocked to see how old a wooden bed looked—not painted as it was when new, but raw battered oak with powderpost beetle holes.

Crazy. Crazy or not, he had to get out of town. The law knew him here. And Pat Garrett would kill him rather than take him in. No asylum for Billy. He brushed snow off a bench and sat down. His cuts stung but didn't reopen and he licked the rest of the blood off.

A huge shifting shape, a boxcar sliding uphill,

stopped in front of him, hissing. A door opened in it. Billy saw a man sitting in front look down at him, then the door, glass-misted, closed again and the thing went rolling off again. As the thing stopped again, Billy decided it was a one-car train. Billy realized he was broke and the hopelessness of it—no gun, no money, no horse, no sanity—hit him.

But I don't give up.

A small steam thing rolled up to him and its driver asked, "Refuge?"

"Buddhist?"

The man nodded and Billy began running. Ten blocks later, something tripped him and he fell, feeling his lips go numb against the cold pavement, unable to move. Men stood around him talking. He feared they had shot him in the spine. *Paralyzed and with the pain to come or am I dying?*

"Jail first for processing," he heard someone say. The men lifted him into a gray wagon. Billy felt himself still breathing but couldn't consciously change the pattern. Then a prick of something against his arm and he stopped worrying. Odd to be dying and not worrying about it, he thought. He waited for the trocar to hit his neck but the truck lurched back into traffic as another one of the men put a blanket over him.

The truck pulled into the basement of a building and a man came down and pricked his finger. "He looks familiar," he said.

Why can't I worry? He heard that Tom

O'Folliard had died, teased by Garrett's men who'd played poker as Tom bled to death. He could almost see it, Garrett's eyes, Tom's eyes.

The black policeman who'd beaten him said, "Al admits this guy didn't have even a transient card when they first met."

The man who thought Billy looked familiar said, "He doesn't test human, so take him to the pound. They can trace the DNA to registry there."

Better to be crazy than dog meat. Dog meat.

CHAPTER THREE

The Purgatory Loop
for Nineteenth-Century Eyes

His gun
            does not shoot real bullets
                                    his death
Being done is unimportant.

Jack Spicer, "Billy the Kid"

WHEN THE ALARM BUZZED, JANE AYERS, WHO'D been awake for the past fifteen minutes, stopped imagining Paris in the 1920's. Her duty at the Abandoned, Abused, and Runaway Chimera Holding Facility started at ten. That Monday morning, the mahogany ceiling with all its boxy angles looked perfect.

How fortunate, she thought, that I'm really literate and have this ceiling to live under.

Like wood jewels, the step pyramids of mahogany dangled from the 1906 ceiling over her one-room apartment, which had been the main parlor until the 1930's depression. On the first Sunday of every month, Jane washed her ceiling with oil soap, then buffed it, working the buffer into every angle. Staring up at it now the day after, she turned on the floor heat, turned off her blanket, and decided she could spend a few minutes being a 1920's rich girl, back from Paris after an unfortunate affair with Picasso. While the room warmed up, she could almost hear the art-deco parties held under the ceiling in its past.

When the temperature reached fifty-five, the thermostat chimed. Jane got up and dressed quickly in long underwear and the Society's uniform, gray rip-proof canvas like a twentieth-century prison jumpsuit. She pulled her winter uniform jacket on over that, but still shivered. *Better get moving.* The stun stick she'd smuggled from work was in her jacket pocket. She wrapped her fingers around that and decided to walk through Washington Park.

Jane blinked at the sky as she left her building. After she walked through Washington Park, she went down a flight of rough cement stairs between hideous twentieth-century megalithic memorials to the third Rockefeller generation. Skaters screamed on a rink set between the huge buildings, cement with frost slabs broken down around them. A crew up on nylon rigging worked at one building face. One of the guys shouted at Jane, "Steal me a girl one, babe," but Jane kept walking and went through maze gates, showed her ID to the door computer, who let her into a small building, mid–twenty-first-century nondescript, on the Hudson.

Why is my job turning into such a bore? she asked herself. When Jane was in high school, the chimera cause appealed to her enough to take the SPCA scholarship. Lately, she wondered if she had been less compassionate than rebellious. Chimeras baffled her. They liked their owners now. Ten years ago when the SPCA got more escaped chimeras, the brain work or DNA had left more behavioral margins. Now, chimeras too often flaunted their elegant clothes and extravagant lives to the pound workers. Modern chimeras understood that humans bred and raised each other cheap enough for routine work. *Them and the rich against the sleaze.* If Jane hadn't joined the SPCA, she'd have never met either—just seen them on TV. Most times, the rich with their chimeras traveled behind one-way glass.

Jane climbed the stairs, switched the computer from voice to alphanumeric, and popped the night log up on the desk terminal. Luna had come back at 4:30 A.M.

"Carl, what's with Luna?" Jane asked one of the wardmen. *Maybe I should steal her for that workman,* she thought.

"Owner pulled a fang while they were both drugging. With pliers. She brought the pliers, not the tooth, dumb bitch."

"Why doesn't she ask us to get a sell order on her?"

"Maybe now. She's upset good."

"Don't order her a goddamn new fang on SPCA expense." Jane checked over the other entries and saw four abandoneds. *Poor bastards, that's the only sad thing left that the builders can't modify—abandonment.* Jane wondered if they could trick the Buddhists at Livingston Manor into taking a couple more senile flesh toys. Then she went into Luna's room.

The chimera lay on her belly with her head turned to one side. Luna looked like a completely human woman who'd been beaten—jaw swollen, black hair tangled down her back—more beautiful than most humans, though. She was asleep in satin play clothes, her hands balled into fists, one arm bent back and down toward the foot of the bed, the other almost touching her swollen mouth. Jane thought she was asleep at first, then heard-saw Luna's eyes were open, silently oozing tears.

Compassion, Jane reminded herself. "What did he do?"

Luna rolled over and bared her teeth. One canine was like a vampire fang; where the other should have been was a black socket. Then Luna began to sob and reached for Jane like a little child.

Jane held her, careful not to touch Luna's jaw on the injured side. Under the sobs, she heard Luna saying, "Andy, Andy, Andy," the owner's name. Jane didn't like learning owners' names, but Luna had been in quite a lot.

"Luna, take refuge in the Dharma. Or at least, let us get a sell order."

Luna moaned and shook her head.

Jane figured Luna was as crazy as her owner—one would kill the other someday. If Luna killed Andy, she'd get a lethal needle. If

Andy killed her, he'd lose the insurance he carried on her, but the police would refund the peace bond he'd put up for her. "Why do you come here?" Jane meant, *Why do you use us?*

Luna pulled out of Jane's arms and smiled, her wretched tooth bared. "It's the only way I have to really scare him."

Jane decided to ask for a sale order anyway. Wouldn't get it if the judge was Corning; would if it were Bruce. She got up to go, but Luna held her and mumbled through her broken mouth, "Fix my tooth?"

"No, Luna, not unless you let us try to get you away."

Her eyes slitted, Luna stared at Jane as if to remind her how much more care went into chimera births than humans, how much more beautiful she was than Jane. Jane tried to feel sorry for Luna, gave up, even more determined to ask for a resale order just to piss off Luna and her owner.

Compassion; they're not responsible for what they are. Jane shook her hands, then her arms, to loosen the tension in her body. Then she saw three wardens leading a human-looking chimera. New York Capitol District cops followed them in.

The chimera could have been a man, vagrant, face bruised or frostbitten, fingers cut. But then Jane noticed the exaggerated buckteeth and the gray eyes. Looking in the eyes was like looking into fog with sun behind it—deep eyes, glowing. But the chimera moved almost as though he were blind. He looked absolutely wretched, smelly.

"He'd been working recon job on a false human ID and squatting with a transient boss on Ten Broek. But he's got skull electronics and the DNA brand is classified," one of the cops said. "And he's recovering from heart-region gunshot."

CIA? FBI? Why would anyone build a chimera for espionage in that shape? Jane wondered. "Have you—"

"We got in touch with Langley, but they claimed he wasn't theirs. Man named Turner at Rockefeller University called back, though, and asked for a DNA full read."

"They didn't want him back?"

"No. He can't see right. If he was a man, I'd say he was hallucinating."

"Programmed vision?" Jane took the chimera's head between her fingers and looked at him. "Do you understand English?"

"And Spanish, ma'am," he said. "My muscles jog me around like there was barriers I can't see." He looked down at her pants. "I can't make out the details of your dress. Al told me I'd gone crazy. I think I may have gone crazy. Pat Garrett . . ." He stopped as if he'd said too much.

"Do you think you're a man?"

"Why, yes, well, I'm young, but I've shot fellows." He groaned and looked back at the cops when he said that. "In self-defense. I say stupid things like I'm made to."

The cops, the pound wardens, and Jane froze. "Where?" she asked the chimera.

"In the guts. I use either a self-cocker forty-one or a straight forty-four chambered for rifle slugs to be sure they stay down. But it was self-defense. I am crazy. I can't be crazy now."

"Where? Town, state?"

"New Mexico Territory, ma'am. Lincoln County. I'm crazy or I'm dead. Something's happened to my eyes." He reached up with delicate hands, smaller hands than a man should have. Jane wondered how he managed to wrap them around a .44-caliber pistol; where would a chimera find such a weapon? Was the chimera confabulating, or conditioned in a holo-tank to remember imaginary gun battles?

If he was a CIA duty chimera gone AWOL, then a CIA assassin chimera was coming to kill him. Jane resented the cops for bringing this lethal thing to her quiet pound. "Well," she said, "you're in Albany, New York, now."

"I know I'm in Albany 'cause I took a train and walked across a bridge. Some say I was born in New York City," he said. "I didn't remember the New York City I left. I got a terrible memory. I'm under arrest, ain't I?" He began sweating.

"Let's call it protective custody," she said. "Where did you grow up?"

"I don't remember." He smiled at her—suddenly the eyes seemed more blue than gray—lips tight over the buckteeth. "Why am I here? You people paralyzed me and I don't remember much after that. Damn. I've got a lawyer, A. J. Fountain, out west, New Mexico, if that isn't crazy."

"What were you doing out on the street?"

"Has Pat Garrett telegraphed you? Governor Wallace promised me a pardon."

Billy the Kid. This chimera thought he was Billy the Kid, back in the 1880's. "We'd like you to stay here for a while," Jane told him, signaling for netmen and sedation.

Luna wandered out of her room then. When she saw Billy, she pulled her play clothes straight. The Billy chimera stared at her—they locked eyes. Both of them kept their lips firmly over their bizarre teeth. Then Luna asked, "Were you a terror chimera?"

"A what?"

"Luna," Jane said.

"*What* is he?"

"I think I'm William Bonney, Billy the Kid. But if you want to tell me I'm not . . . Jesus, help me. Or. . ."

"Be careful, Luna."

"Where were you tanked?"

"Tanked?"

Jane signaled for the wardens to get Luna out. Luna saw them easing toward her and said quickly to Billy, "You're not human, manipulated DNA." The wardens grabbed her and she slammed her injured gum against one's shoulder as they led her out.

"She crazy, too?" the Kid asked.

"We did a . . ." Impossible to explain quickly,

Jane thought, that we know he isn't human because of his DNA patterns, the signature segments. Talking about DNA and identity would get her into an impossible argument with anyone from the nineteenth century, real or imagined. "We'll offer you a room, if you'll talk to us about what you can remember about your past. You don't seem to have a home. And it's getting colder out." That was an understatement—Albany winters were worse than ever, weeks of subzero weather, the frozen Hudson grating its banks like an incipient glacier.

Again that wonderful smile, the shift in eye color. "Yes, ma'am, that it is. I was looking for a horse, but there were none to be had."

One of the cops said, "He tried to take a capitol patrol horse, but Shaka Z and his buddies beat him out of it."

I can't deal with this right now, Jane decided as she put him in a single. She went out and asked one of the cops, "Bring me a whiskey. I think that would be the easiest way to sedate him."

"Miss?" the cop said, meaning no.

She went out herself to the nearest liquor store, about five blocks away, and brought back a sampler bottle of the cheapest whiskey to be had. The cops had left when she got back, but Jake, the senior SPCA warden for the Capitol District, was waiting for her, thawed mustache frost dripping down his chin, his hands in leather driving gloves.

Jake said, "I heard what we have here. And what's that?"

"I'm going to sedate him. He thinks he's gone insane. He may be real psychotic, too, beyond any programming, poor bastard."

"Don't get involved if you don't want to," Jake said. "We both know he's going to be dead soon unless someone's willing to take extraordinary risks."

"I wouldn't do anything to hurt the pound."

"Shit, Jane. I know you wouldn't."

Well, Jake's tone sounds pretty snarky, Jane thought. "Well, let me sedate him."

"Fine, Jane."

"I feel jammed sometimes."

"Yes, Jane, if you're going to sedate him, do it."

"I need the Somnofed. Can you open the cabinet?" Jane knew Jake thought she should be more involved. Two years ago, Jake asked if she wanted to meet chimera underground types, but Jane refused. She suspected that if she even met them, Jake would try to get her to help chimeras pass as humans. They either loved their owners or wanted to pass, these days. Helping them as chimeras was her job, just a job. And the Billy-the-Kid chimera needed to be sedated.

Jake opened the cabinet and handed Jane two capsules. She said, "Don't you think I chose good? It doesn't interact with alcohol."

"Maybe he wants to talk?"

"Jake, he thinks it's the nineteenth century. Did you see him?"

"He's sitting on his bed, just staring. You could have left him out in the dayroom unless he threatened someone."

"Jake, Billy the Kid was a killer."

"Jane, let what's left of his life be pleasant."

"If he's sedated, it won't hurt," she said.

"All right, then."

Jane split the capsules with her thumbnail and poured the powder into the whiskey. Before she took the glass into Billy, she said, "And Somnofed is tasteless."

Just as Jake had described him, Billy was staring into space, trembling slightly. "Hi, Billy," she said softly, "would a whiskey make it better?"

"When am I going to be hanged?" He spoke carefully, with more standard grammar than he'd used earlier, as if he felt he should be formal about his death.

"We're not going to hang you, Billy. Here, drink this."

"I don't drink liquor normally, but . . ." He took the glass from her and drained it. "So, you'll send me to someone who will hang me."

"We're going to try to help you."

"That's what Governor Wallace said. I been lied to before. I'm tired. You gonna sleep with me?"

"No."

"Maybe I'm dead already?" He bent down to take off his shoes, then stretched out on the bed, his forearm over his eyes. "Did Al tell Garrett where I was? I worked good for him."

She came out and said to Jake, "He's completely in his Billy mode now, but calmer. I've never seen one whose brain work put him in a different century."

Jake said, "I wonder if the CIA will let him survive the night. It can hurt to care, can't it? The gene engineers could build us good, altruistic leaders, people who weren't bred into power games. But—"

"That's a stupid idea. They just put sections together. They don't precisely know what gene does what."

"I saw once, at Livingston Manor Dharma Center—"

"A CIA chimera came in and killed a defector. You told me." Jane was tired already and the day had just started.

"We wanted to help both of them. They gas the assassins after."

Billy woke up in what looked like a jail, but his fingers slipped through the bars he saw. He had died, then, poison in that whiskey, or maybe he'd died earlier, frozen to death trying to escape Albany. Kid Antrim, Billy the Kid, William Bonney, Bill Antrim decided it wasn't the Catholic hell, *diablos. Dios. Muerte. Purgatorio?*

He was in a bed, with sweaty sheets. In this Purgatorio, the evidence of his eyes didn't match that of his other senses. When did this begin? He remembered the woman who'd kept him tied in bed. His fingers touched things his body, blind, veered around. Green plants with leaves like wires grew in arroyos too dry for the rain that was falling. Men wearing liquid clothes that veered from the shape of clothes he knew found him shivering in the cave and brought him to the house of a female vampire— yes, he saw the teeth.

And the others, her servants? They treated him as though he was no longer human, but it wasn't in the way of being a prisoner. Different. They were kind—but drugged him. Crazy? Something in his mind kept whispering, *Purgatory*.

He remembered stories written about him, stories that made him into a mad-dog killer. But now there were no flames. He wasn't bad enough for hell. He wondered if Dios, God, the power over the powers that be, finally understood. Billy never thought he was hell-bound bad, but he still felt grateful.

But maybe I am crazy, he thought to himself as he sat on the bed, sweating, wondering if they found his knife, if the knife was real, or an illusion like the bars around him. He stopped himself just before he tried to clang them with the glass left by his bedside. Closing his eyes, he felt the sheets and the blanket—too smooth for jail, for New Mexico. Not *jerga*, not harsh like churro-sheep wool.

"So you're awake?" The man was dressed in those horrible clothes that wavered between illusions. A deputy?

"What happened?"

"Police-found you. You'd been living in a

basement on Ten Broek. They checked your genotype and brought you here when they saw what your cell structures looked like."

The man spoke utter gibberish. Billy slouched on the bed. "You telling me I'm wanted or what? You telling me I ain't Billy the Kid?"

The woman demon he'd seen last morning came in. The jail bars disappeared and the room re-formed as a hospital. Billy's sweat went cold. Hell or insane, Purgatory or insane. "Careful with him, Jake," the woman said, now dressed in nurses' gray, a long dress that squirmed around her legs like pants. "He doesn't know."

"This is Purgatorio, isn't it?" Billy asked.

"Maybe we could modify him," the man, Jake, said to the woman. "Wash out the Billy-the-Kid concepts if we find an uncontaminated core personality."

The woman took his pulse as if checking to see if he was dead. She said to Billy, "No, this isn't Purgatory. It's a Society for the Prevention of Cruelty to Animals holding center. Don't you remember me from yesterday? You were pretty upset, but we'll try to explain things. What we're going to do won't hurt."

He jerked his wrist out of her hand and said, "Demon, I'd have thought Purgatory was more honest." He started to get up, watching Jake to see what he'd do.

But it was the woman who swiftly pushed something against his arm that stung. I shouldn't stopped watching her, he thought as he went limp. Vaguely, he still heard their voices as they bent over him, the woman saying, "Unofficially, nothing is missing from Langley. Maybe we shouldn't do a wash because they want to see what this guy remembers. Some human handler may have . . ." The words didn't register—noises. He sweated, waiting for the stab to his throat. *I've been dead before, or it's all been Purgatory.*

Jane watched Billy sweat and twist as the drug took effect. When he muttered about stabbing . . . throat, she felt vaguely guilty. As his head rolled, she saw one fresh scar on his throat and possible signs of others. And he had a series of scars on his chest, the freshest one a massive healing wound. If Billy were human, Jane thought, he would be crazy, considering the dissonance between his reality and the rest of the world's. Whoever had made him broke two laws doing it—stolen CIA genetic segments and a criminal identity matrix. Hard-wired eyes or visual reprogramming? What the Kid chimera touched with those small hands seemed to be real by the world's standards, but the visuals either didn't register consciously or were transformed into something nineteenth-century, something out of William Bonney's prior life. He'd stepped around the computer when they put it in his way but blamed his motion on muscle cramps.

And whoever made him let him be shot, over and over.

Now the pound waited for Langley, but an

escaped Billy the Kid didn't seem to be too urgent a matter for the CIA these days. A vet came in the second day Billy was in the pound and estimated him to be about nine to eleven years old—not just out of the tank.

He was Billy the Kid—no, a flesh text of someone's Billy-the-Kid research or fantasies. Which alternative, Jane wondered, would make him more dangerous? When her duty time ended, Jane went to the state library. She sat down at a carrel and accessed the Billy-the-Kid entries and sat watching the digital of Peckinpah's *Pat Garrett and Billy the Kid*. An era she hated, Bob Dylan just an example of the fall from elegance drugs and computers brought. She looked down at the keyboard and called up the print-media references. The library had copies of Billy the Kid's letters to Governor Lew Wallace, contemporary newspaper accounts, and court records, but Jane decided to call Pat Garrett's and Governor Otero's accounts, and *Alias Billy the Kid* from the stacks. Then she ordered other books—on the Lincoln County war itself, on Pat Garrett, and on media representations of the Kid. She felt in her gut that this Kid was more poetic than strictly real.

When she got the books, still in acid-free storage boxes, she thought, I'm interested in my job again.

The streets outside were dark, so Jane took an uptown bus, then went in her building, turned on the blanket, and pulled it over her fiberfill cocoon. Warm at last, she began reading. Quite a range in possible Billies, Jane realized as she learned about the Lincoln County range war, Billy the Kid in literature, and Brushy Bill, an old man who in the late 1940's claimed to be Billy the Kid.

I'm going to keep him tranquilized, she decided, and see what the Society wants to do. *We should turn him over to a security pound, but* ... Nobody would claim a walking-around felony—and the CIA hadn't sent an assassin chimera after him, yet. She laid down the book on Brushy Bill and rubbed her neck. The phone rang and she answered it. Jake said, "We've been asked to take him to the veterans hospital tomorrow for a full brain workup."

Three men with sticks and leather thongs surrounded Billy. One said, "We're not going to hurt you," and bound his hands behind his back. He wondered if they were preparing him for his execution. But what can I do? he thought as he pulled against the leather restraints on him. Not leather, plastic restraints, that new thing.

Billy sat down on the bed, trying to compose himself. Jane came in, her with the stingers that brought sleep. She said, "Billy, I've been reading about you."

"Yeah," he said, "and everyone said Pat killed me back in 1881."

"Someone made you to be like him."

"Out of plastic?" He lifted his cuffed hands

behind his back. "It sure looks like everything else, your plastic."

"No. Are you ready to go? We're going to have a hospital scan your brain."

Dead for sure, he thought, but he was too tired to fight off the man who put more plastic around his ankles, tying his feet so they couldn't go more than eight inches apart. In hand and leg restraints, Billy shuffled outside with Jane. A vehicle waited. He got in whatever it was and squeezed his eyes tightly shut. When they got to the VA hospital, he was trembling, so aides strapped him down on a stretcher.

"To Neurological," Jane said. She went with them on the elevator up to a room filled with white-enameled metal and lit with corpse lights—no, some weird gas in tubes that glowed.

"They want pictures of the inside of your head," Jane told Billy as a burly man leaned against his stretcher and tightened restraining straps around his head.

He felt hopelessly beyond them, brain hazed with the drugs she gave him. He said, "Don't do this to me, not tied like a hog." He closed his eyes, feeling his pulse rattling in his ears as the burly man pushed his stretcher into a metal tube with glass knives.

He'd fainted. Jane held an ammonia vial under his nose and held his hand as the man cautiously unstrapped him.

"They say he's an illegal," the man muttered, but Billy heard and sighed.

"I'm a man," he said stubbornly.

"DNA construct," the burly man said, pushing Billy's damp sandy hair off his forehead, "you've got a lot to learn. We're going to try to help you."

"DNA construct?" he asked, sitting up unsteadily and staring at the scanner. "What *is* that?"

"What does that look like to you?"

"A giant cannon, with spikes in it. Inside of my head, with that? I thought you'd saw me open."

The man gritted his teeth and swore softly. "Jane, you should have said more about this. His ventricles have chips swimming in them."

Billy started to tremble. "What are you doing to me?"

"We've looked inside your skull," Jane said. "You have machines in there that control you."

"You ain't split my skull yet."

Jane said, "I'd better call a restraint car."

"You mean you brought him in a cab," the technician said. "What were you hoping, you'd get a Buddhist?"

"I don't like Buddhists," Billy said. He felt like he'd been mocked and he was beginning to get mad.

Why am I getting sentimental about this illegal chimera? Jane thought as she sat in front of the security plastic that Billy kept prodding, leaving oily smears from his fingertips. When Jane was alone with Billy, she forgot the legends, forgot even what he looked like. But around others, she saw the absurdities in the tiny hands, the almost bulbous eyes, the long jaw, and those teeth, like horse teeth in a child's mouth.

"You bitch," he said. "I thought you were taking me to be killed."

"Billy, settle down. It's all right."

"I've been told my eyes are pretty," he said as though he hadn't called her a bitch just seconds before, "but not honest. Why don't you sit back here with me?" He smiled again and his eyes flashed blue. *I never sleep with animals*, she reminded herself, but she felt vaguely guilty that she'd put him behind the restraint barrier.

"Does being behind the barrier bother you?"

"I know enough to know I could be crazy." His fingers smeared the smears he'd made earlier. "Plastic, you people do a lot with plastic, don't you? You put me in this cage." He stared at her reflection in the mirror—eyes utterly cold gray for an instant, then he sighed and leaned back.

"Billy, what I've read about you doesn't say you hurt women."

"I've always given women a damn good time."

Lying on his bed in the pound, Billy considered what was. Somebody he couldn't remember made him to be Billy the Kid, killed him, maybe, and brought him back to life. What he faced now was not hell and a bit too confused to be Purgatory, so he must be alive. And he knew he was Billy the Kid. Plastic wasn't that different from celluloid that they couldn't have invented it in the east sometime when he was hiding. And so what if some inventor got an arc light to fit inside glass? They had to be lying about the time.

The next morning, when Jane came in, she overheard one of the wardens tell Billy, "William Bonney died, killed by Pat Garrett. This is 2067, not 1884."

"Don't," Jane said.

"You, Jane, what date is it? Bring me a newspaper—I can read. You couldn't set type that fast."

These days, Billy, she thought, we could. He was trembling, still in the isolation room. "Billy, we have the medical report. Someone hard-wired your brain's visual center. There's a neuronal overlay—maybe impossible to strip out. I know you don't understand this."

"I can read." He wiped his eyes, then continued, "I'm a literate outlaw. I wasn't a real killer; I was fighting for my friends at the store and Blazer's Mill. Woman, they killed Tunstall in cold blood."

"This present is very different from what you think reality is."

"So you eastern people invented a lot when I was hiding. You're saying I'm crazy?"

"Do you know what the other alternative is?"

"Flesh robot?"

"We'd like to take out what's been inlayed in

your brain. Maybe then you'd see normally, but the operation will hurt."

He reached for her hand, which she let him take. Then he twisted her down before the warden beside them could react. "Tell me, bitch, what is wrong with me that you look at me as if I was worse than a prisoner."

"You are made out of rebuilt animal cells. Rich people have chimeras like you made for companions—and the federal authorities use you for spies."

"Are we owned? Are you looking for my owner?" He released her and wiped his hand against his pants leg, then shook it as though touching her had cramped it.

"You're a felony. No one is supposed to make a chimera like you."

"Is making a chimera think he's a man illegal? No, no, I'm crazy. You're just another crazy." He was sweating.

"The felony was making a criminal reconstruction."

"You read too many damn dime novels."

"We don't know anything about how you were made. You may have less-than-adequate inhibitions about killing." She looked at the warden. He nodded slightly; she crooked her finger to say *let's just be prepared*.

"I told you—"

"If you thought you were Billy the Kid shooting an enemy, then perhaps you actually murdered someone. Chimeras who kill people get lethal injections."

He groaned and squeezed his eyes tightly shut. "Where's Pat Garrett?"

"There is no living Pat Garrett."

He looked stunned for a second, then whispered, "Flesh robot. I kinda grasp things, like from dime novels. Oh, damn, can't I have a lawyer? I had lawyers in New Mexico. I have my rights."

"We're going to have to . . ." She looked over the medical report again. The neuronal overlay obviously caused him to block or think he was in Purgatory when he almost realized the truth.

"Maybe I'm crazy. But if I'm not, then please tell me what's going on."

"First, maybe you are a bit crazy. We're going to try to make you well first," Jane said, hoping someone in the Society could get funding for such an operation on a stray felony chimera. Lying to chimeras was like kicking cats; they were so helpless despite their arrogance, even the terror ones. If none were ever again made, she'd be relieved. But maybe not, maybe she'd be diminished. *Maybe, if he has to be killed, we can reenact a scene from the Billy-the-Kid legend, let him die fulfilled.*

He said, "Whatever you do to me, I want to know who or what I really am," as though he knew what she'd just thought.

"Oh, Billy, that's not always possible, even for humans."

"Flesh-robot brains should be simpler," he said, a flash of ice in his eyes, then he lay down on his bed. "Can I see the other flesh robots, if that's what I am?"

"Are you lonely?"

He looked down at the gray chimera-pound clothes he was wearing. "Yeah, bring me in some other dog-meat robots."

"You pick up things outside the New Mexico frame of reference, I think."

" 'Dog-meat robot,' I've heard it before." He stared up for a few moments, then said, "I was shot dead." His arms snaked out at Jane, but she evaded him and the wardens pinned him to the bed. He was shaking, maybe crying through the sweat on his face. "I don't want to die again. Not go through that again. It hurts . . . it scares . . . it hurts like hell."

"I'm sorry," she said. "We'll give you some company." Jane wondered if Luna would be bad for him—none of the other chimeras could give him a good feeling about how humans treated their creations. Maybe she ought to talk to the Buddhists at Livingston Manor, see what one of the Roshis might suggest, but they'd only take him in of his own free will. "What do you know about Buddhism?"

"I have a gut bad feeling. Let me talk to the vampire."

Whoever made him would have conditioned in or hard-wired an aversion to Buddhism. Maybe his prejudice would strip off with the neuronal overlay?

Jane signaled the wardens to step away from him now. She said to Billy, "Luna just looks like a vampire. Her owner and she have a sick relationship—when she's hurt, she comes here, recovers, and then lets him reclaim her. She always says she provoked him. Judges believe her."

"You don't?"

"He's got her brain-rigged so what she does is what he wants. And he had to have had her made that way, deliberately. Chimera design has gotten lots more precise in the brain work since the first neural-control segments were mapped."

"Like me, brain-rigged. Sick relationship?" He turned his back on her. "I wish I really was Billy the Kid, the real one. I fit in that life."

"In that life, you're killed in the dark, Billy."

He rolled over and stared at her with eyes gone blue. One of his small hands slowly reached for her shoulder, trailed down her arm while she stood, the sudden warmth between them scaring her. He said, "The women loved me in that life, loved me before Pat killed me. Somehow I think he killed me a lot."

Billy lay back against the pillow as the woman Jane left. He was still drugged, his mind leaking images of things he didn't know he'd seen: things he had no words for, things he had words for, but the shape for the word was more primitive than the things he was seeing, had seen. When the door opened again, it was the vampire, beautiful as a dream. He almost hoped she was deadly. Luna, that was her name, wasn't it? "Hi, Luna."

"Hi, Billy. You look negative."

Words change in hundreds of years, Billy realized, even as they changed from east to New Mexico. He asked, "Negative?"

"Depressed."

He figured out the metaphor—down, low-spirited—and said, "Yeah, I'm dog meat."

She sat down on the bed and fingered his sweaty hair. "Your owner will come and make things okay."

"My boss was killed—Sheriff Brady's men blew him away, Tunstall. Maybe he was really my owner. I was stolen." He closed his eyes and saw Tunstall lying on the embalming table, his skull smashed and the army doctor lying about Willie Morton smashing the rifle butt against Tunstall's head after he was dead. The pain hit fresh.

"Don't they make you feel happy when they hurt you? I think it's illegal not to," Luna said.

"I'm illegal, through and through."

"But the SPCA can help you. If I need to get away, I just come here. Then I go home again when Andy calms down. Maybe Andy would buy you?"

"Shit." He wished the *vampira* was a real killer. She'd been built with the wrong bit of bloodsucker, a mosquito's whine, not a good solid bite. Luna was just a woman who takes a beating and runs off to her folks, then goes back to the man, not like Deluvina hustling her way out of Apache bondage.

Luna stroked his chin with her nails as though his jawbone was his cock. He smiled up at her, then saw the wardens' grins. *Like people watch dogs cock-tied in the road.*

"I think like a man," Billy said to them. "I look like a man. Why can't I just be a man?"

"Because your memory is false," one warden said.

"Because you're not human DNA," the other said.

Luna rose from where she'd been kneeling by the bed and said to the wardens, "I want to call Andy. If you won't put in a new tooth, he will."

Billy wondered if they were holding him here to see who'd come hunting him.

Suddenly Jane woke up in her cube, disoriented, as though the whole space with her beloved mahogany ceiling had rotated. A light played over the ceiling panels. "Nice," a man's voice said, "but I bet you call it a cube, not an apartment, not a room. Cube—stupid word for stupid people."

Who could evade block security and her own personal Society alarms? CIA. FBI. "Who is it?"

"That's the last thing he asks, every time, but he asks it in Spanish," the voice said. Something wrong about the voice, synthetic. Eyes gleamed beside the street-side windows facing the park. The man wore a liquid crystal camouflage suit, a lump with eyes in her wall. Lights from beyond the windows obscured him even more.

"I thought you eliminate chimeras who got away."

"He's mine. I want him back."

"He's illegal."

"Illegal to break into a cube, but I'm here, understand. I find a place where Billy the Kid can hide when he shoots people—some of the space in his head. You impressed by him?"

The intruder had spoken of "a place where Billy the Kid can hide when he shoots people" as if he were quoting something. Jane said, "He seems more decent than the legend."

"Have you slept with him yet?"

"No," she said, shocked.

"Extra male pheromones, so maybe you're a dyke or frigid." A light flashed at the edge of Jane's vision—catching the sensitive retina rods. She turned her head slightly and saw a diode flashing by her bed. His unregistered voice in the room tripped an alarm. So he's not perfect, she thought with relief. The man stood in a confused blur as the camo suit re-formed its display. "I want him back." Light shone beyond him. *Damn him, he cut my wall.* Jane found she couldn't move.

"I'll see if there's a way," she said, terrified now, still unable to move, limbs jerking slightly each time she tried. Just talking took too much air—she could only breathe in twitches. "Computer at library . . . trace? Drug?"

He sprayed something at her and left. Her

body writhed, then was finally under her control again. *Rogue CIA, FBI, commissar.* She fumbled for the phone, hit the audio switch, and said, "Police."

"Not yet," his synthetic voice said through the phone. "Wait."

Her neighbors heard her scream. She heard them pounding on her door and went to let them in. The room was freezing cold.

"Chimera problem?" a middle-aged woman asked. Her sleeping cocoon was patched with nonmatching glue-ons, one embroidered.

"Yeah."

"Rough to get between the rich and what they want."

Jane stood up and looked at all her neighbors standing bundled in their sleeping cocoons around her door. "We've got laws."

"Still, it's got to be rough," the woman said.

"He cut a hole in my wall. Bastard. How soon can we have it repaired?" She realized they were talking in the dark and turned on her ceiling light.

The building super shuffled in wearing plastic boots and a fiberfill jacket. He went over and fingered the cut. "You might want to have the walls wired. In case he comes back. That would take maybe a week. You know how it is to get help for nonstandard. We can put up some temporary inso-board, but people from the park can see it's a patch."

Jane felt helpless, angry, the more angry for the helplessness. Just like a richtech, to destroy her security, invade her space. "I can stay at the pound. Fix it real secure." She knew why the CIA hadn't come for Billy. They were using him for bait.

The two building security guards stepped forward, one too young for such a job, Jane thought. "We'll stay with you," the older one said, "until you get your things stored or packed."

Jane stared up at her ceiling and thought about the thousand fantasy parties lost in the past. The middle-aged woman put her arms around Jane's shoulders and squeezed, lumpy fiberfill between them. Jane wondered why she'd never learned the woman's name, then knew she felt superior to people who had to patch their parkas and sleeping cocoons. She said, "Thanks," to the woman when she stepped away. Jane then called the pound.

After Jane explained what had happened, the night officer said, "The Kid is restless. Maybe he smells the man? Sure, we'll put you up here, if you're not embarrassed to sleep in a chimera room."

The two apartment security guards helped her carry her things to the cab. She said, "Take me down to the chimera pound."

"You work with them?" the cabby asked.

"Yes," she admitted, wondering if he was a Buddhist sympathizer.

"The rich make dog-meat doctors and techs to keep us from getting good jobs."

"I don't think they're doing that. Chimeras are too expensive to use even for that."

"Sin to sleep with animals. Bible says."

"Yeah."

"Do you?"

"No," she said, realizing the cabby was an orthodox Fundy, no friend of the Buddhists at all. She hated these conversations, wished she had phoned the Livingston Manor refuge for a Buddhist cabbie.

"They build imaginations and fuck them. It's idolatry. Only God should make things in his own image."

"The Buddhists wouldn't agree. They don't think anything is or isn't."

"Bunch of sickies—rich men and beasts together. Leave their fellow humans in the gutter."

Yeah. Jane thought of Luna and Andy and agreed with the cabbie on how sick fucking chimeras was, but Fundies made her job difficult. "Chimeras have feelings as complex as ours." I am not sleaze, she told herself, not like this.

"Bullshit. Psychologist on TV—"

"Do you have any children?" she asked. Generally, with ortho-Fundies, that derailed discussions of chimeras.

"Oh, children. Let me tell you. . . ." and he did, all the way to the pound. But once there, he didn't help her with her bags, as though he'd been forced to drive to a bad neighborhood. She lifted both of them and wrestled them through the door.

"Jane, are you all right?" Jake grabbed her bags as he talked, looking half-asleep, his hair rumpled, mustache hairs twisted. "We're meeting on Billy in the morning—Sidney from district."

Jane noticed that the wardens wore hypo-guns and Billy and the other chimeras were standing around, awake, out of their rooms. A TV blared anti-Buddhist propaganda in the corner, but no one paid it any attention.

"Jake, the CIA is using him for bait. Pay the cab," she said. "I'll tell you more, in private."

The phone rang and they all—human and chimera—stared at it. Jake picked it up and pushed in a trace code as he handed the receiver to Jane.

"Yes, Jane," the same synthetic voice said, "I know where you went. Sleaze are too dumb to be good rebels."

"I care for these creatures," she said. "I am not sleaze."

"You're just jealous. In the twentieth century, you'd have been hating people who wore fur coats; in the nineteenth, you'd have cut horses' check reins. You accuse us of the cruelties you can't afford. Now it's chimeras. But you're too dumb, out of your league, Jane." He hung up.

"It's real untraceable," Jake said softly.

"Garrett wants me back," Billy said. "To kill over and over."

"Billy." Jane started to say *we'll get him*, but suddenly the synthetic voice, the untraceability, the liquid crystal camouflage suit seemed like a digital in holovision of some real rich life, as though the cameras were watching around her. Jane felt like a secondary character in a program starring the CIA, the FBI, or some spectacularly rich bitch with money to hire any illegality she wanted. "I hope we can help you."

Billy said, "Give me one of those guns."

"They don't kill," she said.

He asked, "What do you have them out for then?"

None of them slept. In the morning, they unlocked the doors and let in Edward Mather, the district Society representative. He dressed rich: asymmetrical lapels in a striped wool coat with all the stripes matched perfectly, black hair slightly long, looking like it grew in a perfect cut.

Jane, feeling utterly grubby, said, "Hi, Edward."

Mather nodded, took off his coat, exposing black British tweed. He hung the coat up himself and said, "You people worry too much."

"We've had two weird phone calls," Jane replied, her legs stiff when she stood up. "One untraceable, to here."

Mather said, "Has the media been kept out of this? CIA's sending a surgeon to recover the internal ware."

"I bet the CIA keeps media out any damn time it wants," Jane said. "Are we going—Jake, get our friends to their rooms."

Billy's eyes changed from blue to gray and

his head turned, glancing at each of them. Two wardens gently took his arms. "Billy, go with them, please," Jane said. The other chimeras, expressions caught, modified, and held in the way of experienced chimeras, left for their other rooms. Billy shrugged slightly, eyes slowly turning back to blue, and let the wardens lead him.

Humans and chimeras all knew Billy was a lethal needle case unless the district supervisor said otherwise. Mather, generally more a fund-raiser than a pound worker, had left his home in the Adirondack Preserve at Saratoga Springs to determine if there'd be an exception. Jane resented his presence. What did rich contacts have to do with this?

Edward Mather took out a pipe and filled it with a nonchimerical tobacco full of tars and nicotine. "The CIA suggests we recondition him very thoroughly if we leave him alive."

"I wanna leave him alive," Jake said in a rush. "If we get out the thing that's making him see the nineteenth century, then maybe he can see like us. He has good insight into his perceptions being distorted, and if we can strip out the nineteenth-century visual distorter, if it's simple as that, then we shouldn't kill him. He didn't ask to be made."

"He can't feel free to kill people," Edward said.

"The real William Antrim—" Jane began.

"He isn't the real William Antrim. He's a my-thoconstruct. You met the man who made him, so disguised you couldn't recognize him. He tore down your wall. Jane, do you trust that man to make a decent Billy the Kid? He has stolen from the government, made a criminal personality."

" 'A place for him to go when he kills people,' " she said, "the guy who came last night in a camo suit using a chip voice said that."

"Sounds like a quote," Mather said. "Trace it. I'll put off the lethal needle until after the CIA surgeon cleans his brain." He signed the order book to that effect and then stared at what he wrote for a second, then said, "We're going to have a couple of CIA people helping us guard this Billy, so make sure everyone's presentable. Jane, couldn't you . . . ?" He didn't finish, but instead walked out the door.

Jane looked down at her pants and noticed a black stain on the right knee, frayed threads over the zipper. She wondered if Mather and his rich might buy her new clothes, knew they wouldn't.

Billy went away easy because the wardens had guns. He sat in his room alone, not even the fake *vampira* with him, and tried to remember his life. He remembered something like this room, only smaller, something thicker than water, warm, then memories of riding across New Mexico, of Celsa, the Celsa of Fort Sumner, not the Celsa with short hair in New York. Memories troubled him—the eyes of the man over him, his head banging against the floor, pimp, pimp, and his gun going off in the man's face.

Billy started when Jake walked into his room. "Sorry I startled you," Jake said. "Doctor's coming to operate on you. I wanted to prepare you. They're going to cut into your brain and try to fix your eyes. I'm on your side. Remember that. If you want to come back out into the dayroom, it's okay."

"You're on my side?"

"I'm trying to help, legal. Maybe we can smuggle you to a refuge?"

"I hate the Buddhists."

"You've been conditioned against them."

"I don't even know what you're talking about." He got up and went into the dayroom where the *vampira* was telling how she'd brought the pliers instead of her tooth when she ran away from her owner.

Everyone laughed, but Billy felt sick. Cut him, they were going to cut into his brain. Jake looked like his clothes would fit him. More guards were coming—he'd heard them with ears that were almost coyote sharp. *Made keen? Can't think about that now, have to get out of here before they hack my brain apart*, he told himself. The guns the wardens had weren't real guns, some drug toys, but if they'd drop a man . . .

He yawned, then slumped down before the glittering glass box whose images eluded him except when they were of his era—"western movies," the fake *vampira* called them—phony like you, she'd told him.

The other fake people liked him. If this really wasn't Purgatory, he didn't think they would try to stop him. He began coughing, hard, as though choking.

The warden who came over wasn't his size, but he grabbed the gun, shot it, then shot the other wardens as fast as he could fire the thing. *They may not be dead, but they are going down.*

"You stupid," Jake said as he slumped to the floor.

Alarms rang. Billy undressed Jake as fast as he could, staring at the zipper that crawled like a snake down the man's pants. *Should be buttons—I'm seeing too much.* Closing his eyes, he grabbed and pulled the little metal tongue down.

Jake said, "Would help you. Promised."

"Yeah, just like Wallace. Damn, damn, damn," Billy said. He got the pants off Jake and turned them back the right way to pull them on himself.

The door was locked. For a second he panicked, fingers scrabbling at it, imagined gunfire echoing through his head, memories of dying . . . then he went to each body, searched for keys. *Nothing.*

He looked out a window into a blur of building and canyon, a tremendous drop, fifty feet, more. Still, he raised a chair and smashed it against the window. The chair bounced back, hurting his hands. Purgatory. "God, I am truly sorry." He tried to remember what the Mexicans said when they were dying, but then he was dead, wasn't he?

"Billy?" It was the woman Jane. She wasn't in the room, but a box on the wall—her voice came from that.

"Yes. Jane?" He remembered her name.

"You can't get out."

"No?"

"No."

"Then I'm sorry I hurt your people."

"Did you shoot them with their trank guns?"

"The drug guns, yes,"

"Billy, we're coming in. If you don't fuss, you won't get hurt. Stand in the middle of the room and put your hands on top of your head." He heard her mutter, "We've got to get a medic in real quick. No telling how many doses."

Then the walls collapsed, sank into the floor. Billy stared at nightmare men with snouted faces and nets. He quickly put his hands on top of his head.

Two men threw a net over him; he tried to stand still, knowing that struggling against this horror was useless, but his muscles coiled up. Just as other men began to reach for his feet, he kicked at their faces. Then he saw Jane, face mottled like pissed-on snow, terrified of him, as the men threw him to the floor and pinned him down, a knee in his throat. They ripped off the shirt he'd taken and put a canvas jacket on him, pulled the straps tighter the more he struggled.

He tried to lie limp. When he could breathe, he called, "Jane, help me, please."

Jane moved from behind the men. "Don't," one said, "he's dangerous."

"Billy never hurt women," she said, coming up and kneeling beside him, but not taking off the canvas jacket with the closed sleeves. Straitjacket, he realized with horror, they've got a straitjacket on me. He knew he could wiggle cuffs off his small hands, but not this. "Billy, we weren't going to hurt you that much."

"Now you're going to kill me," he said, vaguely pleased that his voice sounded almost calm. "I wasn't first to shoot. Charlie Bowdre, they killed him right in front of me. Wallace promised me a pardon. They killed Tunstall, Dick Brewer, McSween, Tom, Charlie, they just kept killing us."

"No, Billy, you aren't responsible. But if you're dangerous . . ."

"I just want to go back to New Mexico."

"The New Mexico you remember was only in your mind."

From the crowd, a man said, "Feels like something Boyle would do, or Hannisforth." The man wore eastern clothes and had steel plates in front of his eyes. Billy saw his face reflected in the steel—no, glass—as the man came closer and bent over him. "We can't let you run loose," he told Billy as he cut the canvas with a penknife and pulled one of Billy's hands free, looked at it, turned it over to look at the palm, and then moved the fingers around. "Quick with your hands, eh, Billy?"

Billy nodded, suddenly exhausted. The man

pushed Billy's hand back into the canvas sleeve
and slapped tape over cloth he'd cut. Billy pushed
his hand against the slit but the tape held.

"We'll have to get in his brain and see what
all's been done," the man told Jane.

Billy thought this was a cruel way to kill him.
"I wouldn't mind if I'd died fighting, thanks."

Jane watched Dr. Morse, the CIA doctor, turn
away from the straitjacketed chimera and fold
his pocketknife. He looked back at the chimera
once more, then said, "Jane, we'll put a mobile
hospital somewhere in the old Concourse, close
it off. Interesting situation."

"Not for Billy."

He looked at her sharply and she remembered
what the synthetic-voiced man had said—that she
was SPCA to spite the rich. Morse said, "Perhaps
he'd be better off put down. It's cruel to keep them
alive when they can't deal with life."

"Edward Mather makes that decision."

"We want to handle this quietly before the
cameras find out," Morse said. "It sounds too
much like a holodigital already."

"I thought you controlled the press."

Dr. Morse sighed, as if saying, *we wish*. They
walked to the wardens' mess while the others
rigged myo-electrical restraint tape around Billy's room. Jane had never met CIA before—she
realized how much of her attitudes had been
formed by the news reports, the government
stories about heroics in Tibet. Very popular
with the *kulturati*, the liberation of Tibet and

all its Buddhist treasures. The CIA were the arms and gauntlets behind the rich, and this man had the sinister elegance she'd expected. She was grubby beside him, dressed in her pound canvas pants and the rip-proof jacket. *Whatever this man wants, he'll get it. If he wants Billy to die, Billy will be dead.*

"Rogue maker," Dr. Morse was saying. "Chimera designers are a bit odd. We just want to clean out the classified hard processors and then you can see what you want to do with him."

"He's illegal. It was cruel to limit his vision like that. And you're using him as bait."

"Much of what we do is illegal, by your standards. And some of it has to be cruel. This was theft of company property. What else might the maker steal from us?" He picked up the phone and slotted in a transfer wire, then opened his bag and took out a graphics tablet, touched it rapidly in several places with a stylus, then punched numbers on the phone. The phone beeped, then he said, "We'll operate tonight. Camera's been spotted around."

"Life like a holoshow," Jane said. "Can I see him before you operate?"

"No, after. You're good with them when they're upset, Edward says. He may still be Billy the Kid even after I've stripped off hard processors and any bioprocessors we can spot. We've brought an extra eye in case he's got retinal mapping, too."

"You can do all this, but . . ." Jane felt resentful—with all the cerebral technology used on chimeras, why did humans have to suffer strokes, age?

"It's terribly expensive. We wouldn't do this to just an ordinary chimera. If chimera research didn't have security applications, the pets wouldn't be as good as they are. Gene work and conditioning narratives are expensive."

"It's cheaper to breed people."

"It certainly is." He dropped his pad and wire in his bag again and said, "I'm staying with friends on a preserve. We'll be back in a few hours to operate."

Saratoga, she thought, remembering the wall, the glittering hoops the maglev train cruised through, from the Mohawk to the reserve. And she wanted to steal all their abused chimeras away from them, the rich.

"You hate the preserves? Don't be jealous," he said, looking back at her from the doorway. "And we won't destroy your Billy unless he proves to be dangerous."

"You're going to use him for bait."

"I'm sure we'll catch the maker from his work signatures."

"Why is the media coming around?"

"You think we're all-powerful. We aren't. Really."

"I think you just sacrifice some of the rich to the media."

"The structure of order is never as simple as some people would like to believe."

114

Jane wondered if curbing her jealousy might be crucial in keeping Billy alive.

Billy was trapped in his fragile skull, struggling to see as the men in green circled and strapped him down even though they'd paralyzed him with drugs already. *Dog-meat puppet ... dog-meat robot ... dog meat.* Everything bristled with revolvers and knives; they'd brought the sun in to stare at him. The man in eastern clothes who'd captured him, the one they called Dr. Morse, like the code, began tightening screws on his head. He couldn't feel any pain, but heard the screw points crunch into his skull bones. *Crueler than Apaches to break my skull and let me feel my brains ooze out.*

"What do you see, Billy?"

"I ..." He wanted to wail, but kept himself calm. "Guns. Sun."

"Okay, we're going to put goggles on you, try to tell us what you see." The doctor lay the goggles over his eyes—blackness.

"Dark."

The doctor muttered to someone else, "Better make sure these holos aren't realistic. Just patterns."

A red stripe floated in the air—no, inside the goggles—he felt them still around his eyes. "Stripe, red," Billy told them. Doc Morse tightened one of the bone screws.

Then as they began to saw his skull, Billy prayed that he was in Purgatory. "Dead," he told them. "Dead." His voice sounded like it was echoing down from a thousand miles away. "Dead."

"Shut him up, will you," Doc Morse said to a nurse.

"Sorry," Billy said, but the nurse touched his tongue with two round pennies and it just lay in his mouth, heavy. Then he lay there, with the red stripe crossing his eyes for hours, more hours, while the doctor cut away a cap of bone from his brain. He tried to scream, fainted, but nobody noticed.

"Conscious?" They lifted the goggles and looked at him. He wasn't in the same room, or was. Somehow he'd seen this before, but . . .

"Are my brains oozing out yet?" he asked, shocked to hear how pathetic he sounded.

The doctor said, "What do you see now?"

"The room's funny, but it's like I've seen it somewhere." He had no names for the amorphous shapes—like the doctor had ripped meaning out of his mind.

"You've grown some new vision pathways, so I'm not surprised."

"What is that, like the sun behind glass?"

"A lamp."

"Not oil? Not carbon arcs?"

"No," the doctor said. "Put the goggles back on. Billy, what you see now will look real, but it's just something played inside the goggles."

The nurse laid the goggles over his eyes again. He thought he felt wind tickling his brains, then saw a woman in pants on a bicycle with a motor—big fat tires, though. "It's like a bicycle, but . . ."

"What's under the seat?"

"Like a funny-shaped canteen, with a screw-top lid."

Then the woman went away and he saw a little glass bottle with a metal screw neck, wire inside. The wire started to glow. "Glass bottle with glowing wires inside."

"That's a light bulb."

"Are we going to do an eye now?" the nurse asked.

"No. He's not retinally mapped," the doctor said. "Billy, we're going to close you up now, but since it will be rather tedious, we're going to let you sleep through it."

He felt them prick his arm, then a snake slithered down into his lungs, a tube, rather.

"God, what an adjustment he'll have to make," he heard the nurse say as he tried to yawn.

When Dr. Morse came out, Jane felt cold. Dr. Morse stripped the surgical gloves off his hands and pressed the fingertips together, wiggling the fingers against each other. "He's got an interesting brain-cell structure—I think he's been dead at least once, since most of the neurons fartherest from the capillaries are new growth."

Jane asked, "But will he be okay now?"

The doctor made fists and continued working the kinks out of his fingers. "I'd like to see how well he adjusts. He . . . the design looks more crude than some of the duty chimeras, but I think the maker went crude to hide his work signature." The man sighed as if he wished he hadn't said that. "But the illusion building . . . someone has a thing for Billy the Kid."

"He's talked about being in Purgatory."

"Since the brain remains capable of mitosis, the maker might have given him a Purgatory to handle twenty-first-century input. Without breaking the general illusion."

"Why?"

Dr. Morse grinned, a face-wiggling boy smile. "Because you can build any flesh illusion you want with about $40 million worth of material and equipment and our budget is rather loosely managed. The maker thinks breaking code is fun. Pure outlaw."

Morse seemed to like the idea of one of his own CIA people going rogue, empathized with him. Jane thought, They're all alike, the willful rich.

"Did you take out the outlaw parts? Can I go in to see him?"

"We want to do a readout to see if we can anticipate his character. Tomorrow, maybe, you can see him."

Chapter Four
The Chimera Underground

Sir

I will keep the appointment I made but be sure and have men come that you can depend on. I am not afraid to die like a man fighting but I would not like to be killed like a dog unarmed. . . . Tell the commanding officer to watch Lt. Godwin he would not hesitate to do anything There will be danger on the road of somebody waylaying us to kill us on the road to the Fort. You will never catch those fellows on the road . . . give a spy a pair of glasses and let him get on the mountain back of Fritzes and watch and if they are there will be provision carried to them. It is not my place to advise you, but I am anxious to have them caught, and perhaps know how men hide from soldiers better than you. Please excuse me for having so much to say and I still remain

Yours truly
W. H. Bonney.

—From a letter to Governor Wallace (Others involved in the Lincoln County killings had escaped jail shortly before the Kid wrote this letter negotiating his surrender to testify against them for a pardon.)

FROST HAD CRACKED THE CEMENT AROUND THE entrance into the old Concourse, eroding the opening out of its man-made right angles. As Jane went through it, she thought it would look like a cave entrance in another two hundred years. In the basement arcade, sculptures abandoned by the Rockefellers rusted below street grates. Beyond the sculptures, fluorescent lights surrounded a white trailer parked in front of abandoned shops. Jane walked between the sculptures toward the trailer. A guard stopped her. She showed him her ID and said, "I'm here to see Billy."

"Wait," he told her. "Here," meaning *don't move*. He held her ID and stepped back from her to a terminal, entered her ID number, his eyes moving from it to the keypad like a man who memorized figures without being truly numerate. As he hit icons on the terminal, she felt both nervous and disgusted.

"Dr. Morse said I could see Billy," she said.

"Tell them at the trailer," he said, waving her on.

A young Oriental man in red leather studded with tiny gold studs the size of pinheads came up to her. She said, "I'd like to see Billy."

"Why?" The man had a slight southern accent, incongruous in that face.

"He is, was, one of my charges."

The man said, "Yes, the rogue talked to you. Tell the rogue, only the rogue, where we've got his creature. You'll see Billy's alive." He walked her toward the trailer. The fluorescent lights seemed set to obliterate shadows. Beyond the trailer, one defective tube strobed almost violently.

Jane went in. A nurse and three guards sat watching the trial of a rich man who'd murdered his lawyer. The oldest guard, a man with stiff gray hair cut so it stood on end, looked up. The Oriental said, "She's here to see the replica."

The nurse got up and unlocked a door. Jane saw Billy in bed, scalp shaved, a halo brace around his head screwed into his skull. The scalp was stitched in two neat circles each about four inches round. His gray eyes, almost vacant, flicked at her, then returned to staring at the barred trailer window and the strobing fluorescent-light tube. Jane wondered why one of the guards didn't call maintenance, or unscrew it himself if security feared a leak. She walked to the window and pulled the drapes so the flicker wouldn't give her a headache.

Bill said, "We're inside a bigger building. Are they that scared of me? Are you real? How can I tell what's lies and what's not?" He sounded like a tired ten-year-old boy.

"I'm real," Jane said, sitting down beside him and taking his hand. Touch, she'd been trained, makes them seem more like fellow creatures.

"Things have changed, but not so much that I'm not behind bars. Now I'm really wounded, cut up in the brain."

"Billy, didn't the operation fix your vision? We're trying to help you. You were made illegally. We're trying to catch the guy who did it."

"But I was shot." His hand pulled away from hers and fluttered over his chest.

"He wants you back, but—"

"Everyone thinks I'll kill a guy just for bumping me on the street. For teasing me about my little hands and feet. The first man I killed, he was banging my head and calling me a pimp."

"Billy."

"False memories? They told me it was 2067—that would mean . . ." His neck flexed as he tried to move his head. Jane realized how frightened he was, but he seemed to notice her own expression and said, "Guess without the screws my skull would fall apart, all the sawing Doc Morse did." He smiled, trying to put her at ease,

123

and she was touched, then annoyed. Even like this, he tries to be manipulative, she thought.

"We're going to keep you alive."

He looked at her sharply, as though he knew what she'd almost said: *alive for now.* "That's an odd thing to say, as though you could murder me without trial for no reason at all other than my reputation." He raised one of his delicate hands toward her and said, "Jane, I need a friend I can trust. If I had such a friend, man or woman, I could learn how this twenty-first century works. I was never stupid, despite what was said about me. Even if I was made to be Billy the Kid out of dog meat, I still don't think I was made stupid."

Jane felt that she'd exaggerated how deliberately manipulative he was and didn't avoid his fingers that moved in gently to touch her left cheekbone. "Billy, it's going to be very difficult for you." She did tighten her neck muscles, no reproof, but no response either.

"Bring me Billy-the-Kid books—I want to figure myself out—what there was to go from." He reached up to tweak her hair. "Now I see so many women with short hair. Or did you get it cut between when I saw you last and now?"

"It was short."

"I want those books, Jane."

"Okay, Billy."

"The newspapers had me all wrong. I was maybe stupid to write some novelist, for Christ sake, but Wallace was governor. He—"

"Billy, that never happened to *you*. Your DNA

says you were made out of government parts."
She wondered how long the media had been
making their own events. Centuries, perhaps.
"I'll bring you the books. The country has
changed a lot from what it was when the real
Billy the Kid was alive."

"In some ways," he said slowly, suddenly pale
against the hospital pillows, "I'll always be Billy
the Kid. I hate Morse for making my head hurt
like this."

"Oh, Billy, don't say that," she said, wondering if he'd earned himself a lethal needle with
those words.

"I've got to rest," he said, not looking at her,
eyes fixed on the barred trailer window. She felt
angry, dismissed by both a chimera and his
maker. They looked at each other again when
she reached the door. "Hard to take, find out
I'm not even being a human man. You help
things like me?"

"I'll be back," she said. "You do need a
friend."

His eyes turned blue again and he smiled.
"Thanks," he said, closing his eyes. "It's been
rough."

Kid, you have no idea, she thought as she
closed the door.

Dr. Morse and Edward Mather stood just outside the chimera's room. "Don't get too at-
tached," Dr. Morse said, his glasses reflecting
the lights over his eyes.

Lethal needle. Edward wouldn't look at her.
"He's trying so hard," she said to them both.

Dr. Morse said, "If the man with the synthetic voice contacts you again, we'll trace the call with better equipment than the SPCA has."

She walked home through the snow in Washington Park, watching the cross-country skiers waxing their skis by the lake. Thinking of the real Billy the Kid, she wondered, Did they have skis then?

"Hi," said a bulldog trotting by itself up one of the cleared paths.

She stopped. It winked at her; the voice was the same synthetic voice. "They're going to kill him after they trap your master," she said.

"And they're following you, so keep walking. I have a plan. You want to rescue him, don't you?"

"Not for you."

The bulldog laughed. "But you couldn't get him out yourself. You're just a little middle-class SPCA city officer, idealistic, you think, but really not terribly loyal to anything. The Animal Protection Underground doesn't trust you. Why, you'd let the CIA kill Billy because saving him would risk your job, bring you down to sleaze level, not that I can see much difference between an SPCA clerk and a hamburger fryer."

She felt as if snowflakes would flash to steam on her face. "I'd try . . ."

"Would try." The voice was very sarcastic about that "try."

They'd reached Washington Avenue now and the edge of the park. Jane saw her building and stopped. The bulldog came up. "Stoop to pet me," he ordered. She did and he whispered, "Take the dime out from my collar and don't spend it."

She felt the collar and found the dime in a slot like those in old-style loafers, pried it out with cold-numbed fingers. It looked like a real silver dime. The bulldog mouthed her hand, ran to two men, and jumped up on them with wet feet. The shorter man grabbed the bulldog's collar, but the dog jerked, muscles in the legs strained into high relief, and scampered into the bushes. The man stood up with a broken collar in his hand, said something to his taller companion. Both then looked at Jane.

When Jane got in her room, she closed the door and leaned against it, staring at the ornate ceiling, not precisely hers, something left from 1908 when this was a different world. The real Billy, if Wallace's pardon had worked out, could have lived until the 1950's. The room was freezing—she punched her bank code into the thermostat and turned it up to seventy-two Fahrenheit. *If I'm fired, my credit rating won't matter.*

The phone rang. "The dog?" a voice asked when she picked it up. "Was it his?"

She didn't know who to trust. "His?"

"Yeah."

"I don't want Billy killed, but I don't want him back in some preserve, either. He gets killed there, too." She stared at the dime, wondering if they knew about that, decided to tape it inside her purse. "Yes, it was him. He wants the chimera back."

"Look, it's nothing serious for him, just a hyper maker running a thrill."

"It's serious for the chimera," she said. "Tell Edward I've got to talk to him."

"Edward's cooperating." The voice cut off, as though she'd been put on hold, then came back to say, "Let us know what the rogue asks you to do. Go see Billy tomorrow."

"Do you really need to know who the rogue maker is?"

"If he's breaking little rules, we can't be sure he won't break bigger rules."

Billy was nothing more than a little broken rule. Felonies among international intelligence agencies weren't so serious, Jane thought. "I don't think I can help either of you," Jane said, wondering if it was safe to hang up on these people. The phone disconnected from the other end, and she asked, "You still there?" before putting the receiver back in its cradle.

The next day, she didn't go see Billy, then wondered if her obstinacy hurt Billy. On the way home, a crow flew up to her and said, "Atta girl, Jane." The men following Jane shot the crow with a drug dart, but she kept walking home. They're all just chimeras, she told herself, the bird, the dog, and Billy.

The day after the bird was shot, Jane went to the pound just in time to see Luna leaving with her owner.

Jake said, "Judge Bruce gave her back to him." As they went to the staff kitchen for tea, he added, "Sometimes, I wonder why we bother with her. And I wish Billy . . . Never mind, Jane, I know you don't want to hear about it."

"Andy'll slip someday," Jane said. "Luna'll kill him. I wish we could save her from a lethal needle then."

Jake nodded and said, "You didn't go see Billy today."

"They're going to kill him, after they catch his maker."

Jake just looked at her, then went back into the men's room. When he came out, he asked, "Were you followed?"

"By both the maker and the CIA proper."

"Do you really want to save him?" He put a plastic bead in her ear. It whispered to her in his voice, "You know some of us SPCA have contacts—I wouldn't use them for Luna, but this boy . . ." The bead seemed to have run out of storage—it was a tiny thing. Jake fished it out of her ear with a sticky stick and swallowed it.

Do I want to know about the underground even now? she asked herself. She felt odd— she'd dismissed Jake as not terribly realistic. Then the bulldog told her nobody in the underground trusted her. No, they did, maybe. She said, "Billy's weird. He shot you. He would have killed you if those guns had been lead-projectile weapons or lasers."

"Something about him."

129

"You're not gay. The maker said he jacked up the pheromones." She began pacing in a tight circle.

"Jane, drop the bitch act. I know you're worried about him. Go visit him even if you do lead the maker into the trap."

"I'd like to see Billy live," Jane said, wondering if she cared enough to risk her career to help. She looked at Jake and knew he was wondering if he'd been a fool to approach her. "I feel he'd be a decent creature if he got a chance."

"Billy's straightforward. Almost dumbly honest . . . for an illegal character."

Jane remembered that the real Billy the Kid wasn't even twenty-one when McSween, trapped with his men in a burning building, asked Billy for advice. *I'd like to talk to this one's maker. Did he try to be historically honest, or is this Billy more mythic?* "So, what are we going to do before he tries something nineteenth-century against the CIA?"

Jake wrote on a pad, *We've slipped in a sympathizer—we'll let you know if we need you.*

Not sure that they do need me, are they? Jane gripped her coffee cup and stared at the oily film on the surface—ersatz cream—while Jake took the pad to the sink and burned both the sheet he'd written on and the next seven sheets under that. "Maybe there's nothing we can do, but I sure wish," he said, staring at the ashes in the sink.

Jane said, "I thought the CIA was omnipotent."

Jake turned on the water tap and looked back at her with an expression between smile and grimace.

Jake's put me out of the main loop. Jane knew she should have been relieved to find out that someone else was handling the illegalities. But she didn't want to be just another groupie at the edge of a digital hologram. *If I wasn't going to be risking my job for nothing, I'd want to be the star of this now. . . .*

Later that day, she realized she hadn't daydreamed about Paris since she first saw Billy in the pound. But she had spent an inordinate amount of time speculating about the real Billy the Kid, caught between Irish cattle raiding and the oncoming twentieth century. And his killer, Garrett, gunned down while pissing after the century turned, a failure at almost everything except killing Billy. And there were Mexicans who denied he did that.

She stopped and realized she was making up her own myth out of raw files, later history, and Garrett's ghostwritten account. But there was this real creature down in the Concourse, a CIA rogue's meat dream of the Kid.

"Wonder if the rogue maker would run me up a Picasso," she said to tease Jake.

Jake pulled his feet under his chair and said, "Picasso wouldn't be illegal."

She said, "Just teasing, Jake, but how factual

131

is his reproduction of Billy? Nobody double-checked his research, did they?"

Billy said to the nurse, "I feel better. Can you unscrew the frame from my head?"

"No."

The law had Billy now, a headlock screwed into his skull bones. Jane visited him, telling him the time, which made him more grateful than he imagined such a little thing would make him. He stroked her chin before she left and the heat of her face warmed his fingertips for hours. About the time it felt like night, not that a man could tell under the maddening flickering light, a guard asked, "Need anything?"

"What happens next."

"Don't know." The man pulled up a chair. "You want the tank on?"

"Tank?"

The man said to the others standing guard, "Hey, we have a tank around here?"

The crispest guard with hair like steel bristles said, "He doesn't need it."

"Hey, he's bored. I'm bored. Little tank, can't hurt."

The tank turned out to be a glass sheet bent round, about one quarter inch thick, a foot high, and two feet across the circle, open at the top, on a black metal stand. The friendly guard clicked a switch at its base and tiny people popped up in the center of the tank. Billy stared at it, not sure what he was seeing, magic or lantern slides.

"It's a holo," the good guard said as if he'd explained something. "Tells a story." The guard with the steel-bristle hair frowned.

Billy felt the spikes dig into his skull when he tried to nod. The good guard turned a knob under the glass cylinder. The words the little people were supposed to be saying came out of the base of the tank.

The tiny people walked into a house and the walls of their parlor materialized on three sides. Jump-cut, like real life. Billy wondered if the walls blocked the view, then saw the good guard watching from the other side as though he could see just as well, too.

As Billy stared at the furniture, some metallic, some furry, he thought, I was always in the future, but couldn't see it.

The tiny woman sat in front of a keyboard. Billy recognized it as the descendant of a typewriter, but all in plastic, as if these people had less metal than in his age. Except for their furniture. He tried to move his head slightly and felt the screws against his skull bones—metal enough. A picture appeared on the tiny screen in the glass tank.

The bristle-haired guard laughed and said, "Isn't there anything better on than a woman's show?"

The friendly guard said, "I don't have any cassettes."

"I've got just the thing for tomorrow."

What felt like tiny muscles tugged at his eyeballs as Billy watched the bristle-haired guard moving around the room. He damned the man for pinning him down by the skull. Olinger, all over again, but Billy couldn't slip these bone screws as easy as he'd worked his wrists out of the cuffs.

That jailbreak didn't really happen to me, he thought, but how I remember taking Olinger and poor Bell will have to guide me now.

The man moved to be in better view when he noticed Billy's stare and said, "Relax, you never were really Billy the Kid."

"He knows," the friendly guard said. "I'd like to let him watch shows, get to know what it's really like outside."

The tiny holowoman and the man whose picture appeared on the screen over her typewriter met by an Oriental gate. Billy's stomach squirmed. He wondered if he'd been knifed by a Buddhist once.

Jump-cut to monks shaving the woman's head, the man's head, a tearful embrace, then the man leaving, surrounded by monks, as if he was going to be taken off and sacrificed.

Buddhist, not a refuge at all. Bare belly and knives with squiggle writing on them. Billy stared at the holotank, waiting for a rescue, but the story was over.

The next day, the steel-bristle man brought a leather sack and shook out a thing the size of a playing card, but thicker. "Enjoy," he said to Billy as he slid the card into a slot on the tank.

There was a white-haired woman in a velvet

swing. She was Jean Harlow, dead, but alive. MICHAEL MCCLURE'S "THE BEARD"—the letters floated in gold trimmed with red over the swing. A man Harlow called the Kid was there.

Billy looked away from the tank at the man who'd brought the cassette. "That ain't me."

"You never were him—this is one of the possibilities. You're a construction—how much based on the real Henry McCarty/Wiliam Antrim, we don't know. Perhaps you're based on this. Maybe what you're based on will give us a clue as to who made you."

"I've been in dime novels all my life," Billy said. He watched quietly until the Kid went down on his knees in front of Harlow. "If hell's giving head all the time, I'd be glad to go."

"You're an image of Billy the Kid, that's an image of Billy the Kid. What sort of image did your maker follow?"

Billy trembled, tried to hide it. A fake past, all of his memories? Not even a man, a lie. Then he got angry and hid his anger. That was part of the Kid program—stay angry, hide it. But he died in the end, over and over. He said, more dry-tongued than he wanted, "I wanna be my maker now."

After three weeks, the doctor took the metal spikes out of his head. Billy began working on his neck muscles, his arms, holding the pillow out beside the bed. He knew his legs had lost tone, too, but he couldn't figure out a way to strengthen them secretly. The urge to escape was so intense, Billy wondered if he'd been programmed to run. So what? If these people were waiting for his maker to come for him, they were using him for bait. Bait dies.

The trick, Billy decided, was to get just a little sick and exaggerate it. Then they'd relax and he could steal one of those shock sticks or drug guns—better with his little .41-caliber Colt Thunderer, but he hadn't seen any revolvers around. Unreal memories, Jane had told him— he wondered if he'd ever shot anyone with a real gun gun.

In his memory, he shot Olinger, the shotgun kicking up. Even from the upstairs jail window, he saw the blood jump out of Olinger's body, felt the memory of the gun stock in his hands, a splinter in the stock under his thumb. He'd worried it with his thumbnail, triumph and dread fighting in him. Escape, but for how long?

How could a man fake a memory like that?

The Buddhists could hide me. But Buddhists—images of incense and sacrifices to a dark copper god rose in his mind—screams under a knife going down into Billy's own belly, a salt smell in his nose, not blood or table salt exactly. Suddenly he questioned his spasm of fear when he thought about Buddhists. Fuck that, he decided, that's a real artificial memory. Then he wondered who was the Olinger that he shot if the memory was real.

About a week after the doctor took the spikes out of Billy's skull, the guards relaxed and let him watch a real news story, about a chimera who was made a miniature of a rich man. The man lost his money, so the man's fiancée broke with him and bought the chimera, who took over the man's social functions.

"Chimeras don't mind being bought?" Billy asked.

The good guard said, "Lots of them don't know any other life," and Billy remembered how the *vampira* loved the owner who yanked her tooth out. The guard continued, "Like you thought you were Billy the Kid. Make things artificial enough and you really can't tell."

Jump-cut in the holotank—the ex-rich man was calling a Buddhist monastery, claiming to be a chimera seeking refuge. He was discovered, but the Roshis let him stay.

"This happened for real?" Billy demanded, not understanding how anyone would let people put his life in a glass cage, make a story out of it.

"It was edited," the bristle-haired guard said. "And he didn't apply for exemption after he lost his money. Psychotic, liked the publicity more than the money."

"Exemption from what?"

"From the media. Rich, they're media targets. Not the Euro rich, but the American rich."

Billy lay back against his pillow, thinking these people were insane. "When I was an outlaw—"

"When you thought you were."

"Then, historically, wasn't it that only the poor guys got lies printed about them?"

"You missed Hollywood," the bristle-haired guard said. He stood away from Billy, as always.

The other guard said, "We followed actors' lives, the stars. Spread to all the rich. Media."

"Would the guys who make the little miniature people for the tank do that to me?"

"Media, the government. Odd relationship," the good guard said.

Billy said, "Always has been." He looked back at the tank and saw the ex-rich man sitting on a black cushion with his sacrificed hair on the floor around him. Images of killer Chinese rose in his mind, but they didn't look as vivid as his memories of the brain operation or the smells and sights of the men holding him captive. The man had phoned the Buddhists for help. The Buddhists preferred to help chimeras. Billy could hide in his nightmares, if the man who'd killed him over and over again had given him those images of killer Buddhists.

Killer Buddhist monks chanted in Billy's mind: *Don't do it, Billy, we'll kill you.*

Bait dies, Billy thought to them. He'd find the real Buddhists somehow. The man in the news show called them. But Billy didn't trust the phones. Telegraph wires had been tapped. He decided to get out in stolen clothes and walk to a Buddhist refuge. *My eyes, are they too weird to be human?*

"Where's Jane?" he asked the bristle-haired guard.

"We don't allow Jane in."

But Billy could find her if he could find the pound again. Dark copper god with an infinity of hands—dark copper god with teeth that bit ... artificial memories linked with memories of a salt smell, wet skin. The other chimeras in the pound seemed to think the Buddhists' refuges were good enough but boring. Images of sacrifices, of a broad knife, going into his screaming belly ...

Bullshit, he told his mind. "Get me some whiskey, you goddamn deputy fart," he said to the bristle-haired guard, since noise drove the images out of his mind.

The man scowled. "No whiskey, Billy." He looked at Billy as though Billy was dead meat already.

"Coffee?"

"You can get it yourself," the bad guard said. "You need some exercise."

Billy suspected he wasn't supposed to go near the electric gismo that heated the coffee water, but he'd made the guy mad. Good. Angry people slipped up. Billy hadn't planned on leaving just now, but here it was—a slip, opportunity.

Jane wouldn't like this, he thought as he threw hot coffee into the man's face and wrestled away his stun stick. He pushed it up against the man's ear and said "Bang" as he pushed the firing stud. The man toppled over. As other guards came toward him, he threw the hot plate and the rest of the coffee at them, before he shoved the trailer door. Pain from the door blasted him, but he didn't flinch, just wondered if wired-in twenty-first-century pain meant the door was flimsy or if he was killing his hands. The hinge screws screeched and the door came off.

They'd put something under his skin in the flesh of his buttocks—first thing was to get that out. How they'd transformed his eyes stunned him: vast tunnels with glowing light tubes, polished white tiles, a humming in the air punctured by random sounds. As sirens went off, he bent low and ran through the tunnels until he saw broken glass glittering under a street grate. He grabbed a shard of glass and bent around under the grate light, saw the scar, couldn't remember any wounds he'd gotten precisely there, and sliced into it, biting on the stun-stick shaft. Through the blood, he saw a tiny obscene black thing, pushed the glass shard under it and flicked it out, then tore his shirt and bound the wound as best he could, sweat dripping from his face. *I had a wound in my thigh once and ran on it.*

"Damn," he heard a voice say.

He turned with the stun stick and limped toward the voice. It was the steel-bristle-haired guard, the nasty one, on his feet again and hunting Billy. Like Olinger. All Billy had was the stun stick. He pointed it at the guard and pushed the button, but the man just stood there. Billy's stomach bent double inside his body.

"Stun sticks don't work at a distance. They were tracking you through that. We were going to get you out soon, you fool."

"Who are you?"

"Friend."

He saw the burns—coffee, not the hot plate—on the man's face. "Bull."

"Seriously, friend."

"You gonna take me to Jane?"

"They're watching Jane. We don't trust her, either. Man, you're bleeding. You need help fast."

"I gentled Jane. I trust Jane now." He wanted the man to come in range of the stun stick, but the man hunkered down, waiting for him to bleed faint. "I need Jane."

"We'll see what we can do."

"Let me go. I'll find Jane." He felt dizzy.

"God, I'm not sure we should. . . . Come with me, give me the stun stick and I'll report that you sliced your jugular and call for a body removal team. By the time they get here, we'll be gone, but you can't attack anyone anymore."

"Be quick," Billy said.

The man pulled out his radio and hurriedly told them that Billy'd slit his own throat rather than be recaptured. Then, as Billy swayed, he darted up and took the stun stick. Billy looked at him, waiting for the betrayal, but the man hustled him into the tunnels and up a staircase to the street.

"Oh, my God," Billy said, seeing the real cars, lights, snow. A helicopter cruised up the Hudson by the huge old dilapidated government buildings. *"Dios."*

"We've got a cab waiting. Hair dye. Shit, man, you almost boxed it. Chimeras who attack people get lethal-needled. You lucky I'm a chimera, too." The man tugged Billy. A metal machine screeched away from a line of other metal machines with rubber tires, then jerked to a stop in front of them. Billy dove into seats that looked somewhat like a stagecoach's, then closed his eyes as the thing leaned up on two wheels to take a corner. The driver and the man who'd found him under the grate talked—doctor, safehouses, Dharma refuge—while he felt sick, almost going crazy from the machine. It made a racket like a steam reaper, like a gasoline-burning water pump.

"Shit, Steve, he's bleeding all over the cab."

Steve, the bristle-haired one who'd found him, pulled Billy's pants down and tried to stanch the blood. "If he hadn't cut the homer out, we'd have them all over us."

"You could have goddamn neutralized it."

"He'd cut it out before I could get to him."

"Jee-sus."

"Went through the pain door, just took it down. Built tough like me, I guess."

They went suddenly silent. Billy knew they were worrying that he was too mad-dog for them to handle. "Jane works at the pound," he said quietly. "If you'd told me you were going to rescue me, if you had of just let me know, I could have pretended to be bad sick like I was planning."

"Sorry, Billy, but if they had a tracer up your butt, you can imagine what they had all over."

"In my time, they made the telegraph carry sound."

"Come on, chimera, that's not real," Steve said.

"Please get Jane to come to me."

The driver looked at Steve in the little mirror in the front window and they shrugged at each other.

"Why were you the bad-ass?" He felt confused, then remembered Pat Garrett, once his friend, hunting him. *Shit, I can't tell anything real, friend, foe. If they're really going to help me, I could use them.* "Don't keep me sedated either," Billy said. "It makes me very cranky." He smiled at them. When they cringed, he remembered his teeth and leaned his head on his hands, covering his mutilated eyes, as the real world or another delusion ambushed him.

"We didn't want anyone to suspect," Steve the bristle-haired one said. "Maybe you can tell us about CIA chimeras, too."

Simon had the Navarez chimera out when Baxter from Ops came in. By now the chimera thought he was Navarez. He turned his Axtecoidal face toward Simon when Baxter said, "The colonel died in a wreck in Chapultepec Park."

The chimera asked, in flawlessly accented English, "Colleague of mine?"

Baxter said, "Colonel Navarez, wait, please. I've got to discuss something with Simon."

Simon followed Baxter out of the room and sealed the door gaskets. *Dismantling, think of it as dismantling. They always get killed eventually.* He visualized Billy with the trocars up his neck veins, dead for three minutes only.

"We've got another possible," Baxter said. He led Simon to the canteen and nodded to the waitress, who pulled a bag of coffee beans out of the freezer. She set them up to grind and put a new filter in the coffeemaker.

"They'd been a bunch of idiots for years," Simon said. "Greasers. Why'd they consolidate when the climate changed? Why do we have to deal with a huge motherfucking country with oil?"

"If the seas sink, they want to hold the continental shelf. They're thinking ahead."

"Greasers, they never thought ahead before." He remembered reading about Billy, the real one, yelling insults out at the Mexicans, begging Pat Garrett to unchain and arm him—*su madre*. He could visualize the scene as if he'd been Pat Garrett. But the book had lied. The Mexicans really wanted to lynch Dave Rudabaugh, not *El Chavito*.

"Racism isn't Company policy," Baxter said. The waitress handed them each a cup of coffee, her face impassive.

Simon didn't answer for a while, sipped the

coffee and stared at the waitress whose eyes seemed vaguely inhuman. Chimera, he decided. Then he said, "I hate losing them."

"So do I," Baxter said.

Behind them, gas hissed into the room where the chimera sat, waiting.

Jane was walking to work down the heated sidewalk on the building side of Washington Avenue when she saw a crow land on a streetlight just ahead of her. The crow opened its beak in a mechanical way, the bird's real eye frantic to be so controlled. "Billy's gone, isn't he?" she said before the bird could speak. A man near her turned his head, looked away when she caught his eye. It was the little Oriental CIA man, dressed in an electric-blue leather suit. He smiled almost at himself and looked back at her. The crow flew off and swerved.

The Vietnamese said, "The crow?"

"No," Jane said. "I saw you." She didn't want to see the crow shot.

"Someone thinks you know where he is."

"I didn't know he was gone until just now." The crow was flying erratically in the sky, the natural bird fighting the controls planted in its brain. Jane watched it, then it flew away fast.

The CIA man walked her to work. As soon as Jane came into the office, she saw Jake. "Jake," she said, "Billy's gone."

"Don't talk to me about it," Jake said. "I don't

know a damn thing. CIA wants you to cooperate. For some considerations."

"Considerations to who? Billy? Can he live?"

The small Vietnamese came in and said, "I'd like your door key. I'll be there when you get home."

Jane thought, a thousand dollars' worth of leather to watch me in my cube. He was younger than her, somewhere between nineteen and twenty-four, she thought, if Orientals didn't age faster than Caucasians?

"Don't worry. I'll keep intruders out better than an electric wall."

"I don't really want this."

The young Vietnamese said, "The chimera may be in the wrong hands. Several foreign agencies have made anomalous moves."

Each night the CIA agent smoked cigarette after cigarette, stubbing them out in one of her saucers and leaving them. He wouldn't tell her anything, didn't come on to her, not even to flirt. The first night, she couldn't sleep. In the morning the Vietnamese followed her to work, then turned back at the pound door with her keys. Probably the CIA had other people watching the pound. The second night, she woke the first time startled by the sound of his leather pants rubbing against each other as he crossed his legs. Later, dreams threw her out of sleep to the sight of his cigarette glowing in the dark, dim highlights on yet another gaudy leather suit.

Jake moved to the night shift.

The second week, she began to relax, accept

the agent's presence, feeling slightly relieved that he never made a pass, but obscurely annoyed, too. Then the third week, she changed her blouse in front of him, not closing herself off in the toilet. He raised his eyes from a magazine he was reading and smiled, then looked back at the magazine. The smile burned into Jane's memory—an indulgent smile as sexually indifferent as if she'd been a dog squatting to piss.

And Billy's maker didn't contact her again either, no funny birds or chip-voice phone calls, nothing.

The last day of January felt to Jane like the first day of the next ice age as she walked home from work. The Vietnamese opened her cube door when she knocked, one hand covering what she feared was frostbite on the cheek the wind had kept gusting against. Behind him was Dr. Morse. She saw the lie probe like a large flashlight in Morse's hand and felt invaded again.

Morse motioned for her to come in. She did, hand still against her cheek until she went to the mirror over the dresser and saw red, not the white of frozen flesh. Then she said, "What do you want? Why won't this man tell me his name?"

"Come here," Dr. Morse said. She went up to him and he pressed the lie probe against her throat. "Do you know where Billy is?"

"Maybe he's dead already." She was glad she

147

had no idea as the lie probe caught messages from her vagus nerve, carotid, and windpipe.

"And the intruder, the guy who claims to be his maker, hasn't been back?"

"No." She almost regretted that as much as she resented the chimera underground not trusting her. Oh, Jake, she thought, they don't even suspect you and they're protecting us against glaciers.

"Ask her about the crow last month," the Vietnamese said.

"I thought it was from the maker," Jane said, "but I didn't want to see it die, too."

Jane had known for a while that the guards who were working a few weeks before quitting were the CIA day-duty officers on Billy's case. A few days after Dr. Morse interrogated her, two young city cops brought a human-sized chimera with fangs to the pound. Jane saw one rub his eyes as though they itched, then he looked at her. Floating on his eyes were colored contact lenses, a tiny rim of blue showing around them. The latest CIA guard twisted out his cigarette and stared at her. The chimera began chattering about the pleasures of tanking when the programs were really esoteric, like the stolen Langley program his owner used.

Jane saw the disguised cop—Billy, she couldn't let the CIA man know it was Billy—brush up against her coat hanging on the rack. Billy, if it was Billy, smiled at her when no one else was looking. His teeth were Billy-sized.

Then the other cop touched her skin with something cold.

She shivered slightly and forgot what it was that she'd just learned, knew still that she'd learned something important. The CIA man asked, "You recognize either cop?"

"No," she said, vaguely aware that cops had brought in a chimera who was still standing in front of the check-in desk, chattering away about the wonderful illusion of being a spy. The cops had disappeared, but Jane didn't remember them leaving. She wondered if she'd had a dizzy spell, or a little stroke. *All this and my health going, too.*

The CIA man began asking the chimera questions. Jane wondered if it was really a chimera and said, "Test him."

"Cops brought him in," the real pound guard said.

"I can get a test team up now," the false guard from the CIA said, already dialing.

Human DNA, implanted teeth. By that time, the Vietnamese had arrived, dressed in a raw silk suit that looked almost like pajamas, his face puffy, marked by a wrinkle from his bedclothes. He looked at the human fake chimera and said, "A distraction, but whose?"

Jane said, "I don't know."

He held a lie probe against her throat and said, "Say that again."

"I don't know."

"But you think you should. Something happened to you. You're under stress."

"Wouldn't you be, with a CIA case officer watching you while you slept?"

Both CIA men turned to the human, who said, probe to his throat, "I was cold, my cube, I just wondered what it was like in here."

The Vietnamese said, "He's partially lying," and called a number, put plastic cones over both ends of the receiver. "Extension 41, please." He paused, then said, "Send us an interrogation team. And stop the police who just left. Damn, they can't have just disappeared."

The other CIA man said, "If it's a feint, then the rogue knows we're taking this seriously. Maybe we're taking him too seriously? Everyone's got to blow off steam some way. He's not necessarily going KGB or *federales*-level rogue just because he made this Billy reconstruction."

The Vietnamese said, "Have you read in archives about the slack discipline around Christopher Boyce last century? Smuggling in even a beer, leads to . . ." He looked at Jane and shut up. She thought, one of the million Vietnamese who stayed angry at her personal slack discipline that lost them their country a century ago. Her visual cortex assembled an image of Vietnamese picketing something—America, her house—thousands of angry disciplined Asians. The Vietnamese—no, the whole CIA— wanted Billy to identify his maker. They weren't just after the maker; but would go on to stomp the undisciplined bastards who'd hire such a maker turned even petty rogue.

Jane nodded at him and put on her coat.

When she got down to the street, she reached in her pockets for her gloves and found a message: *Ski the Pine Bush each Saturday at eleven, my time. They don't trust you. Henry.*

Henry McCarty? Yes, Billy's true name. Pacific Coast time? And who doesn't trust me? CIA? Chimera underground? Probably all of them.

Back at her cube, she figured out what New Mexico time was in Eastern Standard. When the Vietnamese went out on an unexplained errand, Jane hammered the coin the bulldog had given her. The plastic was solid, so she put it in her microwave and burned the message from Billy in her sink. As the coin bubbled in the microwave, exposing glints of microchips, she thought, Oh, shit, what if it was like a dead-man switch, signaling until I destroyed it. I've signaled the maker that contact was made. As she washed the paper ashes down the drain and waited for the coin mess to cool so she could scrape out the microwave, she realized that the Vietnamese would know she'd been contacted, too, by the scorched plastic smell and the mess in the microwave.

And why does Billy trust me?

After she scraped out the ruined communication coin, Jane went in to her bathroom and brushed her hair, staring at her reflection, the sallow unrebuilt face with bones angular in the wrong places. Why go with Billy? she wondered. He was with the underground. She had

151

her job to consider. Maybe in a few years, she could have her jaw done, the nose.

The Vietnamese let himself in. She heard him open the microwave, but didn't get up, stopped her hand with the hairbrush above her left ear, listening to him. He found the coin's remains in the trash bag. Jane said, "I found it. The maker must have left it when he came here."

The agent didn't come into the bathroom, just to the door. "Why did you destroy it today?"

"I just found it today." Jane wondered if he'd noticed any paper ashes in the sink. "You went out to see what I'd do while you weren't here, didn't you?"

"You lie."

"I just want to continue on at the shelter. I don't want to get involved in this spy crap."

The man stared at Jane's reflection. She put the brush down and looked up at his eyes, then looked away. He stared at her mirrored image as if she were the chimera. She said, "I could have gotten an engineering half scholarship, but—"

"You don't need to defend your career choice." He smiled. His tone was condescending.

Suddenly Jane wanted to break into the man's brain, destroy his utter devotion to the dumbest task, like watching her, because he was disciplined, sure of himself. "What else do you do for the CIA?" Stupid to ask, she realized as soon as she'd framed the question.

He kept smiling and said, "Many things," as

he crossed his arms in front of him. The smile made him seem younger than was possible.

"I wasn't trying—"

"No, you'd have been more subtle." His lips twitched and he turned his eyes away from hers in the mirror.

"I couldn't trip you up, could I?" Did she need to think of the CIA as omnipotent? That was an oddly disturbing thought. If they were half as muddled as most humans, she felt the glaciers would freeze America—if not the actual ice glaciers, then all the political shifts the physical ice caused. Why do I need to see them as evilly omnipotent? she wondered.

"Assumptions are dangerous."

Jane looked once more at her uncultivated face, bones unshaved beneath the flesh. "I do have a good job for a person from my background." She stopped herself just before she asked, *don't I?*

Without answering, the Vietnamese packaged the ruined coin in a mailer.

Both Billy's old perceptions and his new vision fought. Steve Bristle-hair, whose clothes wavered between nineteenth-century illusions and this future that had Billy trapped, asked, "Are you only alive when you're stunting? You managed when we gave the message to the woman but you're falling apart now."

"I thought that was dumb, and she hasn't done what you wanted," another man said.

"She's under observation," Steve said. "I

want to get her out because she knows about Jake, despite what, whatever.''

Billy sat up in the bed, feeling his scars. The bullet damage to his thigh, his chest was real, down to the chipped bone. Or so they told him that here to scare him. "Why did you take *me* out?" His head wounds, the scars rawer, had brought on this nightmare. If what he'd seen turned out to be a dream or madness, Pat Garrett still hunted him, could kill him real easy while he was crippled in the head. Somewhere, Garrett oiled his gun and collected his information, slowly, always slowly. Billy needed Jane.

"We got a tip that they were going to dose you lethal," Steve said. "We wanted to talk to you. I've got something in common with you."

"I don't understand," Billy said, but he knew what lethal meant.

"Lethal needle—that's how they execute people and put down chimeras these days," the second man explained. "Steve's a chimera defector. Your maker works for the CIA. Steve's been telling us a lot about how cruel the spy-chimera system is. We're people who help chimeras, believe in equality of structural DNA regardless of the source."

Billy still didn't know how executions were done—stabbing the heart, the brain, with a needle? Or drugs—he didn't want to know how it was done. Always people first wanted to humiliate him, then kill him. This life was no change. "I don't know what DNA is. You know that. And

Jane, you think she knows where Garrett is."
Billy shook his hands to get rid of the ghost
sensation of irons on them. He thought that he
had killed his jailers in this body almost as he
remembered, despite whatever he really was.
There was a salt smell—alkali spring—to memories he was sure were false. *Dog-meat robot.*
"Steve, don't you feel pain? Don't you hold
grudges? I scalded you." Steve made Billy nervous. He needed Jane because her brain wasn't
grown to see funny.

"It's all right, Billy. We'll see about getting
Jane to join us."

"I am a man," he told them.

The second man said, "I wish it was that simple."

"She knows me when I thought I was either
crazy or really Billy the Kid," Billy finally said.
"I need that." He tried to make his eyes see
things the way they were but the room began
to go black around the edges, vision tunneling
to blindness, then he touched his eyes to see if
they were still open.

"That's a pretty stupid reason," the second
man said. "Steve, we can't make her do anything and maybe she's told them about Jake already. Bet she's afraid to lose her job."

Billy gave up fighting his vision and closed
his eyes. "If I'm blind, would they kill me?" He
opened his eyelids, but the room was still dark.
"I can't see now."

The two men didn't say anything, just moved
around the room. Billy heard one come close,

155

then felt body heat. Steve said, "Billy, I'm going to touch your head." The man's fingers—no, the dog-meat robot's fingers—landed on Billy's chin, and Steve said, "Hysterical blindness, the pupil reflex is still there."

Billy wondered if he'd be safe gone crazy. Maybe they were Olinger and Bell? Two of them and he so crazy he couldn't really feel the irons on his legs and wrists, just tickling sensations. "My name is McCarty, but Antrim said I could use his name." He felt his heart roaring and lurching inside his ribs like a caged man gone loco.

"Billy, when you can see again," Steve said, "I'll give you some books that will get you oriented."

I don't want to be oriented. He couldn't tell them that. If he was Billy, they'd kill him. If he was a dog-meat robot, someone else would kill him. He hadn't wanted to die all those times. "What do you want from me?"

"Just tell me what you remember, try to keep the false memories out of it. You must have seen something," Steve said.

The other man said, "Forget the woman. We'll set you up with a false identity after some facial surgery."

Billy said, "Can you give me bigger hands and a smaller jaw?" He doubted he could get his hands out of cuffs then, but those hands and his jaw were his most distinguishing features. And these people bound a man without steel cuffs.

156

"We'll do the teeth tomorrow," Steve said. "We can glue them in in no time."

Late one evening as Jane and the Vietnamese watched the holotank play a digitalization of *Casablanca*, the Vietnamese said, "You can call me Trung."

"Bet that isn't your name, just something to call you."

His lip corners jerked. Jane noticed that his puffy Asian eyelids seemed moist, as though he sweated there when he sweated nowhere else. He said, "I think you've been contacted. No one knows where the Billy chimera is except the people who took him. None of the makers are moving. We'd like you to help us. For Billy's life."

She stared at the tank, the little Bogart bleeding red—would he die, was he just wounded? Could there be resistance today? Against the onrushing ice, when eleven thousand years ago European forests turned from boreal to arctic in less than a hundred years? "Why? I have a nice job. He's just a chimera." If the CIA operatives were merely human, then all the conspiracy theorists were stupid. If the CIA was omnipotent, then the rest of the citizenry weren't failures in their impotence. She almost said, *But you haven't asked me about Jake?*

"We need to find the maker."

"Poor bastard's probably too scared to steal any more segments from you."

"The KGB has moved, not toward anyone, not

away from anyone, there's just more traffic."
He sounded anxious.

"What do you want me to do?"

"Do what they wanted. I'll follow you."

"Why will you follow me?"

"Because otherwise you would look suspicious. You will call us. We will let all our makers know where the chimera is, see who is interested. Perhaps the chimera remembers something, but I doubt it. We can't show him pictures—he may be implanted with false memories. We might lose the wrong man and good makers are not so easy to get."

"And who's listening to us talk now?"

"We're feeding false conversations to the bugs we found."

Jane felt stripped naked. "What can you do for me?"

"You'll have money, a job as good as your old one. The chimera might could live."

"The SPCA—I'd be marked there. The underground is a considerable part of it."

"Relatively harmless, normally." Trung slumped down in his chair and sighed.

"I bet you've infiltrated them and don't want to betray your inside man."

"Ah, Jane, so paranoidly American. I have no idea whose wires we're feeding."

Jane realized that someone from the underground could be listening, watching. Or the maker? Plots within plots. "I can't help you. I'm tired of this. I'm going to go skiing next weekend if you want to come along." She smiled slightly and nodded.

He bowed slightly—almost mocking her.

Simon sat at Langley in an environmental protection lab, fingers on white computer keys calling up segments on file, building a duplicate Brazilian IF agent cum cultural attaché, the real DNA sequences showing in a pop-up. Someone smuggled out the DNA sample in a lap-top battery card.

No one else came in the labs when makers worked with live sequences, so Simon, as his fingers slowed down on the keys, thought about Billy. Simon stared at the Brazilian's DNA readout, then realized he ought to really let Billy go and hope the Garrett template distorted all the views of Simon he'd ever seen. Every intelligence agency had people working on a dead-brain readout, but each brain had systems too unique to read easily—and memory was fluid.

Vision, hearing, and speech could be tampered with, but memories clumped in ways that were never random to the specimen, but might as well have been to the investigator, like Library of Babel bookshelves where only the owner could locate an item—dreams, real time, speculations, readings all rotted together.

He began fitting in the sequences that would grow a biorecorder that could be read when the Brazilian defected—false defector, true chimera. Or was this an intelligence-*federales* trap?

A small benign tumor in the right hemisphere should do it. The man had approached a CIA agent, diplomatic corps, offered to defect but not right away. A chimera agent sent word out that the Brazilian wasn't even Brazilian, perhaps was a chimera duplicate of the original, perhaps not. If chimera, then someone had broken the rule and built a chimera exactly like a man.

Simon called up the Brazilian's brain profile and saw where he could fit in his recorder, thinking how tired he was of designing chimeras who died, hundreds by now. In all of them, bred to a fiercer loyalty than any man had, the adrenal loop was detuned, the concept of time and death blurred. Simon thought, for at least the millionth time, they could take the planet if they wanted to. What revenge they could take if they weren't so self-sacrificing.

But Simon hadn't built Billy that way. Billy could shoot him. Being shot by the Kid would be better than all the slimy pity he'd get from the Company psychiatrists before he was sent off to sit until spy-building technology had gone beyond his present knowledge and after all his agents had died.

How many of Simon's spies still lived? He remembered the KGB woman, a lieutenant when he built her, now a major. The original, after reconstructive surgery, died in a car crash. The Mexican general, the Algerian cabinet minister, the Brazilian industrial chemist—they could live for years.

His heart monitor began murmuring numbers at him as he changed to leave, so he sat down on a bench and meditated the thing quiet.

But then on the train going home to Richmond, Allesandra, her head veiled in blue silk chiffon, sat down beside him and just looked at him, didn't say anything.

100 beats per minute. Simon knew he'd have to report her. Then when the train stopped in Richmond, she said, "Some people are interested in a rogue maker. I heard on the street."

Projected 110 beats per minute.

Simon wondered if she was offering him a deal. Which way? "We might be interested." *110 beats per minute.*

Allesandra touched his cheek with her hand and smiled, then stayed on the train as Simon got off.

I should confess, Simon thought, but he drove home and called internal security to report Allesandra's contact. *120 beats per minute.*

The Langley internal-security secretary said, "Mr. Turner's office."

Simon hadn't heard that Turner was back at Langley now. Hunting him, yes, Turner would be the obvious one for the job since he'd trained most of the current makers. Simon said, "Allesandra came up to me on the train. Said word on the street is that foreign agencies are interested in a rogue maker."

"Was she warning or asking if you were a rogue maker?"

"Trying to ingratiate herself with us, I think."

Simon hung up and wished he could just shoot Allesandra, have her shot. If Turner questioned her, then she'd simply tell the Agency everything. It's so terrible, he thought, it's not just business, but all the personalities involved, too. Allesandra let her skin go after he turned her in. Turner had tried to get away from direct work, but was now hunting his protégés. Was hunting him. Simon took a tranquilizer, then sat staring at nothing until the little heart voice faded.

Steve the Bristle-hair took Billy away from the others one morning and fitted him with boots, mittens, and a heavy jacket before taking him outside.

Billy, who hadn't yet seen where they were, looked out the door onto snowfields, trees, gentle hills, a narrow long lake out beyond them. The snow was deep, but someone had shoveled a long path down toward some woods.

"Haven't been out in a while, have you?" Steve said.

"No. Damn, it's cold." Billy's nose hairs felt stiff.

"About eight below, but we've got a fire in the warming hut. Thought you needed to walk a bit."

"Yes, yes." Billy began walking, feeling the blood and the cold fight in his thigh muscles to see if he'd stiffen or loosen up. He beat his hands against his legs and remembered another cold time. The trail went on for two miles, maybe, before they reached the hut with the wood stove. Billy wondered how they plowed it. The hut was all big slab shingles, roof and siding, with a black metal stovepipe coming out. It reminded him of Stinking Springs, where Garrett killed Bowdre, mistaking him for Billy because of the hat, no doubt. But that had been a rock house.

Steve opened the hut door and said, "You need to rest a little."

Billy was tired, but didn't want to stop moving after all those days of being trapped. Then his thigh that had been shot at least once, for real, trembled. He nodded.

The hut was warm inside, with the windows all steamy. Billy stopped when he saw something like a giant's coffin and smelled the not-quite-salt smell.

Steve said, "You know what that is?"

"I hate it."

"I didn't like it either."

"But I don't quite know what it is."

"Ah, Billy Henry, we know what it is, don't we?"

"I know, but I can't remember."

Steve opened two cocoa pouches into cups and then poured hot water from a kettle on the stove into them. "Relax." He stirred both cups with the same spoon as Billy watched, nervous about drugs and poisons. Steve smiled and said, "Take either cup. I just want you to look at some pictures." He opened a photo album after Billy took a cup, then sipped his own cocoa.

Billy looked at the photographs and recognized Pat Garrett's. Damn odd to think the man had been dead since 1908. Some of the photos seemed more like people dressed these days. "Pat. The others I've never seen before."

"Yes, that is Pat Garrett," Steve said. "But you should be able to recognize the others."

"Don't think so," Billy said.

"Do any of these make you feel nervous?" Steve came up and pointed to five photographs—men and one woman, all modern.

Billy said, "You make me nervous. Did you make me?"

"Enough. I know you don't like the tank, but I promise it won't hurt. We need to find out how to make a new life for you. We'll do it if you cooperate."

Billy wondered how many men surrounded the hut. "You'd force me."

"Well, I'd prefer not. We do have things in common after all."

"Help me be able to figure out what a false memory is."

Steve ran his hand over his stiff hair and smiled slightly. "Does Pat Garrett smell of this room? Epsom salts?"

Billy looked at Pat's photo again and couldn't make up his mind. "I've seen him for real, I think. It's not like the Buddhists."

"Oh, you don't want to go to the Buddhists. Opiate of chimeras and humans alike."

The black tank seemed even more like a coffin. "I won't get in that. If you make me, I'll know where I stand with you."

Steve stood without speaking, then drank his cocoa. He walked around Billy, then asked, "Did he put you in it after you died?"

"I don't want to get killed again. I'm tired of it."

"We want to find the man who made you and keep him from ever doing anything like that again."

"You think that thing would help me remember?"

"Maybe."

"Can I just look inside it?" When Steve nodded, Billy walked up to the black tank as though it was a trap. He lifted the lid, which swung back smoother than any hinges Billy could remember. Inside was thick water, heated, and inside the lid was glass five inches deep. Billy said, "All I remember is Pat Garrett putting . . ." He was sweating. "Stabbing me in the throat. I don't know. It was just Pat Garrett and my blood being pumped back into me."

Steve began looked at the photographs again. After a while, he said, "Did Pat Garrett ever lean on anything?"

Billy said, "He rode horses that talked," and wondered when he learned that.

"But did he lean on things?"

"That's odd, I remember him standing in a door frame, body curved a bit, not leaning against the door."

"Three of them are fat. Garrett was a tall

skinny bastard. Thanks, Billy, I don't need you to get in there, at least not yet." Steve closed the photo album and put his coat and gloves back on. "Maybe we can use Jane as bait? He has contacted her."

"Bait dies."

"Oh, it will be perfectly safe for both of you," Steve said. "If you're not in shape to walk back, I'll call for a snowmobile."

"I'm fine," Billy said. "I'll walk."

"Just as tough as the original Billy, I'll bet." Steve pointed back at the tank. "You a coward of it?"

"I'm not afraid to be a coward in these days."

Each Saturday, Trung in his goatskin suit skied behind Jane through the Pine Bush, singing Oriental songs. Then, on the third Saturday, when she finished duck-stepping up a snow-plow scrape to cross a road, five snowmobiles whizzed out of the woods, whirled around her. Trung flailed across the road, ripping the bottoms of his skis. Arms pulled her up into a snowmobile. Trung dropped his ski poles and fired a pistol at them, two hands on the gun. Then she was jolted across the snow while the person who'd pulled her into the machine held his hands over her eyes.

A sixth machine came up, roaring along beside the machine Jane was in. Both machines reversed treads, snow clods thumping.

"Other one," the man said, stripping the skis from her, shoving her out.

She half fell, half climbed into the other machine, driven by a ski-masked man, and rode with him to a car.

"Last place they'll look right now is your place," the man said as they drove back down Washington Avenue. He stripped off his mask and she saw that he was the bristle-haired guard from Billy's time in the CIA hospital trailer.

Billy was waiting just inside her outer house door. He asked, "Jane?"

Maybe I don't have to betray him, she thought. They embraced and he said, "We had to have you with us, Jane. I need someone who knew me when I really was Billy the Kid. Steve here needs you as bait for the man who made me."

"Billy," she said. "I hope this isn't a mistake."

"They've caught up with the first ski mobile," Steve, the former guard, said. "We'll head up-river—sympathizers on a preserve." He motioned for them to step back outside to the street. Jane looked around for Trung, but realized Trung would be off the case now, having failed to keep up with her. She almost felt sorry for him. As soon as they stepped out to the curb, a cab that had been parked down the street rolled toward them. Steve opened the rear cab door and motioned for Jane to get in. He sat in back beside her and shifted his facial muscles and lowered his bristly hair. Billy got in beside the driver in front.

His face shifted. Jane felt her stomach spit acid up her esophagus. The cab seemed too small, too open to the outside, too crowded with a face-shifting creature beside her. Steve the inside chimera, she thought. CIA?

Billy seemed to know the cabdriver, and joked with him as they drove up by the graffiti-tagged university buildings. "I was conditioned scared of the Buddhists, then I found out how boring you guys really are. Really boring. Sitting on your asses all day. Not knife killers at all."

The cabdriver laughed and said, "Chinese say to be born in interesting times is a curse."

"Yeah, let's not wait to find out how interesting," Jane said. Steve nodded, keeping his face in its new configuration, his hair flat.

"Can't speed," the driver said. "Just relax."

Steve said, "Demon dialers have been working your phone, so surveillance says. Wha'd you do, tip someone about Billy's message?"

"The man who said he was the maker—I broke the coin he gave me."

"Yeah, that'd do it." Steve's hair bristled.

"I wish I knew how trustworthy the memories he gave me are." Billy seemed almost excited about the challenges that humans had thrown him.

"You look good without those buckteeth."

"Doubt the real Billy had such real buckteeth," he said. "I seem to have a quick mind—CIA-custom encephalization and neural DNA segments, these guys suspect. But my person-

ality? That come off a DNA chain or out of tanking? Do I really have to kill people?" He looked
back at her, fine teenage beard showing on his
upper lips and jaw, his eyes gray.

Jane realized she'd been thinking of him almost as if he were really a time-traveling Billy
the Kid, but he was just a chimera, someone's
pet who'd gotten lost. "Nobody's quite sure how
people get theirs."

"Should be simpler with us," he said. "Jane,
you're not a bigot down deep, are you?'

Steve looked over at her and smiled. Was she?
She was willing to help chimeras within the
limits of the law. Now she was doing this—but
how does one treat chimeras socially? She had
a sudden image of them in bed together, but
with Billy relapsing into his nineteenth century
and beating her for being a whore. She wondered if he had supernumerary nipples, a
sheathed cock—*no, the CIA can't afford to have
duty chimeras look like animals.*

Steve said, "The other reason we're getting
you out is that you know Jake was Animal Defense. But you're not really eager to be with us,
are you, Jane? You were beginning to like
Trung, weren't you?"

"Jane, you are going to help me, aren't you?"
Billy asked. She didn't answer; he sighed as if
he was disgusted with her. He said, "I have to
become a man. I always thought I was one."

She said, "That's the most difficult thing for
you, isn't it?"

"Yeah, and I wonder who all the other people

were? It wasn't all holograms in a tank, I don't think. These guys gave me hologram car-driving lessons. I'm good, but my first driving memories smell like Epsom salt. I remember the smell from other times, but not . . ." He clamped his jaw shut.

" 'A place where Billy the Kid can hide when he shoots people,' " Jane said, remembering what her intruder had said.

"Someone say that about me?" He sounded belligerent. When she didn't answer, he turned back to stare at her with his eyes gone deep blue.

"Yeah, but it was said first about the real Billy—no, about a poet's imaginary Billy."

"I need to read that book, that poet's Billy-the-Kid book, all the Billy-the-Kid books. But I tell you I don't kill people unless I've really got to—like to escape."

"And Steve isn't mad because you nearly burned his face off?"

Steve said, "My pain nerves aren't like yours."

Jane said, "Not to speak of your face muscles."

Billy almost interrupted. "And I know that they were using me for bait to catch the rogue maker. Then, lethal needle. Shit, I, the real Billy the Kid, had lawyers, wrote the governor, reporters."

"The library had your letters but I suspected you were built more mythopoeic."

"I remember . . . oh, shit."

"The media plays an even bigger part in to-day's life," the driver said as they crossed the Mohawk, "than it did in the nineteenth century. We've got what we need to give to the media if the CIA won't cooperate."

Jane thought they were naive to think they could blackmail the CIA. Billy would die. She considered that helping Trung might be best. Billy could die in that "might be," too.

Billy stared out at the snowy parking lots and narrow streets as they drove through Cohoes, circling back to make sure they hadn't been fol-lowed. In front of the old Dansk building, he said, "Why can't I have lawyers? Don't tell me. I'm really a dog. Dogs don't get lawyers."

Jane realized she was thinking of him as real again. He looked at her as if he saw the shift inside her mind—real, no, a toy Billy the Kid who really shoots people.

The car turned and left Cohoes, headed for the Adirondacks. "Well, maybe we can relax," the driver said.

"Not with everyone using me and Billy for bait," Jane said. "Are you people using us for bait? Who are you?"

"We could make Jane think she used to be a chimera," Billy said. He slumped down in the front seat, one foot tapping the floorboards.

"Billy," the driver said.

Billy asked, "Humans not supposed to be tampered with?"

"Billy, I'm afraid . . ." She almost talked about Trung's offer—set the chimera up as bait, let him live after they caught the maker, give her a good job. "Who are these people?"

The driver said, "Blindfolds now, ladies and gentlemen, we have to make sure you can't lead anyone back here."

"I hate things messing with my eyes," Billy said as he pulled a blindfold over his head. "They're my eyes, even if they lied to me."

When Jane put her blindfold on, cold wetness hit her eyelids. When the light around the edges of the blindfold faded to black, she realized that the cloth had been drugged and she was really blind now. *Way out of my league.*

The car began to turn, Jane's body shifting from side to side. Mountains, side streets? She was too stunned to panic when unseen hands helped her up steps into what had to be a plane. When the jet engines cut on, she heard Billy say, "What the damn?"

"It's all right, Billy, it's a plane."

"I know what a goddamn plane is, I know what a goddamn plane is," he said, repeating himself in an angry rote way as if saying he knew would explain all the physics. "I seen them in pictures."

The plane taxied a short distance and jumped into the air.

CHAPTER FIVE
A National Park of the Mind

. . . I saw the two Billies the other day &
they say they are going to leave this county.
That was my advice to them for I believe it
is the best thing they can do. . . . I know
of nothing to urge in my favor, now than
that others were pardoned for like offenses.
Experience is a good but slow teacher & I
think if I keep my mind, I will let every man
do his own fighting so far as I am concern
& I will do my own.

Respt
Chas. Bowdre

—**Excerpts from December 15, 1880, letter
to Captain Lea.** (Bowdre was killed when
mistaken for the Kid by Garrett's posse
at Stinking Springs December 23. His last
words were, "I wish, I wish, I'm dying."
The two Billies, Billie Wilson and the Kid,

along with Dave Rudabaugh and Tom
Pickett, surrendered after Garrett as-
sured them that they would not be shot
out of hand as he'd originally intended.
Two Texans saved the Kid when Barney
Mason thought killing him anyway would
be wiser.)

JANE'S EYELIDS STUCK AT FIRST, THEN CAME APART, showing her a flat board ceiling and pale light that seemed like early morning. She couldn't remember exactly what had happened, but she was under an antique quilt nobody she knew could afford.

Some unusual dust made her sneeze, and she remembered. The night before—or whenever—the plane that took them out of New York State had landed, skidding down on a tilted runway. Then, still blinded, she'd let someone lead her to a car. She and Billy, both on the backseat, slid together on the curves. Lots of curves, so they were in the mountains somewhere.

When they'd gotten out of the car, the driver had taken them into a room. Heat radiated at them from a central point. Billy sniffed and said, "Wood heat."

Now Jane got out of bed and realized that the bedroom was warmer than her Albany flat, but she couldn't see any heat registers, only an empty fireplace with smudges where ashes had been swept away. What had the driver told them when they came in yesterday? Yes, the house had electricity, running water, and about a cord of wood stacked on the back porch. He'd said, "That's a good stove—we heat our whole house with one like it."

Jane saw snow outside the windows on hemlocks and leafless trees, too many deciduous trees to be north of Maryland. But then she remembered. As the man had sprayed her eyes to bring back her sight, he'd said, "Billy, we thought the Appalachian Cultural Park would be easier on you."

But what about me? Jane thought, now remembering. "Billy?" She felt as if she'd been kidnapped, as if this couldn't be real. Trung should be down at the other end of the room, smoking his cigarettes. But no. She'd never wake up again under her mahogany ceiling.

She thought, I'm in shock, that's why my memory is so crappy. I'm exiled unless I trust Trung can keep Billy from a lethal needle.

"Jane, come on down," she heard Billy say, his western accent too pure to be real. Then Billy talked to another person, a man.

She remembered Steve shifting his face and shuddered. "Let me get dressed."

"Clothes for you in the chest of drawers," the other male voice said. It wasn't Steve.

As she took jeans, panties, bra, and shirt from the drawers, she heard Billy ask, "What is the Appalachian Cultural Park?"

The jean legs looked too short. As she pulled them on, Jane listened to the other male voice saying, "This is a place where people didn't want to change. We kept it the way it was in the nineteenth century, twentieth century, and tourists and government grants support those of us who aren't self-sufficient."

"What about chimeras?" Billy asked.

"Most of us don't believe in chimeras," the other man said.

Jane wondered in what sense did they not believe in chimeras. Dust got in between Jane's toes as she came down the stairs. Billy said, "I'm not sure I do, either." Jane saw how tense he was—he seemed to have aged five years.

The man with him wore gold-rimmed glasses over his skinny nose. He was dressed in jeans and boots himself, but instead of a plaid work-shirt, he wore an embroidered smock. His cheekbones glistened over his bearded face. Fucking 1966, Jane thought. "Hi, Jane," he said. "I'm Aram."

"Hi and thanks. Where are my shoes?" She didn't mean to have that sound so curt.

"You don't need them right now, do you?" Aram said.

"My feet are cold. And I'm getting them dirty."

"There are some slippers in the closet here," Aram said, going to a closet by the door. He found some quilted cloth ones that looked like they'd fit and handed them to Jane. She dusted off her feet and put them on.

Billy said, "They've never helped a chimera quite like me before." He gave her a quick sideways glance, then went up to the wood stove, a welded black box the shape of a chimera holo conditioning tank, but a quarter the size. Instead of holding warm Epsom-salt solution and a reality-warping hologram projector, this black box contained fire. From his imaginary time, Jane thought. He opened a door on the box and loaded in a few more sticks. After staring at the flames, he closed the door, then squatted by the stove, pulled on a thick leather glove, and pulled down a lever. "I've done this before."

"It's not authentically 1870's to have a catalyst," Aram said.

"Well, Pat whoever-he-was Garrett wasn't absolutely stone perfect, was he?" Billy said cheerfully. "Steve wanted to stay with us."

"Jane, as I was telling Billy, my wife, Yaffe, who's an adjustment ranger, will help you both."

Billy said, "Yeah, Aram said something about retro-countercultural reagricultural development. I could work cows again."

Jane said, "Cultural parks are almost like preserves, except you can pay to get into them. Handicrafts, they throw a lot of pots here." *Retro, utterly retro, and not even to an elegant era.*

178

Jane felt what she was going through now was close to the disorientation Billy must have felt when he learned that his eyes and memory lied.

Billy said, "Park's been this way over a hundred years, so Aram says." He stood up and asked, "You both like coffee?"

"Sure," she said. Aram nodded.

Billy went to the kitchen and came back with a tin kettle, coffee grounds in a paper bag, and three cups. As he put the kettle on the wood stove, he said, "They've got a your-time kitchen, too, Jane." Then he took off his boots and wiggled his small feet without taking off his gray socks. "If the coffee's no use, I hope it's safe enough to sleep. I'm bushed. Couldn't sleep last night."

Jane thought, Even here isn't that easy for him. He went over to the sofa and lay down on it, hands behind his head, feet crossed at the ankles. He closed his eyes and said, "I feel safe enough now."

"Or you're too exhausted to think," Jane said.

"But I promised to make you coffee," he said, his eyes still closed.

Aram said, "We'll take care of it."

Billy said, "I forgot to bring an egg out."

"Egg?" Jane asked.

Aram went to the kitchen and came back with one egg and a quick-boil pot, not looking a whole lot less puzzled than Jane. He poured the water from the tin kettle to the quick boiler, plugged that in, then poured the now boiling water back into the kettle. Billy opened his eyes and slowly rolled himself off the sofa to drop the coffee grounds into the kettle. He set the tin kettle back on the stove and let it boil, then broke the egg into the coffee and threw in the shells.

Jane remembered what her eighth-grade health book had said about boiled coffee. She looked at Aram and knew he also was calculating what doses of what carcinogens they'd be getting with this brew. Billy didn't even look at them as he poured each of them a cup.

The coffee was thick, bitter. Aram said, "Billy, why don't you just go to sleep? Don't try to stay up."

Billy said, "Not even this coffee will do it, to tell the truth." He sat on the sofa before he sipped, more cautiously than Jane had expected, then stared out the window. "Jane, do you know how to use a stun stick?" He reached under the couch and handed her a new stun stick with adhesive from the shipping tape sticky around the trigger button.

"Yes." Jane looked at Aram, wondering why he wasn't in charge of the weapons, then felt ashamed for feeling safer with Billy disarmed. The adhesive residue balled up under her thumb as she rubbed below the trigger.

Billy stretched out on the sofa as he'd been before, feet crossed, hands under his head. "Jane, you lost your job because of me. Could they put you in jail if they find us?"

"Nobody claims you, so I don't know."

"I scare you?"

Aram interrupted before she could answer or lie. "Billy, we'll go back to the kitchen to finish our coffee."

Jane looked at Aram and saw either sympathy or pity. Trung had promised her a good job. Then she wondered what Trung's idea of a good job would be—tending chimera spies before insertion? If the man a chimera was to replace died, what then? And Trung could have lied to her. That was more likely, easier for Trung.

Aram touched her elbow gently and she realized how rigid she held herself. "Jane, let's go into the kitchen and let Billy rest." She moved away from him through the kitchen door and sat down at the big slab table in the center of the room. Dried chilies and garlic braids hung from the rafters. She didn't see any dust on them. *For Billy.*

"Are you going to be okay alone with him?" Aram asked.

"He's . . ." She wanted to say that Billy had extra sexual pheromones—high-test testosterone—but she couldn't chance how stupid that would sound if she spoke out loud. "I don't think he's dangerous."

"And you know how to handle chimeras. We've got SPCA equipment—tranquilizers, nets—for you, if you feel you need to restrain him."

But no shoes. He seemed to watch her as if she were potentially dangerous herself. Jane said, "I didn't volunteer for a lifelong exile in an escapist zone." She jerked after she said that. Aram must be an escapist himself.

Aram just said, "We have contradictions in our system that might make life easier for you. We'd like you and Billy to stay inside for a couple of days. We're debating now whether it's morally correct to use Steve to decoy the searchers away from Billy."

Maybe they do trust me, Jane thought, and the only reason I don't get shoes is to keep me under a roof so satellites don't spot me. "What can I do for a living here?"

"Surely there's some craft you've thought about learning."

"DNA recombinant engineering," she said, only half joking. "Chimera designing." A bitter fluid rose up her throat—Billy's harsh coffee.

"You know what pain they suffer."

"They don't suffer much. Serious. The designs for the nociceptors, the pain sensor nerves, have been improved in the last decade. Billy and Steve don't hurt like we do."

"That's true of Steve, but not of Billy."

"He went through a pain door."

"He thought his hands had burned off but he kept going to keep from getting killed. The real Billy rode with a bullet in his thigh."

Jane said, "They feel enough pain to get out of trouble, but without anxiety of any real memory of it. CIA shop improvements that came down into general chimera design in the fifties."

Aram said, "That's disgusting. Crippling and

unnatural. But I tell you Billy doesn't have that protection. He remembers dying. And you, you must have cared about chimeras very much to have become an SPCA officer."

Jane wondered if she should tell Aram a scholarship was the real reason she'd gone with the SPCA, decided to say instead, "I care when the chimera cares."

"That's what we need with Billy," Aram said. He sounded relieved, happy to take the conversation toward what he'd really brought her to the kitchen to discuss. "Think about how disoriented you are now. It's a thousand times worse for Billy. He has to build a new life beyond those false memories. Think of him more as a child than as the man he appears to be."

And I have to build a false life beyond true memories, Jane thought. She realized how little control she had now. If she told the CIA where Billy was, she couldn't force them to honor Trung's promise. If she stayed here, she'd be turned into park life. "But you're thinking about using Steve?"

"He was very upset when we separated him from Billy, but he's not temporally displaced. We'll help you adjust, too," Aram said, half reassuring, half ordering her to adjust now, and one hundred percent dropping what they might do to Steve out of the conversation.

"I always wanted to live in the 1920's," Jane said. "Silk clothes, crystal pleats, radios, and Stutz Bearcats. Picasso and Braque. Steamships racing across the Atlantic." Her mahog-

any ceiling, all those wooden inverted cubes,
drifted away from her to the future.

Aram said, "It led to technocrats and class
rigidity, all that's out there now."

"I thought it was all right."

"Jane, are you going to be okay with Billy?"

If they left her alone, she could decide
whether to contact the CIA or not. "Sure."

"Read this. It will help you understand us,"
Aram said, handing her a comb-bound book
with faintly rough edges, cheap microperf. She
saw the title, *Appalachian National Cultural
Park Regulations and Systems*. Aram left her
with the book, going around the side of the
house to his gas-burning car. She laid the book
on the kitchen table and looked for a phone.

When she realized the house had no phone,
she almost panicked. *How far can I get in these
slippers?* Then she decided to steal Billy's boots.

When she slid them away from the couch and
tried them on, they were too small for her. She
looked at him incredulously, her breaths jerking in and out. He was sweating slightly, his
fingers twitching from time to time just as other
chimeras' fingers had twitched in the pound.

Is the coffee still hot? she wondered. She slid
his boots back close to the couch and poured a
quarter cup of the coffee that had been boiling
away on the wood stove, then sipped it as if it
was medicine. When she'd finished as much as
she could stand, she hefted the stun stick in her
hand, feeling the weight of all the copper and

batteries inside. *A minimalist chimera pound, just officer and stray.*

Billy's breath hissed in. He opened his eyes and stared at her. "What is it?"

"Billy, I don't hear anything." Had he been listening to her try on his boots?

He got up and grabbed the poker from beside the stove. As he looked cautiously outside, keeping his body away from the window, pulling the curtains aside with the poker, he said, "The guy who's helping us drives a black steam . . . motor truck . . . Yamaha. Looks like the Orientals do more missionary work and trade here than we do there these days." He went to the next window, still using the poker to move the curtains aside.

Jane said, "Billy, you've got to put down the weapons."

"They were going to use me for bait, then kill me. I may be a dog-meat robot, but . . . ah, a deer." He smiled his sunny boy's smile and Jane came up to the side window to look, too. The deer scratched its ears with a hind hoof, then wiggled between two small trees. Snow fell off onto its back and it shook like a dog.

"Oh, Billy." Jane had never seen a free deer before.

"Well, we won't want for meat," he said. He tapped the window with the poker and the deer flicked its ears backward, then bounced off. "Jane, promise me something."

"If I can."

"Whatever, don't let them shoot me and revive me again. Blow my brain apart, don't let this body get tricked again."

"Don't talk about that."

"The real Billy should have gone to Mexico. This is the equivalent for me, and I want to make it work. But if I get caught, then I'd rather die than go back to being a toy."

She said, "But if they do catch you, why have me kill you?" She wasn't sure she could bear doing that, or guarantee that he'd stay dead. "Why not give yourself the chance to escape again?"

"That escape was pure fluke. Now I'm not all Billy the Kid. I'd rather die than go through all the horror again." He looked at the poker in his hand, laughed slightly, and put it down. "Painful, Jane, purely painful. Jesus, how am I going to live now?"

Jane realized she'd sweated wet under her arms and breasts. She started to embrace him, reassure him, but remembered that his maker said he'd enhanced Billy's sexual pheromones. "Billy," she said, "I don't know how either of us is going to live." Sounds like self-pity, she thought to herself.

He rocked back and forth—tiny, stiff motions—then said, "At least you're not humoring me. I must have been a joke to him. To let me believe I was the Kid in 1879, all optimistic that some governor who'd been dead for over a damn century and a half was going to pardon me." His head jerked up, his eyelids squeezed shut. He was crying. Then he sucked in his lower lip and worried it with his new teeth.

Jane didn't know whether to play chimera keeper and calm him down, or to have hysterics herself. "Billy, what you went through was terrible."

He blinked his eyes and brushed away what he'd cried. "No shit."

Outside, snow started coming down in wet clumps almost too big to be called flakes.

The rain chilled Simon's face as he walked through it from the check house to the tube station. Trung, his leathers wet, hair plastered against his skull, caught up with Simon. Trung had lost the SPCA woman—and Simon hoped that Turner really hadn't decided which of the four most-suspected makers stole the Billy material. But then, Turner could know and be waiting for the KGB to approach, to test Simon.

Trung said, "We always wondered why big countries with moderate weather would take such an interest in small tropical countries." He stuck his hand out and watched the rain hit it. "Now we know."

"It isn't necessarily the next ice age," Simon said. "You lost a stupid SPCA clerk, I heard."

Trung turned his face up slightly and grimaced as the gritty Washington rain, halfway to sleet, hit him. Simon hoped his own face was as contorted from the cold. Why hadn't Trung worn microporous—too vain about his leathers, Simon thought, or was a layer of it bonded

187

to this suit? "She wasn't just an SPCA clerk. She was a plant. And she's with Billy, I'm sure of it."

Simon said, "Really?" If Trung believed this, the hunt was still on, but Simon doubted the woman was any kind of plant. Other than perhaps knowing where Billy was, she was an idiot.

Trung said, "She has the illegal chimera, but we're not sure it's cost-effective to keep on chasing them. Except"—he looked over at Simon and smiled—"the Mexicans have a chimera in the park who's going absolutely crazy that the park rangers separated him from the Kid. We need to know more about Mexican chimeras."

"So you are still hunting?"

"If we are, Jane will get the word out. I promised her Billy. You know there has to be something in his memory that will lead us to his maker."

Simon smiled. As they entered the tube building, Trung shook his hair and all the water fell out of it. Simon decided to take a later train to Richmond. He remembered Trung's neighborhood, all the old Hue and Saigon families living with their servants—real human and chimera both—in huge Victorian houses with new sensor-studded ferroconcrete walls overlooking the James River, walls raw gray with black streaks at the joints. *Where we used to live . . .*

"You're not taking this train?" Trung asked.

Simon saw how tense Trung was, like a pointer scenting quail.

"I was going to have a drink, but . . ." Simon sighed. He boarded with Trung, sitting down in the plush seat, feeling how artificial the fabric was compared to Lisa Auschlander's real silk velvets.

Trung sat down beside Simon, but was silent for at least ten minutes. His eyes scanned from left to right and back as if he was reading right-hemisphere intuitions. Simon wondered if Trung was toying with him just because they'd never been friends or if he'd already identified him as the maker and was toying with him in a crueler way.

"Do you still have your bulldog?" Trung finally asked.

"Yes," Simon said.

"Has he lost his collar recently?"

"No." Simon was about to say *he hasn't left Virginia*, but wondered if he had heard from someone else in the Agency about the bulldog in the park.

"There was a bulldog in Albany."

"Someone seems to be setting me up."

"Turner doesn't want to lose a protégé unnecessarily." Trung grinned. He tightened his grip on the armrest, then let the train's deceleration lift him from his seat. The train had passed through the Chimborazo district and was braking for New Hue.

Simon didn't say anything as the train doors opened. As the train pulled away from the station, Simon said, " 'Bye, Trung," but kept his face muscles slack the rest of the trip, not knowing whether he was being monitored or not. He was vaguely surprised that his heart monitor hadn't counted off at him, then realized that he was too depressed to react. Lucky for me, he thought. Until the Agency caught Billy or wrote him off, Simon would assume he was being watched. The watching itself might attract attention. He repressed a shudder and wondered if he'd be best off if he surrendered.

I'll ride it out. I won't break another rule. I'll be perfect. Thinking these things, Simon got off and walked to his car. When he put his card in the lock, he remembered another rainy day in the same car with Allesandra. They'd both thought they'd be married in an almost tribally CIA Episcopalian wedding. Then he remembered the day last month when she'd found him on the train and warned him about street inquiries about rogue makers. Memories made such illogical associations that creating believable duplicates was difficult. Real memory jumped, Simon thought, *bang*, into the private hell you never wanted to recall.

Simon remembered Jane—so scruffy compared even to Allesandra, a mutt compared to the bitch who'd stolen Billy. He doubted she'd do a damn thing to help the CIA if she felt she was safely hidden. People like her didn't trust any official. Trung was slipping, a comforting thought. Or perhaps he'd said Jane was his plant to see how Simon reacted.

His pulse monitor was so silent Simon wondered if it was working. He tapped his teeth twice to get it to subvocalize whatever his pulse rate was—*eighty beats per minute.* Just like he'd thought, too depressed to react, thank God.

I can't afford to look for Billy. I've got to stay here. Damn, who'd have thought the Mexicans—or was it really the Mexicans who sent the chimera guard that helped Billy escape? KGB, Mexicans, Brazilians, oh, shit, I've got to be a good citizen.

And that was so boring.

Jane felt trapped in Goose Creek Valley, March rains leaking through the crazed geodesic dome grafted over the north wing of the old farmhouse. Her room stayed dry or she would have gone crazy, she was sure, but the steep sides of the valley kept the sun time short even when the sky was clear.

Every morning, Aram brought a basket of food, with meat, too, although Jane knew they only brought the meat because Billy was a chimera with an untested biochemistry. Humans, Aram's people believed, should be vegetarians and wear rope-soled shoes.

Today, even Billy seemed sullen as he unpacked Aram's basket. "We been here a week, Aram. You gonna turn us into a tourist attraction—Billy the Kid and the woman who ran off with him?"

"As soon as it dries off, you can dig your garden spot and plant fava beans, then peas."

"Garden, hell," Billy said, opening and closing unlabeled brown paper sacks. "I'm a cattleman."

"After we change your face, we'll see about getting you work. You too, Jane."

"Bet you keep cattle behind barbed wire here," Billy said, sniffing one of the bags. "Fine coffee, though."

Jane remembered Trung promised her a good job if she told them where Billy was. While she had shoes now, she didn't know where the nearest phone was. "What about me?"

"You could go to another place," Aram said. "That might be safer if the CIA is hunting a couple. Seems stupid of them to continue, though, unless they think Billy is really dangerous."

Billy looked up, his eyes gone gray. "I'm not dangerous."

"We want you to start working tomorrow with the adjustment ranger, Billy," Aram said. "Did I tell you she's my wife?"

"You got that Brushy Bill book?" Billy asked.

Aram unzipped the canvas book bag he had over his shoulder and got the book out for Billy, who opened it immediately to the photographs, almost fingering the one of his old scar. Billy asked, "It's the only halfway plausible story of a surviving Billy the Kid, isn't it?"

Jane nodded.

Aram said, "You aren't Billy the Kid anymore. Come help me with the other bags. Both of you, put on hats."

Satellite disguise, Jane thought. As they all

192

went out to the truck, Aram said, "We should explain our goals here. In the nineties, to keep off the developers and polluters, we took control of the local county government and passed ordinances banning population increases in Floyd County." He handed Jane a white canvas bag, then gave Billy another one. "Then when the National Culture Parks Act passed, we petitioned to be included."

Billy said, "That's a century after the first Billy the Kid. How am I going to fit in, being all technologically made and a fake nineteenth-century artifact?"

They went inside, left the sacks in the kitchen, then went back to the living room. Aram rolled some herb in thin paper. Marijuana, Jane realized, fascinated and repelled. It was the *Ur*-drug of the 1960's.

"I'd prefer not," Billy said when Aram handed him the joint. Jane shook her head, too.

Aram sighed and put it out, then tucked it in his shirt pocket. "I thought it might relax you."

"Not me," Jane said.

Aram said, "We preserve several distinct alternate life-styles. One group went back to the nineteenth-century ways of doing things. Our people free the animal side of human beings, besides acknowledging animals' rights and capacities for thinking—including thought modes not normally considered as valuable as human, like deer thinking."

"I'm a city girl," Jane said. Once she did nothing more than sneak a chimera or two a year into Livingston Manor Zen Refugee. Now she was hiding out in a cultural park with a semi-accurate replica of Billy the Kid.

Aram continued to explain things, "Humans didn't evolve in the cities. For thirty thousand years, we gathered our food and used primitive weapons to get meat for seasoning, so the life here is more normal."

Billy said, "No screwier than what I saw in Albany."

Jane wasn't sure whether he was being sardonic or not. "For thirty thousand years," Jane said, "we didn't have enough population to do anything better. Once we had a decent population base, we improved life in a flash. Industrialism spread flat-out around the globe in less than two hundred years."

Aram nodded, but said, "Humans had a mass panic attack. We lost contact with the spiritual—the inventions express a colossal loss of nerve, a denial of eternity, infinity."

"Are chimeras expressions of human lost nerves?" Billy asked, smiling. Jane wondered if Aram knew Billy was teasing him.

"Most chimeras are attempts to control or embody the spiritual."

Billy said, "Interesting. You know things look so real, detailed, since they got those things out of my brain. Listening to you, I was worried that I was still in a tank somewhere." Wetting his fingers, Billy rubbed them against furniture wood, then tasted what his fingers picked up. "Tastes surprising, real."

194

Jane hoped that Aram wouldn't bring up any Zen ideas of illusion just right now.

Billy continued, "Not that I'm not grateful that you brought me here, but what aspect of the spiritual was my maker trying to express when he made me? I . . . the guy he used to model me on was a confused little son of a bitch, so I'm not pure evil spirit, either. So don't give me this guff."

"Aram drives a truck," Jane said.

"My group isn't utterly pure. But the Amish really knew what the twentieth century was about and knew you denied eternity when you saved time with a trouser zipper."

Billy asked, "Do I really belong here if I'm a techno-dog?"

"Nature subverts the technological process that made you. DNA can be rearranged, not created," Aram said. He stood up as if he would leave when he finished his next sentence. "The DNA mix masters can't control reality completely, so chimeras escape their conditioning, come to us or the Buddhists."

Jane decided not to argue a technical point with him there because if he got even more technical, he could point out that the original design was from nature as were all the chemicals that fit in the helix. But Jane thought Aram was too naive, stranded here in a mental park and meeting only the most eccentric chimeras. She said, "Technology wins ninety-nine percent of the time. What the makers do to chimera

DNA, zygotes, and the later conditioning works."

Aram stopped walking toward the door and said, his face stiff, "I'm sorry you aren't more with us, but if Billy trusts you, I guess you're okay. Steve may be one of the ninety-nine percent."

Billy said, "I never trusted him. He was always nagging me to remember faces, what Pat Garrett leaned on, how he fit through a door."

Aram said, "We don't think he really defected. I hate whoever made him for tampering with his mind. At least, the man who rearranged your life gave you freedom enough to be able to change, Billy."

Billy said, "I suspect it was just an accident."

"I won't betray Billy," Jane said.

Billy put more wood in the stove, then sat on the couch. Jane sat down in a rocker. Aram stayed by the door, put his hands in his pockets, and said, "Billy, one more thing occurred to some of us, but I wasn't sure I should mention it. You could be a reincarnation of the real Billy the Kid working out your karmic problems."

Jane thought they were in deep stupid shit if Billy believed that. Then she saw how nervously he looked at Aram—at least he's got sense enough to be suspicious.

Billy said, "I'll die all over again if I fall back into the story. I don't need some dumb reincarnation bullshit to understand that."

Aram said, "If that's not true in a literal way,

then maybe it's a good metaphor for you to consider."

"Woo-woo," Jane said. "Complete woo-woo."

Billy looked at her and said, "I dunno, Jane.
Suddenly all my past turns out to be living yellow journalism, a fraud. Maybe thinking I'm the
reincarnation of Billy the Kid isn't so bad."

"We thought it might give you continuity,"
Aram said. He left then before Jane or Billy
could say more.

The air seemed jangled. They stood in the
room listening to Aram's truck drive away. Jane
suddenly felt pity for the historical Henry
McCarty, who never escaped being Billy the
Kid. His attempts at being honest led him to
Tunstall. When he should have run for Mexico,
he hung around Fort Sumner trying to get Paulita Maxwell, pregnant at the time, to go with
him.

"I kinda would like a shot at the damn bastard who made me," Billy said. "It galls me that
I have to hide all my life."

May be some sense in the stupid woo-woo
karma theory, after all, she realized. "Karma
means, Billy, if you try to take revenge for what
was done to you, you'll keep on dying."

As Billy listened to Aram and Jane arguing
about reincarnation, he wondered if the man
was a fraud or a fool. Buddhists sharpened
their knives for him, smiled at him as they
drove him away in taxis.

Still, Billy felt less jangled now, less naked.

If both Aram and Jane would leave him alone, he'd drift along for a while without deciding what was real or not. Now, except when he slept, he lived in the more detailed world he'd come to see in the last few months. No brain jumps blanked times that didn't fit a nineteenth-century visual matrix, but he couldn't remember every moment and wondered if that was a chimera characteristic.

But Jane seemed less than the competent woman who'd helped him over his initial shocks when he was captured and brought to the pound.

Billy said, "Relax, Jane. If you want to leave, you've got an alibi. We grabbed you off your skis."

"I don't know what I want, what I can even think of having," Jane said.

"But you did come to me," Billy said.

"Yeah," Jane said. She stood in the doorway between the living room and the hall to the kitchen, arms against either side of the door frame. "I did."

Billy didn't say anything; neither did Jane. He heard another truck pass, gravel under the big tires. *But do big tires mean anything?* He said, "Jane, are you planning to turn me in to the CIA? You're so nervous."

"I'm sorry, Billy. You need a friend now, don't you?"

Damn her, Billy thought, she didn't answer. "You're not the only possible friend I've got."

She blinked, then blinked again. "Billy?"

"What do you want me to do?"

She said, "I don't want to feel like I was lured into something by a CIA maker, and I never—"

"What are you talking about?" The Vietnamese agent had lived a month with her—Billy felt jealous, which seemed stupid because she'd probably not only slept with the Vietnamese but made a deal to use Billy as bait.

Jane said, "The maker said you had stronger-than-usual male sexual odors. I can't believe I'm finally . . ." She trembled as she walked closer to him.

At least the bitch had sex more on the mind than betrayal. He laughed, remembering Catholic girls drinking their inhibitions away with him, but realized the second after he laughed that those memories were fake.

"Don't you laugh at me," Jane said.

Billy decided that whatever his maker put into his head must be based on something real enough. "Jane, I'm sorry." He closed the distance between them and took one of her hands. It was cold and clammy. He felt ashamed of how scared she was, so he just held it, then chafed it between his own hands. Her hand was so large and soft. "Look, my hands are smaller than yours."

"Part of the legend, Billy," she said in a voice he likened to sheets rustling. She leaned slightly toward him, then turned quickly and sat down on the sofa, bent over, and cried in her hands.

Billy felt angry with her, confused, protective—all of it swirling in his head. "I guess neither of us knows much about life here," he said, "so we're restarting even. Unless you plan to go back to Albany after you tell the CIA where I am?"

"You plan to pass for human, here?" She sat up and wiped her eyes. "Billy, if anyone tests you, the genome has a twist that says CIA."

"I need to have time to get away from being some dumb puppet Billy the Kid. Jane, help me become a secret man who can live. Come close to dying, you realize how much you want to live on to old age. Maybe I wouldn't mind getting revenge, but not now. Now I just want to be close to someone, forget the lies, and build some real memories. You understand?"

When Jane nodded, Billy felt less aroused and more in control of the situation. He said, "Good. Aram told me I'd better give you space."

Jane looked shocked, then laughed. Billy's face flushed, then he laughed, too. God, he thought, we can be human beings together. The thought gave him immense relief.

Jane was relieved that Billy didn't push her to tell him about the CIA deal. She was afraid she'd sound exceedingly naive if she told anyone.

Aram came back two days later with his wife, Yaffe. She was a dark-skinned woman with glossy crimped hair down her back, long skirt damp at the hem, and a blouse woven of slubby silk. Jane watched them get out of the truck.

The woman wore quilted shoes with rubber soles.

"Hi," Aram said. "This is Yaffe."

"Good to meet you. Billy's digging a test row for our garden," Jane said. The woman smiled as though Jane had admitted to becoming an alternate-culture grub, so Jane added, "I'm not sure I want a garden. That implies we have to stay here."

Yaffe said, "People pay and wait in line to move here. We'll take Billy with us for a while, okay."

Billy came around the house and smiled at Yaffe as if he already knew her. Jane realized he could, then realized Mexican women were dark-skinned and that the historical Billy the Kid had preferred them. She asked, "You're not going to let him believe that reincarnation crap, are you?"

Yaffe stiffened slightly, then smiled a dazzling phony smile, lots of broad teeth too perfect, Jane thought, to be the product of nineteenth-century technologies. She said, "Jane, we just want him to be content enough."

What's enough? Jane wanted to know.

Billy rode in the truck between Aram and Yaffe up to the little store about a mile from the house. The road went flat between hills, with Goose Creek squirming under it from side to side.

"It's not like anything you know, is it?" Yaffe

asked. Aram shifted down and turned off the truck's motor.

"I feel jangled. Who, really, am I? I miss the *bailes*. Jane's afraid of me because of my extra male scent, some trick of the guy who made me. Or else he lied to her."

Yaffe asked, "What were *bailes*?" as Aram went into the store to buy them each a beer.

"Big rowdy dances with Mexican girls who liked men different than their own kind. What Jane said about extra male sex scent, is that true?"

"Enhanced pheromones. Oh." Yaffe laughed, then said, "Tell Jane that extra pheromones merely suggest more thinking about sex. Nothing forces brain-locked creatures like us to do anything."

"Well, nifty shit. You're saying he monkeyed with me like that?"

"Yes."

Aram came back with three bottles of beer. As he handed them around, he said, "We've heard from friends that the CIA decided it's not cost-effective to hunt you. But Steve is causing trouble. Seems all sides would politely prefer that you identify your maker, so maybe it's not over yet, but we can deal. You remember him?"

Billy remembered Pat Garrett, looking just like he did in the books. Every time he tried to remember a father figure, a man who helped him out of conditioning tanks, Pat's image rose in his mind, shooting at him. "Just Garrett, and

I know he's been dead for more than a century."

Yaffe said, "A block."

"Are you more interested in getting me to remember my maker or adjust?" The beer was very cold and foamy.

Aram said, "Billy, this is important. Your maker could come hunting you on his own. You might have flash memories from associations the block didn't account for, like if the maker showed up unshaven one day. And, Billy, we're trusting that your temper isn't as bad as the historical Billy's."

"What about Jane?"

"Don't let her bitch you out," Yaffe said. "She's not as displaced here as you were in Albany."

"You said you'd make me Brushy Bill tapes so I can imagine a life where I survived."

"If you think you need them, Billy," Yaffe said. She drained the last of her beer and stretched, brushing her fingers on the truck-cab ceiling. "We'll work on holding a *baile*, Billy, someday. Sounds like fun."

They drove him back down to the house. Jane stood in the yard by the outhouse, looking like she was annoyed with the fake nineteenth century. Then Billy wondered if male chimeras had come on to her before, maybe too crudely. He stopped at the picket fence around the yard and just looked at her.

Jane said, "I'm not going to fall for a chimera maker's lure."

"Pheromones? Yaffe explained." He felt more appalled than ever that the maker had told Jane about the pheromones. They walked toward the house, with distance between them farther than arms could reach. "Shit, he messed me up, then he told you." Billy sat on the sofa and took off his shoes, wiggling his feet. "They told me in Albany I might not live as long as a real Homo sapiens." He hoped he was speaking the big words right.

"That's if he used recreation parts, not CIA DNA. Spies have to live as long as the people they replace. It takes three years to grow an adult body, say, and you've been Billy for twelve years, out of the tank. Eighty minus fifteen equals sixty-three. Don't try to make me feel sorry for you that way."

He then asked, "How much longer will you live?"

"I'm twenty-nine. Maybe I'll live fifty more years."

He wondered how he could get her out of her moodiness, then thought he'd ask about the usual relationships between chimeras and humans. "Jane, I guess you think of me as one of the creatures you helped in the pound. Did chimeras and humans . . ." It was going to sound too blunt. He could guess her reasons for not treating him as a sexual man—reasons he utterly wanted to destroy, take out of her mind, screw her.

"Rich humans have chimera lovers. I'm not rich." She stiffened as she said that.

"But I always thought of myself as a man, human being, so this is the very hardest thing. The machines are nothing. We had machines then. . . ."

"I think I understand."

"It's so real now, vivid." He leaned away from her, then got up, muscles stiff, and put more wood in the fire, feeling each log, the fabulous differences in each chunk's bark. Wonderful to be so alive, yet he was still a fugitive—and if Jane went back to Albany, the CIA might wring out of her where he'd been. "Oh, Jane, I'm sorry you're here if you're unhappy."

"I've wrecked my career," she said.

"I'll get them to unhitch the excess male odors."

Jane began giggling. Billy couldn't understand why. He opened the stove and poked the fire.

"Oh, Billy, I'm sorry. But it is rather funny, getting sexual pheromones disrupted so you can get me to bed. That's what you want, isn't it?"

Is it? He hung the poker back in the rack and turned around to stare at her. She raised her head and he saw her pulse beating along her windpipe, moisture not quite sweat on her skin. "Jane, I'm going upstairs to my bedroom. The door won't be locked, so join me if you wanna."

"And if I don't, you're going to be grotesquely insulted."

Jesus, bitch woman. He didn't answer her. When he got to his room, he built a small fire in the bedroom fireplace and pulled aside a shutter on the ceiling. The skylights showed bare trees overhead. He undressed in front of the fire, watching the flames flickering, their light against his body. He wondered if his maker really made him out of a dog. Then he decided, She ain't coming, the bitch. But maybe he wasn't doing things right, maybe he was supposed to kiss her faint. He remembered Celsa, then decided not to trust those tainted memories. He'd died between fucking Celsa and now. The man who made him had weird ideas about women, he realized. But at the core, he wasn't just that human's dog meat. *I ought to go down and apologize to her.*

Billy pulled on a robe and went down in his bare feet. Jane still sat in the wing chair, tears drying on her face. "Jane, I'm sorry if I was crude. I don't really know how to act with women. He may have pimped me. . . . I remember some women, I think."

"Billy, don't tell me," she said. He thought he'd come and kiss her gently, but when he sat down on the floor beside her chair, his robe slipped open. She bent over and slid her hand down from his nipples to his navel. "The CIA agent, Trung, was with me weeks and never . . . it was like I wasn't his species. I didn't want him to do anything, you understand. I just wanted . . ." She huffed and put her chin on the top of his head. "So I'm lonely."

"So?" He took her hand, ready to drop it if she resisted in the least. When she tightened her fingers around his, he led her up to his room.

"I was near sleaze," she said, "and Trung was obviously rich. You're a chimera and I'm not some jaded rich . . ."

"Hush up, Jane." He slipped his hand around her waist and wondered if he had normal desires, like a human. His hand trembled.

"You're scared, too," Jane whispered. Her breath reached out and tickled his chest hairs.

His cock squirmed upright. "Damn. Oh."

She touched it and he jumped. "If you're scared, too," she said as she raked her fingers from his navel to the root of his cock, "then it's not so bad."

"Jane, is this the way humans and humans . . . ?" He wondered if he'd go crazy.

"So far," she said. She took his hand and put it on her breast.

The nipple crinkled. He wanted to take it between his lips. "Oh." Death seemed to be watching.

"It's all right, Billy."

Maybe, he hoped, this was his first real fuck, despite all the memories of Celsa with her clothes off, her body always changing. But as he tasted too familiar sweat, a voice from inside his brain said, mocking, *There's honey in the groin, Billy.*

His cock spurted into Jane. *I do this before Pat kills me.* They rolled apart and he said, "Jane, he lets me do this before he kills me. Shoots me and stabs me in the throat with metal stakes. I barely remember, but . . . Jane, he's crazy."

She hugged him tight. "Billy, you're safe now."

He felt trembling going back and forth between them. "I always thought I was safe with the women. Celsa, in different bodies. He pimped me and watched. Damn him, his voice in my head just then."

"Billy, we can get his voice out. Billy, don't talk about him now."

He embraced her, her breasts squished against his rib cage, her heart beating inside her. "He's real, Jane." They lay there, sweat chilling on their backs, so wet between them it was like they'd grown together. Finally she shuddered a few times and went to sleep. Billy managed to drift off, dreams roiling, a face watching as he fucked, taunting him. . . . *honey in the groin, Billy.*

Billy went stark awake. *I know what he looks like—the guy who made me. I'll kill him if I see him again.*

"Jane?" Yaffe called. Jane looked over and saw that Billy was still asleep, eyelids flickering as he dreamed.

"In here," Jane said, slipping away from Billy. One of his hands twitched as she got out of bed.

"Jane," Yaffe said as she watched Jane hurriedly put Billy's robe on. Jane couldn't tell if Yaffe disapproved or not.

"I hope you don't think of it as bestiality," Jane whispered, hoping Billy was still asleep. "Billy was very excited."

Billy stretched under the quilt, then sat up, quilt covering his genitals, his chest pale, almost hairless except around the nipples. The surgical scars on his head showed through his short sandy hair.

"Jane, I had a chimera before I moved to the park. Billy, I'm surprised the top of your skull didn't fly off."

"About did," he answered, hunched over, eyes dark gray. "Jane, you okay?"

Many implications to that question, Jane thought. "I'm fine, Billy."

He said, "I wish I didn't feel like someone else's dream." His tone changed when he said, "But thanks, Jane, that was real."

Jane felt co-opted into a third-rate dream herself. She looked at Yaffe to see if she was enjoying this, but Yaffe seemed to be keeping her emotions off her face. Jane remembered other owners who could control their surfaces oh so well.

Simon decided to wait. If he couldn't get the original Billy back, then he'd make a new one, but the CIA would have to settle down first.

He played the viola to his bulldog, clumsily at first, since he hadn't practiced in years.

"What's so great about fresh peas?" Jane asked Billy, who seemed more excited than Jane could believe.

"I saw them grow all the way," he said, splitting a pod with his thumbnails and lifting it up to rake the peas out into his mouth. "No jump cuts."

Billy said to Yaffe in one of their sessions, "It doesn't matter if I really shot people or if I just thought I shot people."

"The DNA technician made you what you are," Yaffe said. "I was offering reincarnation as a metaphor. You have another chance here."

"I have to get over wanting to kill when I'm pissed. But I don't have the same chances I'd have if I was a true man. Not being a man, that's hard to take."

"Who treats you as a chimera?"

"I don't know how chimeras are treated, do I? And I'm getting bored."

"Boredom is among the highest spiritual states."

Jane was teaching herself how to knit, using three different books, as none of them gave really complete directions. Yaffe came in and asked, "Where's Billy?"

"Out in the garden, getting the last of the peas."

"He needs to come in," Yaffe said. Jane got up and was about to call for Billy when Yaffe put her finger to her lips. So she went out to the back porch and motioned for Billy to come in. He started, then came in, swaying slightly on the balls of his feet.

"Aram found this," Yaffe said, holding out what looked at first like a June bug. She pried the wings apart and showed them a tiny chip behind the faceted eyes.

"Yaffe," Billy said, "is it transmitting now?"

"No, it records and runs."

"Maybe I ought to surrender?"

"We don't know whose it is. Or even what it's looking for." She took the chip out of the bug, opened her shoulder bag and pulled out a binocular microscope and microwaldos and a hand-sized screen.

"I thought you frowned on technology," Jane said.

"Rangers get to use what they need," Yaffe said, putting her hand in the waldo glove and setting the chip under the microscope. She focused the microscope, then worked with the glove. "Let's see if we can read it. I'll try optic code first, since the thing had eyes."

The cursor on the terminal swept back and forth, leaving colored dots behind.

"Oh, God," Billy said, "it's me."

His face first, then a scan to body proportions. The display paused, then swept through the graphic again. Yaffe said, "Since it wasn't a broadcast unit, I suspect the maker sent it."

Billy paced the floor, hands behind his back, then he said, "I almost wish this was Purgatory. I'd survive Purgatory."

CHAPTER SIX
Deals

Gov Lew Wallace

Dear Sir

I wrote you a little note the day before yesterday but have received no answer. I expect you have forgotten what you promised me this month two years ago, but I have not; and I think you had ought to have come and see me as I have requested you to. I have done everything that I promised you I would have and you have done nothing that you promised me. . . .

—Excerpt from 4, March 1881, letter from William H. Bonney, sentenced to hang.

BILLY STARED AT THE DISMANTLED BUG AS YAFFE turned the iridescent wings with her fingernails. *I've got to stop that son of a bitch or he'll hunt me forever.* Billy's memories played him a flash like the one when he and Jane first fucked. The voice, he remembered as if he were dreaming— the man who made him, talking. He could almost see the face, then Pat Garrett blotted it out. But was the voice a lie, a false memory put in to throw suspicion on an innocent man? He remembered the voice saying, *Ah, Langley, give me 406,* then a swirl of western music, nothing.

"Billy, are you okay?" Yaffe asked. "I've got to leave you and Jane for a few hours. If you see another bug, catch it. We'll be back to take you to your next hiding place."

"I'm okay," Billy said. "I was just remember-ing." The next hiding place? An infinity of hid-ing places wasn't much better than an infinity of deaths.

Yaffe swept up the bug's pieces and left them. Billy paced, trying to figure out what to do with his memory. Jane went upstairs. Billy could hear her opening drawers, taking clothes out. Packing, how sensible. He grimaced.

The CIA was in Langley, he gathered that from what he'd heard when he was recovering from the operation. *406* . . . "What would it be to call on a phone and ask for a number?" he asked Jane as soon as Yaffe's car pulled out of hearing.

"A phone extension."

He remembered seeing a phone box at the store about a mile away. "I have to use the john," Billy told Jane. He went to the outhouse and looked around it to see if mud or such would pick up his footprints. Leaves, fine. He turned the wooden latch and wiggled out the ventilation window over the seat. I've done this before but I died anyway, he thought as he straightened the leaves behind him. He began running.

There's honey in the groin, Billy . . . lethal nee-dle . . . Billy the Kid died in the nineteenth cen-tury . . . overlay in the vision center . . . programmed eyes . . . trocar to the carotids and be back shooting in six weeks.

The phone was outside the store, just like he'd remembered it—yeah, honest memories. He picked up the receiver and asked to be connected to the CIA in Langley.

"Will that be on a credit card or collect?" the operator's voice said. He thought a second, then said, "Collect for Extension 406."

The man who answered at Langley had to check to see if they could accept charges. Billy told the operator, "Tell them it's about a rogue maker's chimera. I'm the chimera."

"Yes, Billy," a man's voice, deeper. Not the doctor, but that sort of educated voice. "We'll accept the charges."

"You want to catch the guy who made me. I want you to let me live down here, no hassles and a complete pardon, if we cut a deal. I know I've been tricked on this before with Wallace— I mean the historical Billy the Kid was tricked. He's hunting me. Not Wallace, the guy who made me. He sent remotes like June bugs. If they'd been transmitting, he'd have got me, but they just record and run away. I want him to stop killing me."

"Slow down. Where are you?"

"One of my friends caught the bug. If it wasn't you guys, then it was him. He kills me, brings me back to life. I hate him." Billy saw another June bug waving its antennas at him, lunged for it, missed. It didn't fly, not a real June bug, but scurried off. He almost dropped the receiver to go after it.

"Stay where you are."

"Another bug spotted me. Do we have a deal?

He's going to know where I am if I don't catch the damn bug."

"Stay where you are. Someone will be down to the store soon."

He dropped the phone as though it burned him. *Stupid, you forgot they can trace through the wires.* He realized he'd been too angry to think, a really Billy problem.

Jane waited a few minutes, enough for a bowel movement, then knocked on the outhouse door. Nothing. She used a stick to turn the wooden latch. Billy was gone. *Shit, he's escaped; the bug scared him or made him really angry.* She had no idea of how to reach Yaffe and Aram—their stupid security—and was afraid to call out Billy's name. He'd asked about the phones, she realized, how to get numbers. Was there a phone near? A store?

She left a message for Yaffe: *My friend's taken a walk. I'm going out for a bit, too. He didn't say where he was going.*

He couldn't have picked a worse time to do this. Just like a chimera, she thought, then stood trembling. She'd slept with a chimera, fickle little chimera. Billy and Aram had often gone to a store, not far away. She stood on the road and wondered whether to go up the creek or down. Before she could decide, she saw Billy running toward her.

When Billy got in earshot, he said, "I tried . . . to cut a deal . . . with Langley. They can follow you . . . on phone wires."

Well, he's crazy again, she thought. "You fool!"

"Jane, I didn't know."

"They traced the call."

"They said they'd meet me at the store soon."

"You called from the store?"

"Yes, I ran back. Jane, I'll surrender. Tell them I did it on my own." He gripped his knees and panted, then said, "Do we have guns here? There was another bug. Really."

"No. Billy, we can't outshoot the CIA. You have no idea." She almost told him about the deal she could have made with Trung.

"Then you're going to have to blow my head up, burn the brains."

"Damn, Billy, stop it."

"The real Billy let everyone die for him. I . . . if I'm not like that . . . I was too pissed to think."

She grabbed his elbows and held him the way she'd held other panicky chimeras. When he seemed more collected, she said, "They'll look at the store first."

He said, "Let's try to get away before they find the house. We'll run, just you and me, link up with the Animal Libbers later, but right now, let's get stuff and do it." He touched her hair, then her breast.

At least he'd have some time free, running. And maybe Trung would cut his deal. She said, "Okay, let's run."

They went inside the house. "Hatchet," Billy said, seeing it by the stove kindling, scooping it up and sticking it in his belt. "Canteens."

"Sleeping bags," Jane said.

"I wish I knew how much time we had," he said. "Mountains over to the east—lots of woods, water, too, probably. But I'm not used to this terrain. Flour if we don't have crackers. Wear a hat, sweaters."

She went into the kitchen and found two boxes of crackers, a cloth bag filled with dried beans, and a plastic water bladder. A backpack stood at the back of the pantry closet.

As she filled the water bladder at the sink, Billy opened the cloth bag and looked in. "Beans, matches, crackers, we'll make it."

"There's a backpack, too," she said. She went back and brought it out, all nylon and aluminum, plastic zippers, and also a little gas-cartridge stove.

"Damn, even that's changed," he said, almost laughing as he packed the crackers and beans in it. Jane added brown rice and dried seaweed. Then they tied the sleeping bags above and below the bag. Billy looked at them funny, then said, "You carry the water. Let's run."

They headed out the back door. Jane heard one helicopter, coming from over the store. Billy looked at her and said, "They got the machines in pretty damn fast, didn't they?"

"Billy, we should have dyed your hair."

"Walnut husks, we'll do it."

"I hope what you think you know is true. People walk around these woods. Maybe if we don't try to dodge them, just walk, they'll think we're just hikers."

He pulled his stocking cap down over his eyes and asked, "Like this," sauntering along whistling, with his hands in his pocket.

Chimera, nothing's not quite real to him.

"You look like you're hiding," he said, "so they're more likely to stop you. Easier to get through if you try to appear more relaxed."

"But you were always caught," she said.

"Me, or Billy the real Kid?" he said.

"You, if someone's been shooting you and bringing you back."

"The last time I got away," he said, "at least to here."

"Yeah," she said. "With a lot of people's help."

"Practice relaxing," he said. "Can you whistle?" She shook her head. "Giggle?" She looked at him a little closer and saw the sweat on his face. *Okay, maybe he knows how to do this.* He danced toward her, the pack swaying on his back, reaching for her ribs, "Giggle, dammit."

"Don't look up," she said. A helicopter circled them overhead. Billy looked up and waved. Jane saw that it had PARK SERVICE in capital letters on the belly, not some weird hash that disguised CIA craft. Too soon, probably, for them to mobilize their own men.

The helicopter dipped lower and a bullhorn called out, "Where do you live?"

"Brooklyn," Billy shouted back. "We're down on vacation."

A camera lens swung at them. Jane was afraid Billy would panic now, but he grinned fiercely.

221

She realized he was deliberately exposing his new smaller teeth. The helicopter dipped slightly.

"This can't be that easy," Jane said. Billy looked back at her, then at the helicopter, and kept walking.

"How did you get here?" the bullhorn asked.

"We left our car on the hardtop," Jane shouted up, remembering how the road texture changed at the last turn when they brought her here. The helicopter lifted up and circled above the hills.

"I bet it can't climb rock chimneys," Billy whispered.

Jane remembered something about updrafts, downdrafts, problems helicopters had in the mountains. "Maybe if we just start uphill."

"They look like they're headed for the hard-top road," Billy said. "We better be hid before they realize there's no car."

"Billy, this road would be impossible in snow. I suspect at least one person on this road parks there. I hope."

Billy said, "Let's go up the hill now." He pulled Jane's hand and they began scrambling uphill. The helicopter sounds faded.

"It's too easy," Jane said.

"We've got to get hid tonight," Billy said, "then see if we can find some walnut husks." They scrambled up the steep hills and kept moving.

Just before they got to the ridge line, Jane

said, "They can track us by satellite unless we stay under trees."

"By satellite?"

"Yeah, things that orbit the earth and take pictures from miles out. They can read license-plate numbers from about a hundred miles up."

Billy crouched and began walking along the ridge. Jane followed him, slipping on the leaves. Billy said, "We'll go to the headwaters. Got thickets around wetland." Jane wondered how much Billy really knew about woodcraft, but decided to stay with him. Perhaps her presence would keep him from being killed on the spot when they were captured. She knew they'd be found. The police and CIA had too many tools these days: ammonia sniffers, infrared scopes, and robot snakes that could slither up quietly and give burst transmissions of locations. She'd heard about robot microcameras that could read fingerprints and retinal patterns from ten feet away. *We're doomed.*

They reached ground thick with greenbriar and laurel. Billy stared at the thorned vine tugging his shirt as if he'd never seen such a thing. Jane said, "How are your country memories holding out?"

Billy said, "They're western. Let's keep moving, see if anyone's friendly enough to get word to Yaffe or Aram." He pulled the vine away and went around the spring area. "I wonder what happens if I go off the edge in a tank dream."

"Listen, this is real."

He said, "They aren't chasing us."

223

"Maybe they believed us?"

"No, I don't think so."

"Let's leave messages. On someone's door-step tonight."

"I'd rather be caught for what I am than shot as a thief," Billy said. "Let's see if we can stay out here awhile longer before . . . I dunno. I like being outdoors, moving. Nothing lasts anyway, does it? Not even being dead."

"Shut up about that, Billy."

They kept moving around the valley, back down toward the house where they'd been stay-ing, but on the other side of Goose Creek, just under the ridge top. As the sun set, Billy said, "Let's stop at the next level place by rocks."

Jane wondered if she should tell him all the ways that the law could find him, then decided perhaps it would be better to be taken while asleep. Well, there goes my alibi of being jerked off my skis and kidnapped, she thought.

When they found the right place, Billy slung his pack off and said, "You know how to oper-ate the little stove?"

Jane said, "Let's see it." Billy slid out of the pack and found it. She hoped it worked like a gas stove, turned it on—nothing—turned the gas off and lit a match before trying again. It caught.

"How long will that last?" Billy asked.

"Don't know."

"Well, we can always build a fire."

No, we can't, Jane wanted to say, but she de-cided that if they got through the night uncaptured, then she'd explain. She poured water into a pot that had been in the backpack and said, "Beans will take a long time."

"We've got some coffee. We'll have that and crackers, then look for some horses tomorrow."

"Billy?"

"You saying they don't have horses here or horses would get us spotted quicker?"

"Both." She fixed the coffee, putting it in two little metal cups with wire handles that she found just then as she looked through the other pockets of the backpack. "Did they tell you about this pack?"

"No."

Jane wondered if it belonged to Aram or Yaffe, if they'd stolen something dear to someone else. "I guess it can't be helped."

"What?"

"We didn't ask them what we should do in case someone found out."

Billy sipped his coffee, then said, "Maybe I should have waited for the CIA? Jane, I'm sorry I was so stupid."

The air was getting colder, so Jane pushed herself into her sleeping bag and pulled it up around her shoulders. She stared at the noisy little stove, then turned it off, putting them in darkness. Billy turned his head up and looked at the stars. He said, "If running today is the last thing I do, I have had some pleasure of it."

Jane didn't speak, just sat sipping her coffee. Then Billy began singing in a high tenor voice, some song about cattle and Englishmen and men on the run. She said, "Don't get caught up in the story again."

"If only I could go so far I'd know I'd made it to the real world. Look at us here, circling around. A computer could be generating this valley."

"We don't know where to go."

He gave Jane an almost cruel look, as if he thought she'd made his tank tapes this time. She slid down into her sleeping bag, tossing and turning to find some comfortable position. Billy sat up, eating crackers and singing softly.

When Jane woke up, she was still free and it was daylight. Billy had the stove going already. "I dreamed I was talking to a man named Turner," he said. "From the CIA. You think I've got some real memories?"

"Your maker?"

"No, someone else, Langley 406. My maker knew Turner and that's who I talked to yesterday."

"You want to go back."

"I don't know how honest Turner is. Maybe he helped the guy who made me steal. Eat some crackers, then we've got to find someone we trust."

"Steve. They said he was in the park."

"I don't trust him. If I could just remember."

"Do you know how to steal cars?" Jane realized how stupid that was as soon as she said it, no cars in Billy's day.

"It keeps coming back to horses," Billy said.

"We need horses. We need to get to Fort . . . no, damn, Jane, oh, Jane, I am here, ain't I?"

"Yeah, there's no Fort Sumner, and besides, your model was killed there."

"I've been killed at many a place called Fort Sumner." Billy shuddered and touched his neck over the carotids.

Jane could imagine trocars going in, pumping blood through a heart-lung machine while Billy's heart healed. How much awareness remained behind the eyes two or three minutes after the bullets hit? "Billy, if you want . . ."

He raised a finger to his lips before she could finish. "I smell horses."

Jane wondered if someone had been listening to him talk about horses. Then Billy said, "Helicopters too."

"Well, they gave us a night," Jane said.

One helicopter hovered over the ridge, dancing in the thermals. Two others flew below them parallel to the road, high enough not to tangle in the trees. When they came to a place free of trees on either side, they began to drop, carefully wiggling toward the clear space, and landed. Armed men in two different uniforms got out, formed a line with less than five feet between them, and began working their way uphill.

"Hear anything on the other side?" Jane asked, sure they were surrounded.

Billy sat staring at them, then said, "Jane, I think I shouldn't have run. And I shouldn't run now, but . . ."

"They're armed, Billy," a voice called out from above them. "I'm with your friends, come." A man riding a horse, leading another, came down from the ridge. He raised his hair into a bristly crew cut and shifted his face.

"Shit, no," Billy said. "You're the fake defector."

"You've got a choice between me and a lethal needle, so come on." Steve looked once at Jane, recognized her, and, shifting his face again, looked up at the helicopter. "Code 4566. We've got them," he spoke into a radio.

The helicopter poised above the ridge wobbled even more in the air. "Do you need backup?" the voice that had been on the bullhorn said through the radio.

"No, we've got a team on the ridge."

"No," Billy screamed. He began running toward the men coming up the hill, screaming, "No, I can't go with him. I remember who made me. If you let me live, I'll point him out for you."

The man on the bullhorn said, "Bring him to the chopper. He's dangerous."

"Yeah," Steve said. "I'll bring him to you as soon as I dart him."

Billy screamed, "Keep me from him."

Jane stood, ignored by all of them. She began walking toward Billy, slowly, slowly. Steve looked at her once when she stumbled over rough ground; they stared at each other.

"Enough," Steve said, riding his horse closer.

He raised the dart gun. "Jane, if you make me shoot you, you'll freeze tonight."

Pretend that you've given up, Jane thought, and keep walking. Don't look at the ax on Billy's belt. Not time yet to go for it. "Steve, can't I kiss him good-bye?" she asked.

"Sure," he said, wiping his face against his shoulder. In that second, she reached for Steve's rifle, drew it back against his hand suddenly grabbing it.

Billy pulled his hatchet. The horse jumped. She ducked its hooves and found the drug rifle was in her hands. She pulled the trigger again and again, until she heard a click.

Steve's face writhed around the darts she'd shot into it. A dart in his lower lip flapped as he mumbled and pulled out a different gun.

If he doesn't kill me, it's been terrible fun.

Billy hit the horse with the flat of the hatchet. The man on the bullhorn said, "Ground team. The code the man on the horse gave us was outdated." The horse bucked again. Steve dropped the gun and tried to get the horse under control as five Special Forces police slid down a rope from the helicopter. He fell off the horse, face bloody from the darts.

"Billy, stop," Jane shouted. She grabbed the hatchet. They swayed, both pulling, then Billy let Jane take it.

"Take my brains out, now," he said as the line of men came up the hill.

Jane was amazed that they hadn't shot both of them yet. As the men came close, Billy slowly sat down, heels on dirt, breathing hard, eyes still almost black. The uniformed men grabbed both of them—two on her, three on Billy. They started to cuff him.

Billy laughed and they checked his wrists and hands and held him on the ground, kneeling on his legs and arms.

Another man, dressed in civilian clothes, came up and said, "We need him alive. This is bad business." He checked Steve and said to Jane, "Why did you kill him? *Trabajas tu por México?*"

Jane said, "He was a chimera. I don't know who he worked for, but he wanted to find out who made Billy."

Billy said, "I'm remembering who made me. Soon I'll see him. I remember him calling Turner on Extension 406."

"I am Turner," the man said. "I trained all the suspects. I considered them friends."

"You didn't help him steal parts for me?"

"No. What's his name?"

"Pat Garrett. Shit, I can't say. I can't, but I want to. The bastard."

"Please, let us try to work with him," Jane said. "He was scared."

"I wonder if the maker designed any redeeming features into this chimera?" Turner said. He pulled out a radio and said, "We've got the Kid chimera back in custody. The Mexican one is dead." Jane felt the CIA official's hand touch hers. "Let her go," he said to the soldiers. They stepped back. "Trung said you wanted to trade him for some information. You met the maker, I understand."

"No, don't," Billy said.

She knelt down beside Billy and reached for his hand. The soldier kneeling on that arm eased up. "Billy, I can't, I don't have any power, any twist on them to ... The voice was disguised. I think he was a heavyset man, if that helps. And he thinks Billy is with me."

"Jane, please make sure I stay dead."

She heard cars coming up the road, tanks, tractors. Then she went through what she did know about the Underground Railroad—*perhaps not enough to hurt it*. Billy stared at her; she kissed his hand. *I don't think of him as a chimera anymore*. "Billy, you're more important to me than they are. But I can't kill you. We'll find a way to get you back alive. As long as they don't have your maker captured, everyone will be after you."

He wouldn't look at her, turned his face toward Turner, and said, "How do I know you aren't going to turn me back over to Pat Garrett, whoever. You're not doing me any good putting me in irons like this."

We've got to get your maker stopped. She wondered if she should care more for Billy's defense than revenge.

He said, "Jane, this world of yours is very complex." She sat up and saw the cars had brought Aram and Yaffe, other locals in their hand-spun and antique nylon. The soldiers locked Billy in a waist chain and neck ring, then adjusted the cuffs to fit in over the elbows, tight, behind his back. One of the women put a camera on her shoulder and aimed it at them. A man with a second camera came down the ridge. "Great shots," he said, "so fucking absolutely holo, it's going to hurt to trade the pictels for Billy."

Turner said, "I've got questions to ask you, Jane, if you really want to help."

Billy realized he was doomed as soon as the guards put the neck iron on him. Memories ate his mind. His maker was named Simon Boyle. Boyle was whispering to a woman while Billy cleaned his guns, first the Colt .41 revolver, then the Winchester. He knew Boyle well now, memories coming back, dying in Boyle's arms many times. He didn't want to be dead again. After the man Turner told Jane he needed to ask her questions, Billy tried to say Boyle's name out loud again and couldn't. Camera glass stared at him, prime suspect. "Jane," he said, "this world of yours is very complex." He felt gut-sick that he hadn't managed better, had called the people in Langley to make a deal and brought them here. His fingers behind his back, his forearms tingled—they'd laid in a bar between the upper arm cuffs and locked it to his neck ring—no way to slip this stuff. He wondered again who he really was—Wallace promised him a pardon, the CIA promised Jane a deal. He was a dog-meat robot Billy-the-Kid reincarnation. Buddhists knifed him in the belly to the odor of Epsom salts.

Turner said, "Billy, we want to help you remember as much as possible."

The camera woman, from her circle of protectors, said, "The man's real good, not holo-shy at all. It sure will be a bitch to burn this."

Yaffe said, "Mr. Turner is Mooncrafter's uncle, so be cool."

Billy couldn't move enough to provoke them into killing him. Then, again, they could hand his corpse over to Boyle, or Boyle could steal it, revive him. He tried to say Boyle's name out loud, his tongue froze. "Please don't stare at me like that," he said. "I can't say his name."

"We don't often catch Wild West outlaws," Turner said. "You must understand that it's illegal even for us to replicate a criminal personality. The CIA was not responsible for this."

As more of the park people came up, the cameraman moved close in to Billy. "I'm not a Wild West outlaw," Billy said, "I'm a dog-meat robot, except . . ." Turner didn't look at him as though he was human, so he shut up.

"Trung promised," Jane said.

"But you didn't turn him over to us," Turner said. He finally looked directly at the two camera people surrounded now by their friends.

"No, he called to you, but he got scared when you told him you knew already where he was."

Turner looked at Billy again, maybe more man-to-man, then said, "We'll have to retank him, see what else he might remember. Maybe his maker slipped in other ways."

They separated Jane from him, held her back while they pulled a conditioning tank . . . coffin . . . out of the back of a truck. He began to thrash and dug his heels as they led him toward it. Turner said, "Hold it for a second." The guards stopped dragging him. "Billy, you promised to try to help us find the man who made you?"

"Are you really going to let me live afterward?"

Jane said, "Mr. Turner, he's remembering Governor Wallace. It may be an artificial memory for him, but the government isn't always honest."

Turner said, "Let him relax a bit. You'll walk to it, won't you, Billy? Or did he make you a coward, too?"

"Fuck you and him both," Billy said. He steadied himself—*shit, I'm dead if they want me dead*—and walked to the tank, looked in, and saw straps to hold him down, looked at the lid and the helmet trailing tubes. "Okay, I'm getting in. Hook me up."

He almost panicked when a man pushed the tube down his nose and sealed the helmet to his neck. The lid went down like a coffin, the seal on his neck like a hanging, the tank filled with thick liquid hot as blood. *I've spent most of my life here*, he thought before reality switched off.

He was suddenly in an office, talking to a man

he didn't recognize, a lean man with gray hair, locks of it falling down to thin gray brows.

It's holograms, it's holograms, it's something they do with light, fake, it isn't real, he began telling himself, looking at the detail, feeling that he was still chained tight, forearms throbbing. He concentrated on his forearms, the reality of the pain.

The scene disappeared. The light almost blinded him—he closed his eyes and felt someone reach through the brine and pull him out. They took off the cuffs with him while he still breathed through the nose tube, then pulled soft gloves over his hands.

I can't feel anything! This time, he seemed to go to sleep, no dreams, and woke up to see the man who'd spoken over the bullhorn from the helicopter, Turner, pulling off his goggles.

Is this real? "Billy, come with me."

His legs seemed to be moving. Turner said, "Guess you could feel the cuffs, so you weren't responding right."

"This isn't real, either," Billy said. Jane, the camera people, and everyone else were gone.

Turner gave him a long look and went out the door. Billy remembered this office from the hologram. Not real.

Lights. Someone shot something into his arm, and he was walking into Turner's office again.

I should let myself believe it. I'm fucked anyway.

"You need to use the john, the jakes, whatever they called that in your day."

Billy felt like he did and saw the door. "There?" he asked. Turner nodded. Inside, Billy saw a toilet like the one he'd learned to use at the pound. He pissed—felt real enough, but then he saw the window was open. He ignored it and went back to sit down in front of Turner's desk.

"I guess they brought us out in the helicopter."

"Yes, Billy."

"So you want to know who made me. I can't tell you that." He wasn't sure he should tell them either. They were as nasty as Boyle ever was.

Turner walked away from his desk. Billy saw a rifle cartridge in the ashtray—he became a bit unsteady, *unreal again,* then remembered that he'd pissed and it felt real. "You're tempting me."

"No, Billy."

If I decide it's unreal and it is unreal, they'll do more to me to make me think this is real. Eventually . . .

"Yes, Billy, eventually, we'll convince you that the hologram scenes are real."

"How do you know what I'm thinking?"

"Subvocalization. Most chimeras and untrained people do it under stress."

"But I can't subvocalize my maker's name. You're real, but somewhere else?"

"Yes. I'm thinking that we ought to try to rehabilitate you for duty-chimera work. Your maker must have stolen some interesting coils."

"I want to see Jane."

"Jane was our spy."

"This isn't real."

"But I'm really talking to you. She made a deal with Trung. And she let you escape from the outhouse. Didn't you see the window open in the bathroom here? You didn't want to try again?"

"I figured that was a trick." He got up on Turner's desk and squatted to shit.

The light blinded him again. *Damn them, what are they going to do next.* But this time, Turner pulled off the hologram helmet, gave him a towel, and told him, "Shower's in there. You shat in the brine."

"No wonder that felt real."

He went into the shower and stared at the knobs. Like the pound, he thought, turning on the cold first, then the hot, and soaping up. It was that same green, stinking soap. Not real this time, either, he decided. The bathroom window was still open. *Where the fuck would that lead, Stinking Springs?* He dried off and dressed in the clothes Turner had laid out for him.

When he came back out, a man with a gun on his hip was standing with his back to Billy, talking to Turner. Billy came in without saying a word and tried suddenly to open one of Turner's desk drawers. The drawer pull almost slipped through his fingers, suddenly became real, and the drawer slid back to show a letter opener. I wouldn't have believed a gun, Billy thought, almost amused.

"Turner, I'd like to talk to you for real," he said.

Turner looked at him. Billy dangled the letter opener in his hand and got up, the point between his fingers, and handed it to Turner. "Look, Turner, whether this is real or not, I know if you guys want me dead, I'm dead."

Turner sighed. "This is real, Billy. Jane was our agent."

"You've told me that before."

Jane came in and said, "That's right, I was their agent."

"That's why you wouldn't sleep with me." He concentrated on saying that, not thinking of anything else. Made himself believe it. She hadn't slept with him, the bitch.

"That's right." Suddenly Jane disappeared.

"Goddamn the cunt," Turner said. "She said . . ."

He woke up in a bed; this time Boyle stood over him. "I smuggled you away from them. You didn't crack, wouldn't believe the illusions."

Suddenly Billy believed this. He hated Boyle for mocking him all those years. Now Boyle was going to make a fool of him for all eternity. *Don't subvocalize—kill him. When you can, Billy boy, when you can.*

Boyle helped him sit up and drink some hot coffee. Billy tried to make his voice really whiny when he asked, "Can I go outside?"

"Sure, Billy," Boyle said, helping him dress. "So you prefer Jane to me?"

They walked outside—and Billy saw the mountains he'd been in earlier from a different angle. He noticed Boyle had a revolver in his hand. "This time, will you let me stay dead?"

"Ah, Billy, you cost me too much to do that."

"You stole what you made me of."

"Cost in terms of other things. Your escape—that almost got me into trouble."

"Should have."

They walked by a woodpile. The air was crisp, about as cold as it had been the day before. "Let's chop some wood, Billy, then go back and discuss what I've got to do to you."

Billy knew that if Boyle offered him the ax, this was a setup, fake reality. Boyle grinned, his chin curling upward, and said, "Stack 'um, I'll split 'um." He put the gun in his waistband and picked up the ax.

They worked for a while without talking. Billy felt the rough splinters against his hand and the split oaks gave off their usual smell. Finally Boyle said, "You carry it in."

Billy picked up four or five chunks, wondered if they were a bit too light. Nothing changed. Boyle didn't react either. "We're still in the park," Billy said.

"Yeah, we've got a training camp here."

Billy fingered the rough bark on the logs he was carrying and followed Boyle into the house. "You've broke me now. I was going to go take refuge with the Buddhists, but I guess I'll be your Billy again."

"This time, you'll be as bad as the old pulp books."

Billy saw the holotank then. They must have brought him in that, then sedated him before they took him out. "Let me rest a bit."

"Get back in the tank, Billy."

He saw the poker by the stove, reached for it, saw Simon not moving—frozen like a light display. Billy screamed, biting at the air in front of his face, jerking, biting the air again . . .

. . . which burst and almost drowned him. The tank lid flew up and he saw the guys who'd brought him here, and screamed, "Fuck you, fuck Turner, fuck Simon, fuck the bitches, Celsa," as they pulled him out, pulled off his mittens. He began vomiting brine, salts, and felt the salts working on his bowels.

Turner walked in while they dragged him to the toilet, held his head over the bowl. Billy was in the clothes he'd worn that morning when he and Jane had fled the cabin, but they were wet, smelly. He held the bowl's enameled sides and emptied his stomach, then sat up and pulled down his pants—loose turds slopped into the water below.

"You're killing me," he told Turner, who just looked at him as though he was a spiteful dog. "Don't give me back to Boyle, please." He leaned his head against the cool china-bowl rim and breathed hard.

"You can say his name now, can't you?" Turner said. "Or are your memories of Simon false, too? Interesting problem you've given us,

Mr. Antrim. And you'd kill him if you had a chance. Or do you know better now than to try to kill in a hologram?"

"Why don't you do me so I don't kill to protect myself?"

"Billy, did he give you any redeeming feature?"

"I can be fooled forever. Just like now."

"Billy, this is finally real."

"Maybe none of it's real, even the stuff about getting the surgery, escaping. I kept telling Pat what I really wanted was to be married and have a little ranch. Really. Or maybe I can lie under Epsom salts?" He got up off the bathroom floor, reached toward Turner. "Can you get me dry clothes? Can I take a shower?"

Turner stepped away as if Billy's touch could be lethal and watched him wobble. "Sure, but they'll be chimera pound clothes."

In the room beyond them, Billy heard someone say, "He got his teeth on the air tube and bit through—man, he really doesn't like Boyle—blood pressure and pulse went way up."

This time, the soap tasted of alkali and fat and smelled vaguely of pine. *They're getting better at putting in more details*. He stripped while Turner went out. Billy turned on the hot knob of the shower, saw the steam, and stepped under it.

The water didn't hesitate to burn him. When he heard shouts, he began to beat his head against the tiled shower walls, hoping to spill out his brains and cook them under the heat.

241

Arms grabbed him, a needle went into his arm, almost cool in the burning skin. A hand snaked up and turned on cold water, turned off the hot. They let him fall under the cutting chill.

Billy mumbled, "Thought it was another hologram." He was dizzy, head aching, shoulders raw.

Turner came in and said, "Poor little Billy. Maybe we shouldn't have stopped you?"

Another voice said, "Shock like that could . . ." He passed out, terribly unsure about whether even the pain was real.

Simon had mailed his small recorder bugs to various post office boxes in the Blue Ridge Cultural Park. Thirty of them looked for Billy; the eighteen set to find the SPCA woman.

At each post office, the bugs would cut through the paper mailers and go toward light. As they looked like June bugs, Simon knew he'd lose some of them, maybe most of them. Then after forty hours of moving toward light, the tropism would switch frequencies and the bugs would hunt warmth.

Most of the survivors crawled up car exhaust pipes. Simon hadn't realized how many alternate-life people ran combustion engines.

After twenty days, one bug turned around and crawled out of the park, taking thirteen more days to reach Simon's pickup point in Winchester.

He put the chip in a reader and found out that Billy was in the cultural park at a store on

Goose Creek. At least he had been thirteen days earlier when he was captured.

No one from internal security even talked to Simon. He still worked on the Brazilian. Maybe, Simon hoped, they won't believe whatever Billy might remember of me, thinking the real maker was sophisticated enough to plant false clues.

Simon waited weeks for someone to do something. In July, Turner called him out in the hall. Simon saw two orderlies wheeling Billy down the hall on an ambulance gurney. Turner had called him out to see that. Billy looked nearly dead. Simon forced himself to ask Turner, "Who's that?"

"Rogue chimera maker's illegal," Turner said. "We're sending him to Winchester for further tests. Have you seen Allesandra lately?"

"Not since she talked to me on the train," Simon said.

"Allesandra thought what we did were child's games," Turner said.

"Do you know who made it?" Simon asked.

"No," Turner said. His lined face looked grayer, his nose longer, as if it grew like Pinocchio's from all the lies he told. "Well, if it begins to get to you, then let me know. Sometimes a designer would like to keep one alive."

"What do you think about that one?" Simon said.

"He seems to have a pretty serious concussion, maybe some brain damage. I think he's harmless now. We couldn't get anything out of him before he damaged himself."

Simon just shrugged. Turner looked at him again—*nothing we don't know, Simon*—and went down the hall through the door where the gurney crew had taken Billy. Simon heard tires twisting on the gravel.

But maybe Turner wasn't lying?

Billy woke up and saw Turner looking at him. "You look more like Pat Garrett than Simon Boyle does," he said. His vision was blurred—his head ached. "Is this real now?"

"What's real," Turner said.

"But you know now." Billy looked around and saw a window covered on the outside with steel mesh. He wondered if he could break out and walk away, or if the window was the edge of the tank, a speck in the goggles over his eyes.

"I have to consider the possibility that another maker set Simon up. But I'm afraid it doesn't look likely. We're watching to see if enemy chimeras approach him. If the pressure gets too great, he might come after you again. I can see that killing and reviving you might ease his tensions."

"I want to kill him if he does."

Turner pushed at the skin below his eyes and sniffed as if he had sinus trouble. "What if he wants you to do that? He's not so stupid that he doesn't know we suspect him."

"Are you going to hurt my friends?"

"I've got a niece there. The park is a necessary escape outlet for people who can't take discipline. It would be a bit awkward to hunt down all the tapes they made of your capture."

"Did you always know where I was?" Billy asked. Turner didn't answer. Billy's vision blurred again. He sniffed the air and smelled Epsom salts. "I'm still in the tank, ain't I? I smell that smell."

"Billy, you've got a good nose. Lots of tanks here," Turner said. "You're in one of the mother buildings of false realities, but what I've told you is real enough, in tank or out. Believe me. You have several options. If you want to be dead, permanently, that can be arranged."

"I don't think so," Billy said, wondering if they could kill him while he was in a tank, or just make him think he'd died. "Could I go to the Buddhists? Simon tried to condition me against them, so I trust them. I met some."

"The park rangers want you back. But we don't know if you're stable enough to have running free."

"You could make me think I was free when I was really in a tank. So what's this?"

"Would you be happy enough if we restricted you to the Appalachian Cultural Park for life?"

"Well, haven't I agreed to that already? Will Jane be with me?"

"If she agrees. We can arrange work in Roanoke, so she'd be self-sufficient. If that's what she wants."

Billy was about to say, *Make her*, but he decided that would sound too much like the historical Billy the Kid. "I would like to become

245

just a little weird guy in the mountains." The room went blurry.

Turner said, "You're sick now and captive, but when you're better, then are you going to be satisfied with park life?"

"Make me be satisfied. Why am I alive, anyhow?"

"Billy, perhaps because I am curious. But I promise that if you so much as steal one hen, I'll kill you myself, as painlessly as possible, and make sure that you stay dead."

"Deal," Billy said, raising his hand from the sheets and seeing for the first time a tube draining who knew what into him. Turner shook with him anyway, cautiously, so as to not disturb the needle stuck in the back of Billy's hand.

The next time Billy woke up, he heard Turner saying, "What we're doing is passing a park ordinance making you, Aram, and Yaffe responsible for what he does." Billy opened his eyes and saw Jane by his bed. She had gone mottled in the face, like she'd gotten in deeper than she wanted to.

"Hi, Jane, I feel terrible. Is this another hologram?"

"No, Billy."

"You'd say that either way." He tried to wake up more, but was too tired. The CIA knew about Boyle. Now they could toss him back out to see what Boyle'd do about it.

Turner said, "I'll drive down with you. This would be a good opportunity to visit my niece."

* * *

As they left Billy still in the hospital at Winchester, Jane asked Yaffe, "How did you do it?"

Yaffe crossed her ankles and looked down at her wool socks and sandals. "We've got pretty arcane connections, too. Like Turner's niece and a lot of other rich kids who just couldn't stand the hypocrisy, the war economy. How do you think we rated a national park?"

"Billy still wonders if this is another trick in the conditioning tank."

Yaffe said, "Tell him as long as he's even tricked, he's still alive. Maybe he'd like to organize an outlaw show for the tourists?"

Jane said, "I hope not."

CHAPTER SEVEN
Memories for Brushy Bill

It will never be known whether the Kid recognized me or not. If he did, it was the first time, during all his life of peril, that he ever lost his presence of mind, or failed to shoot first and hesitate afterwards. He knew that a meeting with me meant surrender or fight.

—From *The Authentic Life of Billy, the Kid*, by Pat F. Garrett (with the help of Marshall A. Upson)

BILLY DIDN'T WANT TO RIDE FOUR HOURS IN A CAR with Turner even if Turner was putting him back, alive, in the park. Those instants when Billy believed the scenes he was in weren't projections in holo-goggles, Turner made Billy himself feel like a hologram gone out into the real world. Billy lacked the small memories about nieces and football games that Turner used to flesh himself out. As Billy got in the front seat of the car, he decided he might still be trapped in Turner's tricks. Turner said, "Seems warmer than usual for July."

Billy said, "I wouldn't remember."

Jane and Yaffe got in back. Yaffe said, "Maybe we should just adapt to the cold, if the glaciers are coming. Yang and yin, heat and cold."

"The Virginia Appalachians weren't buried under a mile of ice," Turner said. "Billy, I think you'll find this drive has too much detail for a hologram."

"How would I know?" Billy asked. "I've never been in the twenty-first century before this year that I knew about."

"Don't try to play Billy the Kid anymore," Turner said. "We know about the man you robbed in New York City."

Billy wanted to explain that he'd panicked over being trapped, but then the historical Kid used that as an excuse.

They drove through fir and spruce at two-to-three thousand feet, stopping at the overlooks. Finally they saw Roanoke, maglev tracks, freight tubes, power lines, reactor containment facilities, apartment buildings going up to the very ridge tops, square ponds glinting oil rainbows. The wind stank of human bodies, electricity, alcohol, and scorched car tires.

Jane said, "What will I do down there?"

Turner said, "We've arranged a data-processing job, running notes through an optical scanner and correcting data when the scanner can't make sure determinations."

"An illiterate could do that." What Turner had told Jane seemed like gibberish to Billy, but she understood and was insulted.

"No, you have to reconfigure data when people send in data written out of pattern. Scanners get confused by squiggles and arrows."

Yaffe said, "Jane, a friend of mine has an

enclosed recumbent bike you could buy cheap. In a while, you could probably afford an alcohol car."

Billy looked down at Roanoke and wondered if it would stay there if he walked down to it. What territory, ever, had he really traveled over? "Can I go down there?" Billy asked.

Turner said, "Never. That's the deal."

Turner took Jane to her new job the next day. Jane hated Roanoke compared to Albany, even if it would be free of summer ice when the glaciers came. It sprawled uphill and down, exposing too extreme vistas—uphill and down—geometric apartments, tiny houses with yards against the interstates, shopping malls beside factories, tubes running at ground level or overhead. Unplanned, unzoned. Suddenly an early-twentieth-century neighborhood would appear by the road, next to it, ferrocement office towers.

Turner turned off at one of the towers and parked the car. Jane knew she'd be working for the Roanoke Valley Planning District, running paper through an optical scanner, notes turned digital without human hands, just her eyeballs checking to see that the scribbles went in correctly, calling to check what she couldn't read.

Grunge job, and the supervisor would probably prefer Jane was only numerate. Jane followed Turner in, feeling like a whipped outlaw in her cheap shoes and print pants suit. "Is the job a guaranteed thing?" she asked Turner.

"The district will want to see how fast you learn," he said, as detached as if she were a chimera herself. They took an elevator up to a midlevel floor where Turner said into an intercom, "We're looking for Mrs. Stanley."

A heavy woman in a black synthetic dress printed with green and yellow triangles came up, unlocked the wired glass door, and said, "I'm Mrs. Stanley. Is this Jane?"

Jane nodded.

"Call me Irene. You literate, right?"

"Yes, I've—"

"No need to explain. Whatever you been through or did, now you just need to keep the data flowing through the Cray. Mr. Turner, I'll take her and show her."

Turner said, "Thanks. I'll be back in an hour."

As Jane and Irene went through more glass doors into a room filled with computer screens, optical scanners, and pneumatic tubes, Irene said, "The managers could speak the data, but they claim they can handwrite it faster. That's okay, it gives you a job. But they grouch when you have to clarify things, so be tactful. Sit down at this one."

Jane sat down and began running pieces of paper through the scanner, watching her screen to see that the data was being entered in appropriate cells. Irene said, "The bosses say they make less errors if they handwrite than if they try to keyboard-entry, and they like having us around to get coffee. There's your first hash."

She pointed to random characters appearing on the screen.

Jane pulled out the sheet of paper and tried to figure out what had been written. She couldn't even make out the name signed at the bottom.

Irene said, "It's Gerrard, you'll learn the names. Call her, then put in what she meant by keyboard."

Jane looked for a phone book, then saw a sheet of paper sealed in plastic. She called Gerrard and heard a young voice on the other end. "Hello, Ms. Gerrard, it's Jane in data entry. I've got your figures for glass recycling but neither the reader nor I could—"

"Hey, shit, yeah. Should be ... damn, can I call you back, I've got to refigure that myself. I shouldn't have sent you the sheet yet."

Irene said, "Flag the file. If this wasn't a test, I'd say get back to her in an hour. You'll have to set up your own tickler file."

Jane looked at the keyboard and saw a key marked "not all entered," and asked, "Do I hit this key?"

"Smart girl. Yeah, then you can shift and hit the key again and the machine will scroll all the incomplete files."

Jane pressed the key, not feeling all that smart. "Do you have a manual for the computer, how we enter this?"

"Oh, you'll pick it up. Just keep on going." Irene went to another work station and began feeding paper through her own optical scanner.

Jane pushed one sheet in too fast and it crumpled. On the side was a button marked "Refeed," so she pushed that. A bell went off. Irene said, "You only get five refeeds an hour, so be careful. Smooth the paper down and put it in slowly. If it's too crumpled, raise the feeder head and lay the sheet in manually. But you need to reach a rate of twenty sheets a minute even with calls for clarification. The machine can do more than an item a second and it's a slow machine."

"What do they need us for?" Jane asked.

"To make sure it isn't hash. And in the morning, you'll take coffee around to five offices, get to know the bosses personally. We'll trade off emptying the pneumatic tubes. Come on, you're behind."

Jane began pushing paper through the scanner, checking each screen to make sure it was realistic enough text. She made two more phone calls, got clarifications on one screen, no answer on the other item, and flagged the incomplete file.

At the end of the test hour, Irene came over and said, "Oh, the machine was smart today."

Jane brushed back her hair and asked, "And we do this five hours a day?"

"Coffee duties take about ten minutes, more on the days you make it, and you get two ten-minute breaks. I remember my mother telling me about eight-hour work days, double shifts, no overtime."

She didn't say anything to Turner on the way

back to Goose Creek except to ask, "How do I get there?"

"You ride your bike to the train at Copper Hill, then transfer to the Number 8 bus which stops in front."

Jane figured she'd never be able to afford a car. The Vector she was buying used was going to cost her twenty dollars a week, a third of her take-home pay, for three years.

When Turner parked the car, she saw the Vector in the yard, a ten-foot-long blue fiberglass bullet with a glass head. Two bicycle wheels were embedded in it. She went up closer and saw two keys taped to its door.

"Take care," Turner said. He turned his car back on and drove away. For good, Jane hoped.

Billy came out then and stared first at the bike, then at Jane. "Are you okay?"

"No. The work."

"The machine looks interesting."

"I've never had to ride a bicycle to work before," Jane said before she realized Billy wouldn't have any idea of what that might mean to her.

Billy said, "Can I ride it, too, if I help pay for it?" He sounded excited.

Yaffe came out of the house and said, "Jane, we may have work for Billy when he recovers from the surgery and the head banging he gave himself."

"That's nice."

Billy lifted the Vector by the nose, raising the

front wheel off the ground, and said, "Jane's pissed about her own job."

Yaffe said, "It isn't necessarily permanent, is it?"

"Nothing's permanent," Jane said. "Life's a flirt."

Billy lowered the Vector and said, "If this is real, I must say I'm amazed. This thing only weighs about sixty pounds, Jane. Come on, try it out."

She pulled off the keys, opened the fairing door, stretched herself out on the Vector's seat and pedals, and began to pedal as she hadn't since she was a child. The thing was so low to the ground, she could get her feet down fast when it threatened to go over. She went bouncing down one of the weir bridges, then up the other side so fast she thought she'd go airborne. Shaking, she turned it around and braked down the dip to the overflow bed on the bridge, then walked the bike up the dip on the other side. When she got back to the house, she felt she could manage the thing, but would never let herself love it.

Billy said, "Yaffe says I shouldn't ride it until I'm recovered."

"You might enjoy it," Jane said. "It's weird."

"Bicycles are very ecological," Yaffe said. "We're going to hold a referendum to see if we should mandate them inside the park."

Jane ran piles of hand-scribbled executive notes through her optic reader day after day.

At three each day, she took the maglev to Copper Hill, got into her Vector, and pedaled home, an hour or so of up-and-down hills, the chain whizzing through the gear changes, the fairing booming if wind gusted against it. Rain streamed off the clear plastic nose, no need for wipers.

They were poor now, but Billy had no idea.

Billy doubted he was in the real world yet, with people like Yaffe babbling about national parks of the mind, a place set aside for simpler life supported by tourists. Then, after the first week with Jane, her driving up every day to a job in Roanoke, Billy wondered if the CIA was trying to provoke him by boring holovisions.

He worked a little garden plot with a spade until Jane rented a tractor for him and Aram showed him how to use it—jolting, fumy, noisy, lots of fun, actually, with a double plow, the left share raised when the right one cut a furrow.

The next day, Billy began plowing the strip across the road on Goose Creek. Then the whole plow lifted up when Billy pulled a lever. On the return furrow, the left share plowed. Billy felt vaguely familiar with plows and steam tractors, but he wondered if the real Billy the Kid would have given up and gone back to rustling if he'd had to plant wheat.

His eyes broke bad when he started to take the plow off and put the harrow on a hydraulic lift. The world rippled. Or what seemed to be real rippled. He wondered if Goose Creek wasn't more unreal yet than some actual park preserved off from the twenty-first century. When the world straightened out a second later, he wondered if that was due to improved holo-product. Still, he hitched up the harrow the way Aram had showed him the day before and cut the clods fine with the steel disks.

An old man came down the road and said to him, "Waste of time work that hard in this valley."

"Why?"

"Too dark here, really. National Park Service didn't steal much of nothing when they took this country."

Billy said, "Guess I don't know much about farming."

"None of you do. That's why you came here."

Billy said, "I'm not really like them."

"No?" The old man didn't seem too interested in what Billy might say.

"They moved me out of another national park."

"Yeah, they think we inbreed," the old man said, "but most of the time, we don't breed at all. And your woman?"

Billy said, "She's from Albany, New York."

"She's on public work, ain't she?"

"Goes to Roanoke every day."

"They don't give many of us that option, now, do they? Saving our culture like it wasn't always our way to send kids off to cities. Damn government."

Billy reminded himself that this all might be some sort of phony hologram test. "Well, I don't know about that. Seems like this place gives folks some options."

"Didn't volunteer for 'em," the man said, "but had to accept 'um to keep the land."

"I guess I did," Billy said. The man walked away. Billy realized he had seen him before the CIA took him away, walking down the road, then walking up about an hour later, enough time to get to the hard surface. Billy wondered if that meant the man was real or if Goose Creek had always been a fake valley for a fake Billy the Kid. He took off his shoes and threw wheat seeds by hand, the dirt cold between his toes.

That night, at the dinner table set with enameled tin plates and big white pottery mugs, Billy said, "Jane, I'm having trouble seeing things."

Jane said, "Yaffe's coming tomorrow. Call her tonight and see if she can bring a doctor or something."

Billy didn't remember having a phone installed. But it was sitting on the cupboard behind Jane. He went to it as if his fingers would poke right through it and stared at the numbers showing through holes in a disk. "When did we get this?"

"When we came back from Winchester, it was here. It doesn't call outside the park."

"I don't remember seeing it before."

"I had it up in my room until today," Jane said, if the image talking was really Jane.

Billy lifted the receiver and heard some odd

tone. Truly in the tank, he thought, but he said, "I don't know how to use one like this."

"You stick your finger in the number holes and dial." Jane came over and demonstrated. "This was the way phones were until the phone companies went to voice chips as people became less numerate."

The world wobbled again, but Billy found Yaffe's number and dialed it, very slowly, making sure his finger felt the edge of the metal stop below the figure *one*.

Billy heard Yaffe's car between blows of his wood-splitting maul.

"I trust that your vision isn't so blurred that splitting wood is dangerous," she said, holding a black bag as she got out of the car.

"What happens happens," Billy said, not sure he wanted to voice his speculations when Yaffe might be no more than a holographic image.

Yaffe said, "Let's go inside so I can set up this equipment." They sat down at a table in the front room. She pumped air into a cuff around his arm, listening to his arm veins. The nurses and doctors had also done that. "What is that?" he asked.

"Taking your blood pressure," she said, frowning. Next, she looked in his eyes with a little light—telegraph electricity heated the wires white-hot inside the glass bulb. "All that surgery and then smashing your head against the tile caused damage in your visual cortex. If you didn't have those weird neurons, you'd be permanently fucked up."

"I'm beginning to understand the way things work," he said to her cautiously. He knew if he left, his three human friends would be arrested. But then, if he was still floating in Epsom salts, he couldn't walk far enough.

She took his blood-pressure reading again. "And some of this blurring might be due to stress," Yaffe said. "Your pulse is erratic. And I got two different blood-pressure readings."

"I'd like to see more of this world than some preserve simple enough to . . ." . . . *to fit in fake holograms*. He caught himself, but still wanted to tell someone he felt unreal.

"Billy, you can travel from Cherokee to Monterey here."

"Monterey?"

"Monterey, Virginia, in Highland County."

"Amazing."

"Turner said the horses you rode were real. One of the old settlers has a cattle farm and is looking for a hand who can drive a tractor, check fence lines, and help with winter calving. And he has horses. He doesn't need you until September, but that will give you time to recover."

Tangled in barbed wire, floating in Epsom salts, or really in a semireal world, a fake past built for tourists and rich kids? "You know, Yaffe, I think I'm really the reincarnation of Brushy Bill."

"How so?"

263

"We both really thought we were Billy the Kid."

Yaffe left him. He wiggled his nose to see if he felt tubes up his nostrils.

When Jane came home, Billy asked, "Can I ride the bike?"

"Help me get the groceries in," Jane told him. He took her sweaty face in his hands and almost kissed her, but she was frowning. He rubbed his thumbs on her cheeks, then picked up two sacks. When they got to the kitchen, he sighed, then started putting groceries up with his small quick hands.

"Are you bored?" she asked.

He told her, "I still have trouble with what I see." She didn't instantly know how significant that was to him, he realized. He was hurt that she seemed to have forgotten what he'd told her when they'd first met: *My eyes are not honest.*

"Billy, we can't afford more surgery."

"It's all right. I'm growing back inside the brains." She'd bought that weird meat in plastic again, the kind that stored without ice. He put the two packages in the pantry, then asked again, "Can I take the bike out?"

"Sure." She handed him the key to the fairing door. "But it'll be dark in an hour."

Billy took the key and went outside. He unlocked the fairing, then climbed in, legs stretched out in front of him on the pedals, hands on the steering wheel, back against the seat. He pushed it with his feet until he felt how it balanced, then pedaled. He watched the mountains through the clear polycarb. *Can I go to the end of the hologram?*

The Vector wobbled a bit, then steadied as he picked up speed. Billy suspected he'd ridden a bike before, but utterly couldn't remember when. Another of those little fleshing-out memories was completely missing, but his body knew what to do. His unremembered skill made him feel considerably unreal.

They've done a good job with the sun, he thought, seeing the long streaks of gravel shadows when he stopped at the stop sign on the parkway. Then he pedaled the sweaty climb up the mountain toward Roanoke.

From the crest, he saw the city sprawled below, tubes running out in all directions. This is no hologram, he decided when he smelled the city air coming out of the valley—reeking of electricity, men, scorched steel and rubber tires, and damp coal.

The lights went on in the shadowed places, and he turned around and rode down the mountain, coasting, leaning into the turns as though the bike was a horse. Then he turned on the fairing lights. *So much real detail—out there, Roanoke. This park is artificially simple—that's why I wondered if it was real. It isn't really real, but it isn't a hologram either.*

When he got back, Jane had stew cooked from the meat she'd bought and yesterday's beans. Billy loved the smell, but wondered still why the meat didn't rot in the plastic bags—like bladder bags, they were, but then he realized the bladder bags he'd known were probably these.

"You gave up a lot for me," he said, realizing that he'd never thanked her, but then until to-night, he had thought that this life was computer-generated lights inside goggles inside an Epsom salt bath inside a tank, tubes up his nose like trains taking supplies to a city.

"Yes," she said, looking at him, her pants and shirt covered by an apron, a lank bunch of grown hair falling over her left eye. She pushed it back with her wrist, still holding a potholder in that hand.

"Thank you." He wanted to hold her. His arms twitched and he looked down at them. They'd done that on their own. *No hologram.*

"Hard, isn't it, Billy, after high adventures, life-threatening situations, to just live? I always resented the chimeras going back to their own-ers, but—"

He interrupted her. "I don't want to go back." His face flushed when he thought about what he did want to do. "One thing missing."

She put down the potholder and came up to him, so close he felt her body heat. "What's that?"

All the blood and heat in the universe ran into his cock. "Take the stuff off the stove," he told her.

"Can't you wait until after dinner? I won-dered if they stopped Boyle," Jane said as she put the soup pot on the cooler part of the cook surface.

Billy's cock lost blood—he remembered Boyle telling him, *There's honey in the groin, Billy,* a quote from an old poem, Jack Spicer. "Oh, shit, I remember him watching me and the women I thought were Celsa. Let's eat, then turn all the lights out. I'll be real boring to him if he's been watching from the cracks."

She got the bowls out and ladled up the stew. As they sat at the table bent over their stew bowls, Billy asked, "Jane, what does it mean to you that I'm a chimera?"

"I . . . I don't know. You weren't brought up chimera."

"Yes, but you were brought up—"

"Billy, please."

"Okay." He ate awhile, then said, "I saw Roanoke today."

"You say that like it was a revelation."

"It was." He decided not to explain. "It's interesting what Simon gave me: literacy, knowledge of wood stoves and voice-operated telephones. Eyeballs, a brain that can heal itself. Life. Poor bastard."

"You still want to kill him?"

"Turner's probably right. That's how Simon would like to end it." He grinned at her. "Too much like the historical Billy for me."

On August 28, 2068, Turner and Trung came into Simon's office. Trung was in a dark blue suit with a cravat, a white collar's points bent over it, looking, Simon thought, even more sinister than he did in leathers. Trung sat down, ankle over knee. Turner stood, his lower eyelids loose on his eyes, looking almost like a hound's eyes.

Accelerating to 110 beats per minute.

Trung said, "We'd like you to go to the beach with us. Down in North Carolina."

Turner said, "Over Labor Day weekend."

Trung said, "You don't have other plans," as though he had checked.

Simon was glad he hadn't smuggled out any parts yet, then realized that he'd have to get rid of the equipment he'd stored in the miniware-house at Amelia Courthouse. *120 beats per minute.* They'd know what his pulse rate was. He said, "Sure," then wondered if perhaps he would just hide the keys.

Trung stood up and looked at Turner who wouldn't look at anyone. *Minor fibrillations.* Simon said, "I've got to walk around a bit. Been behind the desk too long."

Trung smiled when Turner said, "You'll get to walk on the beach."

Trung and Turner changed into jeans and art sweatshirts before Simon and they left Langley on Friday afternoon. The match in their clothes made Simon feel isolated. He became even more uneasy when Turner's driver drove them to an unlogoed twelve-passenger jet at Dulles. Simon climbed up the ramp and looked inside. Only the first four seats were visible. Raw steel plates crudely bolted in walled off the back of the plane. As he put his luggage in storage, Simon tried to remember whether or not the plane had another door in the rear.

Trung was swaying gracefully to music from his earphones, putting his own luggage up. Seated already, Turner was reading the *Washington Post*. He looked up and nodded, then focused on the paper again as Simon sat down in front of him. Their calm exacerbated the anxiety Simon'd felt when he saw that the back of the plane was sealed.

A chime rang. Trung sat down and buckled himself into a seat on the other side of the aisle from Turner and Simon. Simon felt trapped in front of Turner, wished he'd sat behind Trung. The chime rang again and the plane began taxiing. It jumped suddenly into the air and flew out to sea.

100 beats per minute. Simon heard paper rustle behind him. He resented that Turner had left Billy running loose in the Appalachian Cultural Park, but had trapped him. Maybe they decided the real maker constructed a false memory of Simon? Maybe. He should have had Billy remember Quist as his maker, but Simon hadn't been that bad, then. *That bad, then?*

Trung seemed to be sleeping, or listening, loose-limbed, to music. The plane dropped. Simon looked out the window and saw Hatteras, then the plane passed that and landed at Sunny Point on an abandoned airstrip.

"Nice about STOLs," Turner said, folding up his paper. Trung sat up.

"Where are we going?"

"Quiet place, started as a fort, then was a Baptist retreat until we bought it."

"Fort Caswell," Simon said as they got into a blue car with local plates. Trung drove.

Trung drove. Turner said, "If we get bored, there's always Wilmington." Trung laughed.

They bought groceries just east of a historical marker on the capture of the eighteenth-century pirate Bonney, Blackbeard's companion. Simon remembered a facsimile of Bonney's letter he'd bought in Charleston as a boy. The man had begged the royal governor from the bowels of mercy not to be hanged. Was it Bonney or another eighteenth-century pirate who strangled on the rope so quietly that his death bouquet didn't slip from his hands? Simon knew now the man, whoever he'd been, had to have utterly despaired to have died so.

Bonney, a gentleman planter gone wrong. William Bonney, one of the Kid's aliases. Simon hated the parallels and analogies he was seeing today.

Turner said, "We've got a lot to talk about, Simon, while we're down here."

The drive to Fort Caswell was long, by the Southport dredges fighting the sinking shoreline and around the marsh that had been part of Southport's harbor. Out on the road paralleling the ocean, Simon saw a preserved lighthouse striped like nineteenth-century convict clothes and wished his mind hadn't found that analogy. Maybe he should tell them that he had built Billy and was sorry? No, or not yet. They hadn't asked.

He knew, though, as they drove between sea grass and groves of myrtle and live oaks, that this was more than a holiday at the beach. Here and there, he saw pilings where houses had been, well inland. "Ocean's dropped here," he said.

"The ice in Canada ties up about a foot, but the current shifted, too," Trung said.

"Used to be more people here, though," Simon said, wondering if they'd been removed by eminent domain.

"We're preserving the wetlands," Trung said.

Turner asked, "What did you do with your dog, Simon?"

"My vet's boarding him," Simon said. That question terrified him.

Then there was Fort Caswell, rubble and rock buildings, with gray wood buildings inside the fort wall. The gray boards had been painted white once. Paint chips still curled away. Then Simon saw the double-wide trailer sitting incongruously new between the old buildings. Red enamel, windows not sand-etched.

Trung said, "We'll be staying there. And going to Wilmington when we're bored."

Neither Simon nor Turner replied. Each man carried his own bag to the trailer. The back rooms weren't laid out shotgun style. A tiny narrow hall led between bedrooms on either side. Turner said, "That one's yours, Simon."

Simon went in and saw a wall five or six yards

271

from his windows. As he hung up his clothes, he could hear an air conditioner humming and the random sounds of the other men unpacking.

Turner finished first, or had he brought his clothes earlier? He said, "Please join us up front."

Simon felt his windows—plastic, not glass, and immobile. He closed his door behind him when he went to the front room. It was large, for a trailer room, and the kitchen equipment was open in one corner. Trung followed Simon into the room.

Turner said, "We want you to defect."

Simon wondered what this meant, and sat down without speaking.

Trung said, "We're going to interrogate you with tank and drugs."

Simon said, "I'll tell you now. I did build the Billy-the-Kid chimera."

Turner said, "We know that. And that actual people died. Drifters found shot at close range with a load of dimes. Simon, that . . ."

Simon knew the dimes in the shotgun shell weren't authentic. "Are you going to charge me with murder?"

Turner sighed. Trung said, "We'd prefer that you cooperate with our plan."

Turner said, "Both the Mexicans and the KGB were interested in discovering who our rogue maker was. We had other indicators that you were he. Allesandra, for one."

Simon asked, "What about my chimeras that are still working?"

"We'll fix that," Turner said. "Believe me, we can."

Trung said, "We have to make this look like a grade-six interrogation. Your blood will show traces of the interrogation drugs."

Simon was excited—fieldwork at last. "Fine, then. I'll do anything for the Agency."

Turner said, "Well, that's settled. Let's take a walk down the island."

Trung didn't get up. Simon followed Turner out onto the beach. Ghost crabs scuttled across the dunes dimly lit by the moon. Turner went down a boardwalk to the intertidal zone and then began walking where the sand was hard. Simon followed him, neither talking. The beach looked abandoned, but to the east Simon saw a glow that was Southport on the other side of the Cape Fear River. "So you want me to defect? They'll obviously try to replace me with a chimera."

"No. They're going to try to embarrass us with your Billy chimera. Decadent CIA and all that."

"How is Billy?"

"Behaving. You care?"

"I . . . I could always bring him back to life after I killed him."

Turner said, "Not like the others."

"No, not like the others."

"The Catholics say that they're not sacred life."

Simon said, "I'm not Catholic, but I'd bet that the Church says not to make them."

"Church doesn't say that. Just says that they are animal order. That's the Buddhist position, too, but they don't kill animals, either, so." Turner sighed.

"I conditioned Billy against Buddhists."

"He broke through that. That's why I decided to take a chance on him. And he'll be alive to prove your story."

"When do I defect?"

"First, we're going to interrogate you, to be sure we understand you."

Simon thought of the tapes defectors made. Turner and he walked down to the lighthouse. Simon's heart monitor suggested a rest there. Turner kept the rest short.

The next morning, Simon lay down on a hospital bed set up in the front room. Trung inserted an intravenous drip into the back of Simon's left hand. Simon began counting backward.

Sometime during the day, he vaguely heard Trung ask, "What does he remember about the Kid chimera?"

"I don't know yet," Turner said. "Give him a bit more. He's . . ." and the voices faded.

When Simon completely woke up, the trailer was empty with dishes drying in a rack by the sink. Trung and Turner had breakfast only minutes earlier, Simon decided as he felt water still on the plates. He looked outside. The sun was high in the sky. There was another trailer just like his five yards away.

Simon saw a mirror image of himself—no, a duplicate of himself—walk out of the other trailer.

140 beats per minute. Simon began running anyway. His duplicate, recently fed with his drugged-out memories, followed him, but didn't run any faster than Simon did. *180 beats per minute.* Simon wondered if it also had a heart condition? A monitor wired to the auditory centers?

I am human. I don't deserve this.

Stop, the voice from his heart said.

Simon stopped and faced his double. The double spread his arms and hands and began swaying slightly. It said, "Run. If you won't die, I'll have to strangle you."

"Why couldn't Turner do this himself?" Simon cried as he began running again, the heart monitor screaming warnings at him. *Fibrillations.*

Then the monitor stopped. He knew his heart was still beating and clicked his teeth, no reading. He ran even harder, slower. He saw Trung and Turner ahead of him, as if his double had herded him toward them.

Is this really happening? An electric current seemed to go through his body. He was so close to them, no, not close at all.

Then he heard Trung ask, "Don't you want to hear when he dies?"

Turner said, "No."

Simon's heart stopped.

CHAPTER EIGHT

The Surface of Things Bounces You Back

Billy the Kid
(In spite of your death notices)
There is honey in the groin
Billy.

Jack Spicer, "Billy the Kid"

In September, Billy began to work with cattle again or for the first time. He rode Jane's Vector to the farm on Saturday because he didn't want to commit to buying on time until after he met his boss and knew he could do the work. As he pedaled out of the Goose Creek Valley and over into the Little River drainage, he felt almost afraid, remembering—false remembering, he had to remind himself—Brewer with his brains splattered, lariats, and red-hot pokers searing through cowhide to rework brands.

The farm behind its barbed-wire fences looked small—tiny enough to fit in a conditioning tank? Beside a raw plank barn, Angus cows too heavy to range-graze hung around a metal feed trough. Shelled corn poured into it out of a pipe. Down below the pasture, Billy saw the white frame house and pulled into the driveway. A man about forty-five, chunky and red-faced, wearing blue denim overalls and a plaid flannel shirt, came out to meet him. "Name's Billy McCarty," Billy said. "I'm supposed to report for work."

"Woman called said you could drive tractor."

"True. And I've had experience with cattle when I was a kid."

The man smiled. "The AI man's come and gone. We've got to get the hay and silage up, then we'll inoculate and cull as soon as we can get sign."

AI man? Billy said, "I was out west. We didn't have AI men."

"Range-bred then?"

"Yeah."

"Too fucking authentic for words. I won't let them do that to me all the way, even if I have to play hick for the tourists. Land's been ours for eight generations."

"Yeah, the park sure tries to make us all into characters, don't it?"

The man looked up and down at Billy and said, "Call me Sam."

"Yes, sir."

"Can you spike hay?"

"Haven't done that, sir, but I can drive a tractor."

"Silage auger?"

Billy wondered if Sam was trying to humiliate him. "No."

"Branding?"

"Yes."

"Bet they made you use a campfire to heat the iron out there," Sam said. "You poor bastard."

"Look, I can learn. I do know cattle." As Billy said that, he wondered how real the cows in his memories had been.

"Pull calves with chains?"

Billy's memories threw up a memory, more tactile than most, of his arm inside a cow, the odor of blood, the calf nostrils, like wet liver, against his fingertips, feeling his way up the slimy hair to the poll and upper jaw. *Simon sure was a weird fuck.* "I've turned one manually, but it wasn't full breech," Billy said, using the words that his mind gave him without fully understanding.

"I'll run you through on Plastic Elsie," Sam said. "Now, let's get you on a tractor with a blade and you can pile silage."

"I'll need transportation to get here. Thought about buying a Vector like my girlfriend's, but if you could loan me a horse . . ."

"Where you living?"

"Goose Creek about a mile from the store, hard-surface side. House has a hippie wart dome one side of it."

"Got someone who pick you up, okay. Got three quarter horses for exhibit, but I don't let new help ride them."

"I know I can ride."

"But you don't know my horses," Sam said.

"Let's get to work. Put this in your ear and I'll tell you what to do with the little dozer." Sam handed Billy a piece of plastic that looped over his earlobe with one bit that swung down and into his ear.

The little dozer had a small enclosed cab with twentieth-century air-conditioning and tape-deck. Billy had never seen a tractor with metal belts instead of wheels, but it seemed to work just the same as his. He sat in the cab, not liking feeling shut in, not liking the thing stuck in his ear, and tried raising and lowering the blade. Then Sam spoke: "What you want to do is keep the chop piled on the concrete pad. Then we'll cover it with plastic and you'll pack it in by running over it a few times."

After about a half hour, Billy could feel the blade tip through the controls, could almost feel the texture of the chopped corn stalks.

Then, the pile built and plastic laid over it, Billy ran the bulldozer up the height of the pile, slowly, carefully, the blade hanging in the sky, then dropping. As he went down, he raised the blade. Sam's voice in his ear said, "Good boy."

Billy looked out and saw a couple of other men standing with Sam, their smiles fading. If he'd run down the pile with the blade lowered, the blade would have jammed against the ground where the pile ended. The men had been waiting to see that.

When the first silage pile was packed, Sam said, "Take a break, Billy."

Billy got out of the cab and looked the machine over, grinning like a fool, he knew, but the machine was almost as fun as Jane's Vector. "So, cows eat this?"

"When it's ripe," Sam said.

Billy had a vague, sight-only memory of loading a wagon with pitchforks. He knew enough from garden work what a pain that would be. "Not too primitive, Boss Sam."

The other men who'd come to see him hang the dozer by the blade smiled again. Sam said, "We'll get another bunker packed and then get some dinner."

"God, it's good to be back at work again," Billy said. "Even if I'd rather be on a horse doing it."

One of the other men, a young blond with huge boots, said, "You try to stamp out all the air with a horse, you'd be a week doing it."

The local park radio was playing a song about Vitamin C and cocaine and someone with Jane's name who was living off them. I almost wish, Jane thought as she wiped what felt like a cup of sweat off her face. Hot canning jars sat on the table by the kitchen stove. As she listened for the pings of seals being made, Jane figured out on a calculator what Billy's garden had saved them. Some. Yaffe suggested that they get a freezer, but Jane wished they could just jerk the plants from the ground with all the vegetables still hanging, and send everything to a processor-sterilizer and get back vegetables in room-temperature storage pouches, with the inedible parts composed and neatly bagged.

One jar didn't ping. Jane walked around the table touching the jar lids to see if one was still springy. The lid on the beets bounced under her finger. She shuddered. They had two quarts of pickled beets from earlier jars that didn't seal.

Yaffe said that technology beyond what was common in the 1950's was limited to rangers. Maybe Yaffe could take our vegetables off to a sterilizer, Jane thought as she opened the beets and put them back in the kettle to heat up for dinner.

Billy came in and asked, "What's for dinner?"

"Beets. Beans."

"Jar didn't seal?"

"No, and it was beets again."

"I bet cows would eat them," Billy said. He smelled sweaty, not quite human sweaty, though, as he came up behind her and reached around for a breast.

Jane didn't move, let him rub against her. She asked, "How was your day?"

"Farming the way it should be done. Machines, augers, tractors called bulldozers, milking machines." He squeezed gently and she laughed almost against her will.

"You like your work then?"

"Yeah. Made me forget."

Jane thought, I need some work like that.

Billy pulled a pot of beans out of the refrigerator and set them on to reheat. "I like the guys, the machines, the cows. They got beef cows so stout they couldn't run."

"How are you going to get there? I'll need the Vector Monday."

"Guy's going to pick me up. We don't work Sunday unless cows are freshening. Dropping calves. Boss has crew enough for milkings."

Since the canning jars had to sit until they cooled, Jane and Billy ate in the front room, watching flat-screen television from a station in Roanoke that translated holosignals into a broadcast for the park people.

On the screen, hikers were pissing on a dirty patch of snow found on the north side of Mount Washington in New Hampshire. Our first State-side glacier, Jane realized. She remembered her grandparents telling her about the time in the late 1990's when everyone was so optimistic.

"I saw snow like that somewhere," Billy said. "When I thought I was breaking out of jail and killing Olinger and Bell."

"The last ice age never completely went away out west," Jane said. She had wondered if the CIA was really going to leave her and Billy alone, if Billy would eventually revert to his prototype, get bored and hire out to fight for some cause. She had an edgy feeling herself sometimes that the world wasn't helping her, but rather hated her. She'd moderated her own defiance when she went to work for the ASPCA, but now? Jane realized her dread wasn't that Billy would revert to type, but that she'd die to find a way to really right them, that cold Vietnamese, pinch-nosed Turner, and all the indifference they had for her.

In late November, when the snows began, Yaffe sold Jane a spinning wheel and wool and taught her how to spin. Spinning made television bearable, those edited glimpses of the outside world beyond the park. Jane and Billy contracted to buy a used snowmobile on time and the man who drove Billy to work came in a larger snowcat if the snow was deep enough.

We're here because we're here because we heard too much, Jane's mind began chanting at her as she plied knitting yarns, too poor to buy a loom.

Then in January, when the snows had crusted, Turner came back, alone, knocking on her door on a Saturday while Billy was working. He looked at her from his thin lined face and she felt terrified.

"Why are you here?" she asked him. She wondered if he killed in his CIA work—his skull seemed waiting behind his face.

"I have unfinished business with Billy."

She felt her belly spasm, then let him in. Turner said, "He seems happy here. He hasn't done anything more than play a little illicit poker."

"No, he hasn't. I'd hoped you'd leave us alone."

"I've got two phage injections for him."

"Phages? Why?"

"To stop his brain cells from regenerating and to mask the CIA code."

"Not lethal?" Jane noticed for the first time that Turner was wearing cross-country ski boots.

"No." Turner took off his glove and held his hands, palms facing the stove. "I was afraid he'd think that. You think we're that terrible?"

"Yes."

"He's human fertile, did you know?"

Jane swayed and then remembered she had another year on her implant. "No, I didn't." Then she wondered if she would want Billy's child—chimera human. "But is the sperm really Billy's?"

"Chimera spies have to have human-equivalent biology."

Jane stood for a while staring at the stove, then she sat down. Turner stretched his arms, one at a time, over his shoulder, then twisted his torso before he sat down, too. Jane said, "You can take him away at any time."

"He's a test for us."

"Of what? Oh, I know, it's classified."

"As long as he behaves, he is safe. I'll allow for cockfights, gambling, perhaps some distilling."

Jane wondered if Turner knew that she was the one on the point of rebellion. She'd been getting bored with her old job—the new one was terrible from day one. "So when are you going to inject these phages?"

"Tomorrow. After you tell Billy today."

"If he thinks you are really going to give him

a lethal needle and runs? It's another damn test, isn't it?"

"If we have to fight him to inject him, he could die of shock, thinking we were killing him."

"He's not that fragile."

Turner said, "If he runs, I'm not sure what we should do."

"You'll be rid of an embarrassment."

Turner stared at her, then looked away. "The ice makes new geopolitical realities. No one wants to lose, but we don't want to become inhuman."

Sick bastard was trying to justify himself to her, Jane realized. "So you kill chimeras."

"Not only chimeras."

"Let Billy alone."

"We can afford to leave him alone if he can't be traced to us."

If only she'd rigged trip wire between the dirt road and the hard surface, she could sprain Turner's ankle as he skiied back and leave him to freeze. "Okay, I'll tell him the injections won't be lethal."

"It's for his own good and yours, if you care for him." Turner pulled his gloves back on and went out. Jane followed him and watched as he stepped into his skis and adjusted the poles. As he skied off, kicking backward and gliding as though his skies were giant skates, she went back inside and wondered if she should have offered him tea and poisoned him.

When she heard the snowcat drop Billy off,

Jane began crying. He came in and hugged her. "What is it, Jane?"

"Turner came back. He says he needs to inject you with some phages that will change your DNA so you can't be traced to the CIA again."

"Injection?"

"He says we've got to trust him. I'm so tired of all this, Billy."

"What? You said you didn't even have a whole house before, just one room and a kitchen alcove. We've got a garden. I'm working with cattle again."

"Again?"

"Yeah, that son of a bitch did give me that much." He looked down at his jeans, which were filthy. "Better go change."

"You trust Turner?"

"Jesus, Jane, if the son of a bitch wanted to kill me, he didn't have to give us any warning." He left her wondering.

Billy wasn't as sure of Turner as he'd made it seem to Jane, but she was so edgy lately. He went into the bathroom, stripped, and showered, remembering burning himself on a shower to see if that water was real.

If he ran . . . if he ran . . . the park had guarded boundaries. The tourists had to pay to come inside. Jane got out every day on a train, but the trains were locked in tubes except at the stations.

Stop it, he thought. He wondered if the headaches he got when he was very tired were residual brain damage that hadn't healed yet. If the phage—something tiny used to edit DNA, he remembered—kept his brain from regenerating, the headaches would be permanent. I did it to myself, Billy thought, when I banged my head against real tiles thinking they were just pictels.

Billy changed into fresh clothes and put on his black vest and frock coat, the outfit the store on the hard surface sold mainly to musicians. The black coat reminded him of being Billy the Kid, which was amusing some days. He wasn't so amused now when he saw himself in the mirror, puny shoulders just like the old tintype, but if he stalled around to change again, Jane might worry.

When he went back downstairs, Jane looked at his coat and said like a question, "Billy?"

"Looked silly once I put it on, I know."

"You look too much like some dead westerner in it."

"Poker? Monte?"

Jane looked at him without replying, then said, "It's too much in character, Billy."

He went to the stove and loaded more logs in it, poked the embers to get air to them. "Jane, I've been so happy." He realized she could never understand how good it was to be able to live outside Billy-the-Kid legends and the tank. "I enjoy not worrying every second."

"I guess I was used to more drama than this," Jane said. She sounded more like an outlaw than he did, Billy thought.

"Gambling's enough excitement for me," Billy said. "We play poker at the barn for lunch."

Jane didn't say anything more, but turned on the television and Billy sat in a chair by hers and watched some show about a real chimera and her master escaping Mexicans.

"I'm glad to see things improving for the Mexicans," Billy said. "I understand the historical Billy really did like Spanish-speaking people."

"You're not going to run?"

"No, Jane. I'll believe it's what he says it is, and if it isn't, how far can I run with CIA brands on my chromosomes?" If Turner's phages worked and he couldn't be traced back to the CIA, Billy realized, he might could run, if he wanted. He smiled at that and seemed to remember being in irons, kicking his toes against a stone floor to keep them warm. A few days after that, he must have shot two men who were disguised as Bell and Olinger.

Billy sighed and shuddered. Jane looked at him. He said, "Bad memories. Can't go back to them." He wondered how many times he shot Bell and Olinger. His head throbbed.

Jane said, "He said if you were terrified of the injections, you might die of fright."

Billy knew he'd never die of fright after all the times he'd been aware enough to feel the trocars jab him in the neck after he'd stopped breathing. "If he lied to us, I'm dead. One thing I am sure of is that he's listening to us now." He went up to her and wrote with his fingernail against her arm, *If he does kill me, then you can kill him.* Then he licked her forearm where he'd made the letters and began giggling around her fingers. If the bitch says, *too much in character,* he thought, I'll bite her.

She hugged him as if he was going to disappear like a hologram if she didn't squeeze. God, Billy realized, she would kill him if he kills me. He was slightly afraid of her then and loved her harder still.

The phone rang in Billy's dream of chopping his irons with a miner's pick, the phone masked by the sound of the chain breaking, then waking him. He left Jane behind him in the warm bed and went downstairs to answer.

"Billy? Turner, here. We'll be there in about an hour."

"Jane explained."

"Fine. I'll tell you more when I get there."

Billy said, "Fine," back and heard Turner put down his receiver. The floor was freezing his feet, not as bad as the stone floor in the jail— his past, the historical Billy the Kid's past, it didn't matter. He began to think of the Historical Billy as a ghostly brother, with a capital H in the Historical. Nothing to do now but load the wood heaters and run them high to burn out the creosote, then fix breakfast. Let Jane sleep, he decided, she sure was tense last night, almost hysterically clawing him.

Run? No, he was tired of that. The Historical

Billy had only run and died one life's worth. He'd been through it too many more times.

When the stoves were roaring, he went upstairs to dress. Not the black outfit, he decided, something ordinary. He pulled on corduroy pants and a sweater over a thermal top, then shaved. More beard, he thought, than he'd had last year. "I'm going to grow old," he said to Turner's bugs. Then he brushed back his hair. In the mirror, he saw Jane sitting up in bed.

"Turner called. He's coming in about forty-five minutes."

"You look nice in that."

"Thanks."

"I'm glad you're not wearing that nineteenth-century suit."

"I thought it might not be best." He looked back at her and grinned. She reached around under the covers until she found her robe and put it on. He added. "I got the stoves going."

She sighed and began pulling a bra and panties out of her chest of drawers. "I hate waiting," she said.

Billy said, "It's the way it is sometimes," and turned back to the mirror once more before going back downstairs. He turned on the television. The station was running a program on Picasso and Billy was a bit jealous, but he said, "Jane, you'd like this."

By the time the program was running end credits, Billy heard a snowmobile. It stopped at their house, so he got up and watched from the front stoop as Turner came in with a large medical bag. I should help him with that, Billy thought, but he decided not to in case Turner was going to dose him lethal.

Turner put the bag by the couch in the living room and asked, "What do you have on under your sweater?"

"Long johns."

"I've got to get to the veins at your elbow."

Billy took off his sweater and pulled back the sleeve of his underwear made of polypropylene invented between the death of the Historical and his own fabrication. Turner said, "Good, it doesn't look constricting. Lie down on the couch."

"Turner, I'm sorry if I shot people. Do you believe me?"

"Chimeras under conditioning aren't legally responsible." Turned pulled out a plastic bag already full of clear fluid and a stand for it, then inserted the tube into a needle.

"Well, whatever this is."

Turner paused and said, "You don't trust me."

"Don't trust, don't doubt. Don't know, do I, what you are going to do to me."

Turner took Billy's arm and inserted the needle, then adjusted a valve under the plastic bag. He pulled out a vial and inserted a syringe into it, then injected the valve. "You'll be sick for a while."

Jane said, "So there's a risk."

"I have to send the phages on a virus."

"So, how sick," Billy said, not sure he should

have been so cooperative, but glad he hadn't helped with Turner's bag of tricks.

"Maybe pneumonia, but probably no worse than a cold."

Billy wondered if pneumonia killed men these days. "You got the house surrounded?"

Turner didn't respond as he adjusted the valve once more and then sat down in a chair by the sofa. Billy asked, "What happened to Simon?"

"He's all right now."

"I don't know if that's good or not," Billy said.

Turner said, "I don't know either."

"So when I can't be traced to you, will my DNA still tell everyone I'm a chimera?"

"There'll be residual branding, but I doubt it can be traced to us."

"So if I live, I'm not supposed to walk off." Billy wondered if he was getting sick or if he was just imagining pains inside his bones, like bruises.

"Have you considered that?"

"I go to up Bent Mountain a couple times a month and watch the lights go on in Roanoke. Makes a man curious." He felt vaguely sleepy, but fought that when he saw Jane's face stiffen like a witch's.

Turner prepared another syringe and injected that into the same place in the valve. Billy's bladder began to feel full. He put a pint of juice in, Billy thought, so I should have to piss something out. "You're not sleepy?" Turner asked.

"Jane's worried," Billy said, realizing he had been drugged beyond whatever the phages would do. "You doped me."

"It's quite mild," Turner said.

"I trust you enough, I guess," Billy said, "it's just that Calamity Jane ... sorry ... there would scratch your eyes out if you killed me."

"I would have been a lot less conspicuous if I wanted to kill you."

"Don't criticize him on trade craft," Jane said.

After that, Billy, Jane, and Turner watched the bag drain down into Billy's arm. When the bag was flat, Turner pulled the needle out and laid a piece of wet cotton in the crook of Billy's arm. Billy asked, "Can I get up and piss now?"

Turner, packing up his equipment, nodded. Billy got up and lifted the cotton away from his arm. The area around the hole was inflamed, the needle hole itself bleeding. He put the cotton back and bent his arm again, picked up his sweater with the other hand, and went to the bathroom. After he pissed, he taped the cotton to his arm and pulled his sweater back on. Then he put his hands on the basin and trembled. *Why did I trust him?*

Outside he could hear Turner talking to Jane about decongestants and secondary bacterial infections. He looked out the window at the snow and wished Turner had waited until spring to make him sick, but then realized that Turner wouldn't be too upset if he did die. He went out and didn't speak to Turner. Turner nodded to him and went back out to the snow coach. Jane's face looked like piss on snow. Billy tried to remember when she'd looked like that before.

As the snowmobile sounds faded, Jane said, "It's a terrible time of year to be sick."

"Yeah. Cows start calving in February. He put some sedative in that fluid."

"I want to get Yaffe."

"None of Yaffe's business what happened. Jane, I don't feel like he dosed me lethal, but I didn't sleep well last night. So don't panic when I stretch out like this," he said, lying down on the couch again.

When he woke up again, Jane was holding his hand and crying. He tried to speak and found out how hoarse he was. And he was sweating. The sedative had left him completely.

"I feel jittery," he said.

Jane said, "You sound terrible."

"I can hear."

"I don't want to leave you alone tomorrow."

"Shit, Jane, I can't work tomorrow. You'd better."

Billy lay in bed, vaguely detached from life, listening to his lungs bubble. He heard knocking at the door and got out of bed. It's cold but I'm not shivering, he thought as he went downstairs. Need to get some logs while I'm up.

Before Billy could open the door, he had to cough. Spasmed, hacking as if he were going to throw his lungs up, Billy still managed to turn the key in the lock. Clyde, the man who gave Billy his rides to work, opened it.

"Lord have mercy, man, you need to go to the emergency room," Clyde said.

When Billy finally caught his breath, he said, "Where?"

"Look, when you called in sick, I thought we ought to check." He stopped and didn't explain why.

"I've got some decongestants. But when I take them, I feel so fuzzy."

"Bill, I'll call Sam to tell him I'm taking you to emergency and we'll go right now."

Billy wondered if Turner would kill him for going to an emergency room. If he could get out of the park with Clyde, then he'd been a fool not to run before Turner came to inject him with his phages and viral pneumonia. If Turner caught him, so what? He felt like death anyway. "Okay."

"Man, you need more wood in here. It's freezing-ass cold." Billy began coughing again, air wheezing through his pipes, and just shook his head. Clyde opened the door to the stove and said, "Get dressed, Bill. I'll call and set the fires."

Billy pulled on long underwear, then wool pants and a wool jacket, two pair of socks, and Jane's boots. He had to cough again before he could get back downstairs.

"Look, didn't they have hospitals at your park out west? They make us stay here and live weird if we want to hold our land, but they don't carry it so far that we have to die of the old diseases."

"Out west," Billy said, "was different."

"Sons of bitches. Well, leave a note for your woman."

Billy pretended to. He wouldn't leave evidence for Turner. Let's see, he thought, how big a fool I was not to run earlier.

Clyde drove up to a road gate, but the man on duty seemed to know him and didn't check either his or Billy's IDs, just raised the barrier. "Men around here help each other around the most rule-constricted rangers," Clyde said.

Roanoke seemed like a dream, Billy floating in a taxi with Clyde, headed through traffic, the dazzle hurting his eyes. But Turner was waiting for him at the emergency room. Billy felt obscenely relieved. Clyde said, "He's got pneumonia and didn't know he could come in."

Billy watched Turner almost speak as a nurse brought up a wheelchair for him. They left Clyde out in the waiting room and went behind double doors. "You can still trace me," Billy said. "I don't feel so stupid"—he coughed again, chest against his knees, feeling the mucus shifting inside him—"about not running."

"It was a test."

"You planning to let me die?"

The nurse said, "Billy, because of the situation, we can't treat the viral infection, but we can give you a few days' rest here, which might,

Mr. Turner, keep his friend out there from suspecting anything."

"Reasonable," Turner said.

Billy was too depressed to care. The nurse pulled out a plastic package full of tubes and said, "Billy, if you'd get up on the table."

"I'll drown if you lay me flat." He wished Turner would go away and stop watching him.

"We'll make you comfortable, at least," the nurse said. Billy moved over to the table and she began feeding a tube down his nose.

Turner left then. When the nurse hooked the tank up to the tubes, Billy did begin to feel better. Maybe Turner wasn't trying to kill him after all, he thought just before the nurse brought him a pill that made him sleep.

When he woke up, Jane was sitting by his bed, crying. "Shit, Jane," he began, but couldn't finish saying how he'd been worse before Clyde brought him here. He went back to sleep.

When he woke up, his lungs were empty and his throat felt dry—a better decongestant, he suspected. Jane was gone. He got up and went to the door. It wasn't locked, but Turner didn't need locks on him. Turner could find him wherever he ran.

Then Billy realized he did feel better, more than what the decongestants did for him, and that he'd probably live. He felt better enough to be overwhelmed with relief and sat down in the armchair by the bed and trembled.

The nurse who had admitted him came in and

said, "Mr. Turner will check on you in a few months."

Billy leaned back in the chair and giggled. He knew now why the Historical Billy had been so excited and chatty after Garrett brought him and the others out of the rock house at Stinking Springs. The Historical had been sure Pat would shoot him down on sight and was happy as shit to find that he could surrender and get dinner, too. Billy said, "I can live with that," and tried not to laugh more because the nurse looked at him funny.

Two women were sitting in a car in Billy's pull-out the first day the roads were scraped down to pavement or gravel. He got out of Clyde's truck, bloody from the calf he'd pulled from the black heifer. One woman got out of the car. He recognized her. She'd been a Celsa and now was so beautiful he couldn't believe she was real.

"What did they do to Simon?" she asked. "And, God, you're so bloody."

"Fixed him," Billy said. He didn't recognize the other woman, who was a rather crystalline-looking blonde in her forties. "I knew you as Celsa, but I don't remember the woman in the car."

The woman in the car said, "Simon asked me to help find you once."

"Shit. When?" He hated the idea that Simon might still want to recapture him or build another Billy the Kid.

"Over a year ago. But the CIA found you first."

Billy said, "Turner told me they fixed Simon."

The Celsa woman said, "He didn't remember me."

"Good, then," Billy said. "Maybe he's forgot me."

The woman in the car said, "He remembered me, though, but, Billy, it's not Simon. I think they killed Simon."

Billy realized Simon could have been rebuilt just as he was. So the original Simon was with the Historical Billy. He felt almost as if he'd just heard his brutal father died. Simon had killed him, watched him fuck many woman, but Simon did give him real skills and a love for work with cows and horses. His craving for a normal life was Simon's little joke then, but it kept Billy sane now. "Life's like that these days, isn't it?"

Jane came out on the porch and Billy looked at her and at the Celsa woman. He said, "Jane, one of these women played the part of Celsa in Simon's last game with me." He looked at the Celsa once more, briefly, then at Jane, wondering if he was going to continue the Historical's ways.

The Celsa woman said, "Do you stay with her out of habit?"

That broke him of the bitch. Billy said, "No." Jane looked like she wasn't reassured.

The Celsa woman said, "You don't seem as innocent as you were, as fresh."

"I'm not. I'm just a guy who works with cattle. The Historical was really just the same. I've got everything he wanted, little spread of my own, money, a tough woman like Charles Bowdre and McSween had. But I do thank you for getting me away from Simon."

The woman looked more real there for a second, then she sighed and said, "I wanted to do it again, but I forgot about the blood."

"What, see me killed?"

The woman in the car said, "Come on, we've spent too much time here as it is."

Billy said, "Really, thanks."

The Celsa woman said, "God, you're just another scut."

Jane said, "Thanks for saving Billy."

The Celsa woman said, "Well, at least you didn't get anything out of the deal." She opened the car door and stood looking—at the outhouse, at Billy again, and not at Jane.

Jane didn't speak. Billy came up to her and put his arm around her waist. She was trembling. He didn't try to ease the rage out of her.

The car door slammed. The women drove away.

Billy said, "Let's go in and I'll tell you about how I learned to pull calves on the Plastic Elsie."

They went inside. Jane sat down in a wing chair and cried. Billy asked, "What's the matter?"

"I'm so sick of my job. I'm so bored with all this phony twentieth-century life, all this crap, wondering if Turner is going to change his mind and kill you. Wondering if you're . . . never mind. The politicians are corrupt, the CIA murdered Simon and put a clone or reconstruction in his place. That woman looked at me as if I were scum."

"Jane, stop worrying about what she thinks," he said, shifting the smoke path to run it through the catalyst, not wanting to bitch at her now about letting the stove burn without pulling down the bypass lever. "You have to find something to be happy about."

"Are you really happy?"

"Yes. What do you want to do, really?"

"I wanted to live in the 1920's."

"Fool bitch, you're bad as ... Jesus, Jane. What 1920's?"

She got out of the chair and went to the stove and checked the catalyst. "I couldn't have had more than one life then, could I have?"

"Jane, even this park is bigger than a whole shelfful of Billy-the-Kid books."

She didn't look convinced, but later in the week she bought breeding pairs of exotic chickens and a chicken genome map.

Billy and she built fighting cocks better than the park had ever known, but Billy never trusted to go to a match himself. He figured Turner was always listening to him, even if it was logistically impossible for one man to spend all his waking hours monitoring the complete movements of another. Even, years later, after he read Turner's obituary, he never quite believed the man wasn't watching.

CODA:

Why Is Henry McCarty Still Remembered by the Wrong Name After All These Years?

AFTER READING THE VARIOUS CONFLICTING AC-
counts of Billy's life and death, I went to sleep and
woke with a headache. Just how bad was that boy?

Billy the Kid was a little Irish punk caught in
the middle of great illegalities that killed people
before and after him: his bosses, his foreman, his
lawyer, three of his closest friends, and the sheriff who shot him. Some of the most guilty disappeared. Albert Fall, who defended those accused
of killing his lawyer, wasn't busted until the Tea-
pot Dome Scandal in the twenties.

During this killing time in America, even the
lawmen were ambiguous in ways that don't
seem to happen as much in English outlaw stories or in accounts of Depression-era bank rob-
bers. The paradigm movie western resolved the

307

ambiguities into good guys and bad guys, wrapping total fiction around the times.

The terrible ambiguities seem typically American: lawless lawmen, slackness or corruption at the governor's office, the military used as cat's-paws by one side against the other. The real Henry McCarty, alias William Antrim, alias Billy the Kid, who told the 1880 census worker he was twenty-five and a cattle worker, got warped by legend making while he was alive. But still he had enough sense that the whole Billy-the-Kid appellation seems to have made him nervous:

> Q: In addition to the names which you have given, are you now known or styled in Lincoln County as "the Kid"?
> A: I have already answered that question. Yes, sir, I am; but not "Billy the Kid" that I know of.

> (from the Dudley Inquiry)

The real Billy, before his death, didn't handle the mythologizing process as well as did the Earp family, who managed their own transformations from the ambiguous to the heroic by the early twentieth century. Doc Holliday and possibly the Earps were acquitted for doing as much as Billy Bonney/Henry McCarty died for.

Not that he wasn't rustling and pushing counterfeit money, okay. He started with laundry theft, killed a man who'd thrown him to the ground, and then rode with real bad guys before trying to become more honest. Then, after his deal with Governor Wallace fell through, he rode with Dave Rudabaugh, a guy so bad a whole Mexican village was forced to behead him.

Both sides of the myth began while he was alive—ruthless killer, social bandit, killer of Mexicans, friend of Latinos. Surviving friends claimed that he wasn't armed with more than a butcher knife when Garrett shot him. Some even believed that he didn't die in Pete Maxwell's bedroom, but then surviving death is what an Irish solar hero is supposed to do.

The historical man wanted a ranch and said he was twenty-five and a cattle worker in the 1880 census. He didn't understand how badly Pat Garrett wanted to kill him after he killed Garrett's jailers. Garrett described one jailer as a decent, humane man, the second as being a man who hated Billy and who Billy hated (Olinger killed a friend of Billy's). Other sources claim both men were from the other side.

Billy, thinking it was hard that of all the people involved in the various killings only he was going to hang, shot his jailers, shook hands with many Lincoln townspeople, took a horse but promised to return it (and it was sent back), and went to visit friends around Fort Sumner. Both before his trial and after, people urged him to go to Mexico. He didn't, but he talked about it.

Governor Wallace, that almost-not-a-hack writer, seemed not to care what it meant to offer the Kid a pardon for testifying against Jesse

Evans and Colonel Dudley. Rather, he abandoned the boy so as to concentrate on *Ben-Hur* and his own career (the gravest temptation for writers is to think morals in our words are more real than our actions with flesh people). Later, Lew Wallace postured for historical purposes with Mr. Henry McCarty, whose real name has been obliterated except in books. In the 1920's, Lew Wallace remembered many things about Billy. The Kid was a Zen shooter, if Wallace's account is true, a man who pointed his gun as if it were his finger because a man never misses at pointing.

Garrett, however, didn't think the Kid was a great marksman and claimed Bell died of a ricochet. One of the great debates in Kid studies is whether Billy had his gun out when Garrett shot him. Billy had gone to slice up some steaks and was in his stocking feet. I hadn't thought that Garrett might have been lying until I read in another book the impossibility of beating a man to the draw if he had his gun in his hand. But Billy thought himself to be among friends.

And who was his lover? Celsa Gutierrez, generally identified as the woman, was Pat Garrett's sister-in-law, but Paulita Maxwell, who kissed Billy good-bye with extraordinary ardor after his arrest at Stinking Springs, was the one who claimed Celsa was Billy's lover, not herself. Billy had other lovers, mostly Spanish women but possibly Sallie Chisum.

Two theories. First, Billy stayed in Fort Sumner to try to get Paulita, pregnant with his child, to ride off with him. Pete, her brother, betrayed Billy and married Paulita off to José Jaramillo (Billy was killed on July 14, 1881; child born January 1882 shortly after the marriage). Second, Celsa was his lover (or one of his lovers), and Garrett's wife thought something ought to be done. After the killing and the criticism, Garrett left his wife to live with another woman.

Evans, leader of the first outlaws Billy rode with and later one of his enemies, disappeared, avoiding numerous indictments and sentences. Fred Waite, a college-educated half-breed Indian, had planned to go into partnership with Billy before the Tunstall shooting. By December 1878, he'd gone back to Oklahoma. The other Billy, Billie Wilson, captured with the Kid at Stinking Springs, escaped to Texas and made a new life for himself, and finally, with a character reference from Garrett, was pardoned.

In 1950, an old man approached the governor of New Mexico for a pardon. I've read Brushy Bill's account several times and believe that he was sure he was Billy the Kid. But I have become less convinced. Cops who generally ignore all sorts of street crime will clean the streets in half an hour if one of their own is killed. Garrett felt responsible for his jailers' deaths. Taking a chance in the dark isn't an option I believe in.

So Billy died and his women friends buried him and tried to scratch out Garrett's eyes. Deluvina Maxwell said to one of Billy's biographers, Governor Miguel Antonio Otero, "They killed my little boy. I hated those men and am glad that I have lived long enough to see them all dead and buried."

Historians who don't believe Garrett lied wish Otero had been able to do his research earlier while those hostile to Billy still lived. Garrett's revenge for his jailers' deaths is just; Billy's revenge for the killings of Tunstall, McSween, Brewer, O'Folliard, and Bowdre is murder.

The law then was bloodier than it seems to be now (still I knew a prison captain who seems to have delighted in hunting escapees with a .22 and bringing them in bleeding around the knees). My county's sheriff, Jay Gregory, who has arrested a drug-turf war killer, an Aryan Nations member wanted in the Alan Berg murder, and numerous little burglars, murderers, and drug dealers, has never shot a man. Once when a prisoner went for his carotid with a letter opener, the sheriff kept his gun away from this prisoner and managed to wrestle him back into handcuffs. Had it been the 1880's and out west, the prisoner would have died. Jay Gregory said, "I knew he was worthless to society, but someone might have cared." Before I read the Billy accounts, the statement seemed humanistic. After, merely practical.

Why was Billy, out of all those killers, sentenced to death? Perhaps because out of all of them, he least seemed to understand the politics beyond the killings, took all those business machinations personally.

So Billy is an emblem of American attitudes,

our terrible national ambiguity, a nation settled by people who left because folks were against them in the old countries. We are the people Garrison Keillor described as folks who find no one in the old family neighborhoods in Europe will take our checks.

So many of those involved in the Lincoln County war were immigrants and second-generation Americans—when I read about the Irishmen McCarty, Murphy, Dolan, and Brady, the English Tunstall, and the Scottish McSween, I thought about fifth-century Irish cattle raids. Except for improved weaponry, nothing had changed among the Celts. Maybe Billy was a marked man because he went against his fellow Irish? However, Billy seems to have also been involved in a more modern crime—counterfeiting paper money. It was the end of the nineteenth century, with horses and wood heat, the beginning of the twentieth, with trains and telephones. Horses and changes of venue.

The popular image of Billy is the charming sociopath who killed a man for every year he lived, but further research destroys that story even as it increases one's fascination with him. Why should such a small-time gambler and rustler become possessed by so powerful an archetype?

As the legend became polarized between Hispanics who loved him and Anglo ranchers who hated him, the fictions created about The Kid obliterated the real Henry McCarty, who'd become an outlaw after stealing a sack of laundry in 1875.

Was McCarty ruined by the *Police Gazette* and

dime novels? A teacher described him as "artistic" and friends remember him as a reader. In his teens, he killed a man who had amused himself by ruffling Billy's hair, who just before the killing knocked Billy down and called him a pimp (The *Oxford English Dictionary* suggests that word meant more than a procurer).

Henry/Billy felt misused, wronged by the legends, and attempted to refute the newspapers' depictions of him. But while he hid at Fort Sumner and various sheep camps, his friends brought him newspapers. He'd been reading a newspaper when he got hungry and went out to cut meat off a slaughtered yearling hanging in front of Maxwell's bedroom.

That night in July 1881, Mr. Henry McCarty was fatally caught at the intersection of some powerful problems that extended far beyond his own lost case.

So we still remember Billy the Kid, in the way of corruption or progress—we're not sure which. Billy the Kid was impractical. Billy the Kid is what we feel like when we smuggle guns in television movies. He's the stud male to Jean Harlow's female. Billy the Kid could have done anything he wanted to do if he'd only stayed away from bad company.

Billy the Kid has to be dead but we will rebuild him.

Rebecca Ore
Critz, VA
1990